A FAMILY AFFAIR

BY

JANE STUBBS

Published by New Generation Publishing in 2021

Copyright © Jane Stubbs 2021

First Edition

The author asserts the moral right under the Copyright, Designs and Patents Act 1988 to be identified as the author of this work.

All Rights reserved. No part of this publication may be reproduced, stored in a retrieval system or transmitted, in any form or by any means without the prior consent of the author, nor be otherwise circulated in any form of binding or cover other than that which it is published and without a similar condition being imposed on the subsequent purchaser.

ISBN
        Paperback   978-1-80031-436-8
        Ebook   978-1-80031-435-1

www.newgeneration-publishing.com

For Anne who did wonderful things with her life

SUNDAY 5TH JUNE 1887

Do not fall asleep, John Truesdale told himself as the Reverend climbed the steps to the pulpit. Or snore. Usually, he relied on his wife to dig him in the ribs when his eyelids closed during the sermon. Today she was staying at home. Florence did not wish to toil up the steep hill twice in the same day. The weather was warm and they planned to take their daughter, Margaret, down to the park in the afternoon. She would feed the ducks while John showed off his exciting new purchase.

The sunny weather must have affected the Reverend; his sermon was brief and his smile wide as he shook the hands of the departing parishioners.

'Mrs. Truesdale not with us today?' he murmured. 'I trust she is not indisposed.' John felt the women clustered round the Reverend prick up their ears and give their own meaning to the word 'indisposed'. They sniffed a pregnancy. After all, his daughter had passed her second birthday.

'Margaret,' John improvised. 'Bilious.' He had no idea what the word meant but often heard it applied to children. While the Reverend wished her a speedy recovery John, thinking only of his shiny new possession, made a swift departure. As he laboured up the hill to his house, he was struck by a sudden doubt. Perhaps Florence was right? The money would have been better spent on a sewing machine.

When he arrived at his house, John stood for a moment to recover his breath. Down to his left lay the town of Atherley sprawled across the floor of the valley. It did not wear its customary wreath of swirling clouds of black smoke. The great engines and furnaces of industry remained cold and silent on the Sabbath day. To his right the top of the hill was crowned with leafy green trees. Dotted among them were the mansions of the wealthy.

After a hasty meal, John set about some mysterious preparations in the back-garden, while Florence did the pleasantly small amount of washing up. No greasy roasting tin from the traditional Sunday joint. John had foregone that pleasure to concentrate on the main event of the day, the public unveiling of his new purchase.

Florence dried her hands, put some stale bread in a paper bag and handed it to little Margaret who displayed no signs of ill health. They went out into the street to wait for John to appear through the alleyway next to their house. It was a source of satisfaction to Florence that she lived in the end house of the terrace.

Outside on the pavement, mother and daughter enjoyed such sunshine as their shady bonnets and long skirts permitted to reach them. John soon appeared wheeling his prized new possession – a safety bicycle.

'I had a bit of a practice in the garden,' he said sheepishly. 'I think I'm getting the hang of it.' Florence said nothing. She thought the bicycle a ridiculous extravagance for a man who walked to work and lived on a steep hill. On the other hand, a sewing machine would earn its keep many times over. In her mind she reviewed the balance sheet of their marriage. The bike went into the debit column on John's side. She put her refusal to complain about it, into the credit column on her side. As far as Florence was concerned, John's expensive new toy had put him in moral debt to her; she had every intention of calling in the loan one day, but not yet. There was something Florence wanted much more than a sewing machine, but she was not ready to reveal her heart's desire.

Man and wife stood side by side and looked down at the town. For an eerie moment they both had a vision of John on his bicycle plunging helplessly downhill until he hit the ground in a pile of twisted metal. John patted the handlebars for reassurance, much as he would a friendly dog. 'I think I'll just wheel it down the hill. This first time.'

The wrought iron gates of the park were wide open to allow the townspeople to stroll among the lawns. Like the jockey of the winning horse at a race, John led his bicycle through them. It caused a sensation. The men abandoned their wives and girlfriends. They flocked to examine the revolutionary machine, so unlike the penny-farthing, occasionally spotted on the cobbled streets of the town. These were men who worked with, and understood machines; they quickly grasped the superiority of the design to the old high-wheelers with their front wheel drive. The safety cycle with its chain mechanism to the back wheel left the front wheel free for the important function of steering. Even the bone-shaking combination of solid rubber tires on smaller wheels did not discourage them. It was not long before they were hinting that a chance to ride it would be much appreciated.

As the Registrar for Births, Marriages and Deaths in Atherley, John had come across most of them before. They came to his office as grief-stricken sons, nervous bridegrooms and proud new fathers. Today he was the owner of a wondrous invention they wanted to explore. He soon agreed to their riding it. Each man mounted the machine, raced at top speed round the lake and slithered to a sometimes less than graceful halt near John's feet. Then the next man took his turn.

John felt a sneaking envy of the efficient way they handled the bicycle. These men earned their living by physical toil. Their hands were skilled and their bodies strong. John was more accustomed to holding a pen and separating papers. In time the crowd of men dwindled; Their wives summoned them with beckoning fingers as they grew tired of restraining restless children. John looked to the edge of the lake where Florence stood with two small girls in sun bonnets, giggling at the antics of the ducks.

'Excuse me. D'ya think I could have a go?' said a man in a brown suit that had seen better days. 'I've got a new job over Tilton way. Something like this'd save me a fortune in bus fares.' John looked more closely at the man. He saw a ginger moustache but found nothing familiar in the face. He wasn't a miner. The Saturday night bath never got rid of the tell-tale traces of coal dust that clung alluringly round their eyes and eyelashes.

A humble pen-pusher like himself, John decided. One who had seen better days.

The man in the brown suit saw the doubt in John's face. He gestured to the lake where Florence was laughing with the two girls. The other child must be his. John offered the handlebars and watched as the man mounted the bicycle. He expected to see a false start and much wobbling. He was wrong. The man grasped the handlebars, stood up once to test the pedals and set off like a rocket.

A sudden female shriek split the air. All eyes turned to the lake where a small boy was thrashing about in the water. Several men went to the rescue. John was close behind. He saw Florence and Margaret were safe. The stranger's child was with them. He watched as the wet boy was returned to his mother who relieved her feelings by walloping him on the bottom before clasping him to her bosom, and telling him he was a naughty boy who deserved to drown. When the drama finished, John scanned the park, looking for his bicycle and the man in the brown suit. He could find no sign of either the man or the machine.

Surely, he had not gone and left his child? John dashed across to Florence to identify the children whose hands she held. He tweaked back the brim of a sun bonnet, to find the grubby face of a small girl. Florence confirmed the other infant was definitely Margaret. John felt a giant fist had hit him in the solar plexus and knocked all the air out of him.

Stern notices from Atherley Town Council forbad you from climbing on the park seats. John ignored them. He needed a vantage point to survey the whole of the park. He stood tall, stretched his neck and screwed up his eyes. In vain. There was no sign of the man or the bicycle.

A great roar and quite a few swear words emerged from John's throat as he realised that the man in the brown suit had stolen his expensive bike. He jumped off the seat and blundered about in noisy complaint while struggling with a strong desire to hit somebody. People stopped their leisurely strolling and rushed to investigate the hullabaloo.

There were plenty of witnesses. The man had gone through the front gates, the side gate, into the rhododendrons and behind the band stand. He took the road to Manchester. Or was it Burnley? Several people claimed to know him personally. He used to work at a builder's yard. His dad was a butcher over in Tilton. He wasn't from these parts.

A police constable in uniform arrived. He was confident he could catch the thief if he had the use of a motorbike and knew for sure which way he'd gone. He started to write the details in his notebook and take names and addresses from the eager witnesses.

Florence tapped John's shoulder and told him she was going to take Margaret home. It was late and the child was getting hungry. She would take the other little girl with her since no-one seemed to be making any arrangements for her. She set off briskly, leaving John to the commiserations of the townsfolk, a great many questions and some sniggering at the police station.

By the time she was home Florence was in possession of a perfectly formed plan. She fed the girls and warmed the water for a bath. Margaret first. The other girl was none too clean. A spare nightdress and some work with the hairbrush and there were two little angels ready for bed. She said a brief prayer as she tucked them up.

John returned feeling foolish, angry and deflated, Florence gave him hot soup and ham sandwiches and nodded as he justified his part in the events of the afternoon, and vented his annoyance at the failure of the townspeople of Atherly to agree a description of the thief or his direction of travel. The only hope for recovering his bicycle was a telegram sent to the police in Manchester. John did not look optimistic.

Florence brewed tea and cut a slice of fruit cake for him to eat sitting in his favourite armchair by the fireplace. He stretched out his legs and let out a huge breath. Florence did not ask questions. She kept busy in the kitchen until she judged he'd had long enough to settle his thoughts. Then she put her hands on his shoulders and looked into his eyes.

'Well, I for one, am very pleased that you won't be risking your life on that dangerous contraption. I love you too much to risk losing you.' He opened his mouth to protest. She touched her finger to his lips, kissed his cheek, and whispered seductively in his ear, 'Time for bed.'

His face flushed at the memory of the last time she had summoned him to bed with such a voice. Her hair shining in the moonlight, her body naked under her shift and her hands, oh her hands, roaming his body and her lips pressed soft against him.

'Oh Florence, we agreed. No more babies. Do not let me forget myself again.'

'Don't worry. Your virtue is safe with me. I just want to show you something.' She led him by the hand into the tiny bedroom at the turn of the stairs. Holding the candle over the bed she showed him the two little girls sleeping there. Margaret was curled up with her thumb close to her mouth in case she needed it in a hurry. Her brown hair glinted with gleams of gold in the candlelight. Next to her slept the stranger's child, her hair fanned across the pillow in rippling waves the colour of bright autumn leaves.

'I gave her a bath. She was pretty grubby. And thin. And hungry. She ate most of the bread for the ducks.' Florence kept her voice calm and emotionless. This was not the moment to play on John's heart strings. She would do that later, if necessary. In bed she held him in her arms until he drifted off to sleep.

Florence stayed awake; she had much to think about. She'd give John time to recover from the theft of his bicycle. She suspected he was already beginning to feel secretly relieved. He had quailed at tackling the hill on a fine summer's day. How would he manage in the treacherous snow and ice of winter? It was not the bicycle that preoccupied Florence. It was the little girl.

Florence's sole experience of childbirth had been horrific. The doctor claimed she had nearly died and had warned her against having another child. John was taking his advice very seriously. No more babies.

Now fate, or the stork of legends, had dropped a little girl in her lap; the child could be the sister Margaret would never have. But how to keep the flame-haired girl? Better not to ask John outright. The answer would be No. She would have to do it one step at a time. Perhaps the girl could stay with them this week? Just while the police made their enquiries? The father – and the bike - might be found. There must be a mother somewhere. The authorities would not act swiftly if there was a family member to take responsibility. They would be only too happy to save the cost of feeding the child.

Time was on her side. Florence knew how quickly little girls could enslave a full-grown man. After a few weeks John would grow ridiculously fond of her; he would not want her sent to the workhouse orphanage. With silence and cunning she could contrive to make the child their own.

There was one small flaw in her plan. Florence really wanted a son.

Four years later, In March 1891 Florence Truesdale wrote to her younger sister, Anna, with some important news.

Dear Anna,

Thank you for your letter. I am sorry Papa is not well. On the bright side, it means you get to work in his Post Office. Will he give you your wages in a brown envelope at the end of the week.? Or will he tell you it is a daughter's duty to help? At least it is a chance to meet more people. By people, little sister, I mean, gentlemen.

I hope you fall in love like I did. It's a sort of magical chemistry. The next thing you know you want to make babies – which brings me to the most exciting bit. I am going to have a baby, sometime in September. I am so happy. When John gets used to the idea, I'm sure he will be too.

I wish you could see my girls. I daren't say daughters in case the man on the bicycle comes back to claim Jenny. She is taller than Margaret now but is still skinny. Perhaps one day you and papa will be able to see them. The rail fare is much cheaper now.

Grumpy old doctor Holmes has retired, thank goodness. The new doctor is a great improvement. I am confident it will be much less of an ordeal this time. I confess I am hoping for a boy. John loves the girls, but I think he would like to have a son.

In the meantime, love from your sister, Florence

The Atherley and Tilton Advertiser
21st September 1891

Announcements

Deaths

On 12th September Florence Truesdale (nee Jones), beloved wife of John Truesdale, Registrar of Births, Marriages and Deaths in Atherley and Tilton. She is survived by two daughters and an infant son.

NOVEMBER 1897

It was Jenny's turn to lay the table that evening. She set about the task with the speed and silence of a hungry heron. No clattering the dishes, no clashing the cutlery. When she came to her father's place she stopped, frowned and looked around the room for guidance. Tommy was no help; he lay on the rug, like a dog in front of the coal fire. Her sister, Margaret, had her nose in a book as usual. Jenny prodded her gently in the shoulder with the handle of a fork.

'Which side?' she asked, waving it in the air.

'Left.'

Jenny continued to wave the fork in the air. Margaret saw her problem. 'It's the hand the teacher takes a ruler to when he catches you writing with it.'

'You mean the hand that does the Devil's work,' said Jenny, quoting one of their more obnoxious Sunday school teachers.

'Ambidextrous. That's what you are. Ambidextrous.' Margaret rolled the word round her mouth with pleasure. 'It's Latin,' she explained.

The memory of stinging knuckles told Jenny which side to place her father's fork. He was determinedly right-handed and would mutter if he had to swap his knife and fork round. No sense in looking for trouble. There was enough to upset him that evening.

For a start, it was Friday. Friday meant fish. It was his least favourite meal of the week. Hannah, their servant, always cooked fish on Friday. Then there was the letter, lying ominously on the hall table. Jenny slipped out into the cold hall to pick up the letter. She was sure her father would rather open it by the warmth of the fire. Tommy spotted it from the hearthrug.

'Put it on the table,' he told Jenny. 'So, he'll open it and put us out of our misery.' Although he was six years younger, Tommy, as the only boy, felt he had a right to give orders.

Jenny ignored him; she had rights too. She took the letter into the circle of golden light that radiated from the paraffin lamp and scrutinised the handwriting again. 'I'm sure it's

Aunt Anna's writing,' she said and looked round, challenging the others to deny it. 'She sent a letter like this to tell us when our grandfather died.' All three gazed at the envelope with its black border, that tactful warning to brace yourself for news of a death.

'With any luck it's her beastly husband who's dead,' said Tommy.

The girls pretended to be shocked. They knew it wasn't right to wish people dead, not even inconvenient husbands. Tommy was unrepentant. 'If he's out of the way, she might come and live with us again.' There was a mother-shaped hole in Tommy's life that only his Aunt Anna could fill. The sound of the front door closing put a stop to their argument. Their father was home.

In the narrow hallway John Truesdale, Registrar of Births, Marriages and Deaths in the town of Atherly, hung up his damp overcoat that smelt of the fog and coal dust that lay like a cloak over the town. He wiped his hand down his face to erase the memory of the sad queue of people who had come to his office that day. November was a bad month for Deaths.

The smell of fish in the hall dampened his mood further. Bracing himself for a flabby white supper he headed for the warmth of the fire. His first glimpse of the room told him something was amiss. The children faced him in a semi-circle. Only a major crisis could reduce them to such silence.

He took a step further and saw their eyes were fixed on his customary place at the table. Where his dinner plate should be, there perched a letter with an ominous black border, like a crow on the white tablecloth.

He checked the children. Jenny. Margaret. Tommy. They were all there. No blood, no bandages, no obvious signs of injury. There was only one person dear to his heart who was not safe under his roof that night. That person was Anna. His soul screamed out silently, 'Dear God, please don't let it be Anna who has died.

Her name rang in his ears as the children competed to assure him that it was Anna's handwriting on the envelope.

Jenny brought the paraffin lamp so he could see more clearly. Margaret laid a reassuring hand on his arm. Tommy made his contribution with inexorable logic. 'As it's Aunt Anna's handwriting, she can't possibly be dead,' he said.

'Proper little Sherlock Holmes,' said Jenny and scowled at him.

Their father lifted his hand in a gesture that commanded silence.

'Go into the kitchen. All of you. Help Hannah finish. Tell her she can go home now. Wash your hands and get ready for supper.'

Once John had the room to himself, he examined the writing. The ink was as black as Anna's raven hair, the letters as firm and shapely as the woman herself. Without doubt it was her hand. Relief swept over him. He rested his arm on the mantlepiece and pressed the letter to his chest, against his heart. Then he raised the envelope to his face and inhaled deeply, hoping to catch her scent.

Anna was alive and writing to him. John pressed the letter to his lips and kissed where her mouth had touched to wet the seal. Finally, he opened the envelope and scanned the contents. As the children surmised it was indeed Anna's husband who had bid this world goodnight. John started to breathe again. A wild exultation began to build up in his chest. He just managed to stop 'Hallelujah!' bursting from his lips.

When they were all seated at the table, John arranged his face in the expression of professional concern that he used for dealing with the newly bereaved. His voice solemn, he told them their Aunt Anna's husband, George, had died. A quiet rumble of satisfaction went around the table as the youngsters savoured the rare pleasure of being right. There was a certain amount of elbow nudging. Crowing whispers of, 'I told you so,' and, 'I said it first,' travelled between them.

Their antics reminded John of his responsibilities. The world of Queen Victoria took death seriously. There were rules of behaviour to follow: special black clothing, long faces in public, hushed tones and damp handkerchiefs. He rapped on the table to call for order. 'Show some respect,' he told his children – and himself.

A savage glee boiled up inside him. The fact of the husband's departure from this world gave him as much satisfaction as if he had taken a pistol and fired it into the man's chest, himself. When Anna wrote to tell him, she intended to marry George, John had ground his teeth in silent rage. He saw the husband's abrupt end as an act of divine justice, God's punishment for stealing Anna from the man who really loved her.

'It's not as though she had him very long,' said Tommy. 'She can't have got too fond of him.'

'She'll still have to wear all that black and keep dabbing her eyes, won't she?' Jenny knew how widows behaved.

'Poor Aunt Anna. She's not very lucky, is she? First our Mama, then her father and now her husband. She seems to spend all her time looking after people who die.'

'It's not fair,' said Jenny. 'Aunt Anna keeps having to do things for other people. She never had time to play the piano; she was too busy doing the domestics. That's what she called it.'

John thought wistfully of the seamless efficiency of Anna's housekeeping. When she had lived with them, meals arrived on time and clean shirts appeared in the cupboard. He did not have to bother his head about ordering coal or the price of meat. His home ran smoothly and economically, exactly as it should. The man went out to earn his living in the rough world of work and business. The woman stayed at home and maintained domestic harmony. With a sigh he turned his attention to his supper.

It was the girls' task to wash up while Tommy cleaned his father's shoes, a job he enjoyed as it licensed him to spit. In the kitchen Margaret stood at the wooden draining board, a tea towel in her hand. 'Do you think Aunt Anna will come back to us now she hasn't got a husband to bother about?'

'Dunno.' Jenny swirled the hot soapy water for emphasis; she always claimed the sink as she was the tallest. 'Papa doesn't like to talk about her.'

'He must like her,' said Tommy, spitting enthusiastically onto the black polish. 'Everybody likes Aunt Anna. I didn't want her to go.'

'She didn't want to go. She was crying,' said Jenny.

'Her father was ill. I'd cry if I got a telegram in the night to say papa was dying,' said Margaret.

'She left me that blue rabbit she made,' said Tommy as he whooshed the brush up and down the leather.

'You were very little then.'

'Huh,' said Jenny scornfully. 'You two didn't even wake up. I came down when I heard the telegraph boy banging on the door.'

'Afterwards Papa kept saying it was her duty to go. Said she didn't want to leave us. But it was her duty.'

'Well now she's a widow it's her duty to grieve. Like Queen Victoria,' said Jenny as she scrubbed an enamel pan. 'Let's ask Papa if she can come here to do her grieving.'

While the children were busy in the kitchen, John poured himself a glass of Madeira to soothe the turmoil of his emotions while he studied Anna's letter.

She wrote that George's death was very sudden. One minute he was there, the next he was gone. John noted with guilty pleasure that the letter in his hand showed that George's widow was not exactly deranged by grief. The paragraphs were organised, the handwriting flowed and the ink was not splashed by tears.

When the washing up was finished, the children came to enjoy the warmth of the fire before facing their chilly bedrooms. Girls were supposed to sew of an evening. Margaret felt no pang of envy as Jenny's skilful fingers quickly threaded a needle and set about her task. Margaret had mastered the art of pretending to sew. Her needlework lay in her lap, concealing the book, open on her knees, for her last surreptitious read of the day.

John sat in his favourite chair and opened his newspaper. That evening he did not follow his usual custom of falling into a doze after the first few paragraphs. He scoured briskly through the contents, rattling the pages as he went.

'Are you looking for something in particular?' asked Jenny.

'I'm hoping that blasted Parliament in London has come to its senses.'

Jenny did two back stitches and snipped the thread. 'There. That's finished.' She handed him a shirt, with the worn side of the collar now concealed. It was a technique Anna had taught her. It seemed a good moment to ask him if Aunt Anna might come and live with them again.

John exploded. 'For goodness' sake, have you children no respect? A man is dead. We must leave a decent interval for mourning.' He got up and poked the fire ferociously, rattling the hot coals and sending sparks flying over Tommy.

'Time for bed, young man,' said John and prodded the boy gently with his toe. He always took Tommy up to bed; he was too young to be trusted with a candle. Through his work as a Registrar John knew that falling asleep with a lighted candle by the bed was the frequent cause of a spectacularly horrendous death. He led the boy gently up the stairs. Halfway up was a tiny landing with a white painted door that opened onto a bedroom that floated above the scullery. It was designed to accommodate a servant, some unfortunate tweeny, her hands reddened by toil and her heart sick for home. Now it was Tommy's room.

The light from the candle revealed a child's bed. On the pillow was a well-loved soft toy that might once have been a rabbit and might once have been blue in colour. When Tommy lay on the bed his feet dangled over the end. The problem of the boy's schooling made one of its frequent visits into John's mind. He told it to go away; he had more urgent things to think about.

Tommy sat up in bed and hugged the blue rabbit. 'Why did Aunt Anna get married?' he asked, his blue eyes wide. 'Because some bloody-minded bishops in London wouldn't let me marry her, John thought but did not say. He smoothed the boy's hair while he worked at acceptable answer.

'It's what women do,' he said. 'They get married.' He paused, 'They get married. There's not much else for them to do.'

The girls were lined up at the foot of the stairs, waiting for him to light their candles. He spent a few moments contemplating the smooth skin and shining hair of youth. Jenny's tumbled down her back in auburn waves; Margaret's was a sedate walnut brown. Then he kissed them lightly on the cheek and patted their heads. 'Goodnight, Papa', they murmured,

To Margaret, as she turned to leave, he said, 'I think you've forgotten something.' He held out an open palm and raised a quizzical eyebrow.

Margaret sighed, fished the book she had hoped to smuggle upstairs from her pocket and handed it to her father. Satisfied, he gave them both a final pat and wished them goodnight.

Jenny and Margaret had two flights of stairs to climb to reach their chilly bedrooms in the attic. On the second flight, safely out of earshot, Margaret wondered how old they would have to be before their father stopped being so stern about candles. 'He was like this even before the school burned down,'

'Perhaps one day we will have gaslight. Then you'll be able to read in bed.'

'That's about as likely as my learning Latin,' said Margaret, the frustrated scholar.

'Why do you want to learn Latin. Girls don't learn Latin.'

'That's exactly why I want to learn it. Boys go away to boarding school specially to learn it, so it must be important.'

There was a more pressing question on Jenny's mind. 'Do you think Aunt Anna might come back to live with us?'

Margaret screwed up her face in thought. 'She won't come if we don't ask her. You can't go anywhere if you're not invited.'

'I bet Aunt Anna could persuade Papa to have gaslight,' said Jenny. 'Then you could read in bed.'

'How long will that take?' grumbled Margaret. 'You know how he hates anything new.'

'We'll be so old you'll be speaking Latin fluently by then,' Jenny told her.

'And what will you be doing?' asked Margaret.

'Oh. I don't know,' said Jenny. She lied. She knew the path she intended to follow. Her future was mapped out. By then I'll be married, she thought, and she was pretty confident she knew the name of the lucky man.

As a careful householder John followed a nightly ritual to keep his home safe. He locked the doors, damped the fire and turned down the wick on the paraffin lamp. With a single candle he climbed the stairs. At the door to Tommy's room, he peeped in and listened to the lad's noisy breathing. Blocked noses and bad chests were common in a mining town. Very gently he closed the door. His caution was unnecessary. It would take more than the creak of a door to disturb Tommy. John doubted the boy would wake for the Last Trump.

A few more steps took him to the first-floor landing. Darkness and silence from the floor above told him the girls were asleep and their candles safely extinguished. He turned to the door of the main bedroom, a room he seldom entered. Every now and then he forced himself to check for mould, spiders and signs of gnawing rodents. It was always an ordeal for him. It was in this room that the two women he loved had slept. And one of them had died.

The brass doorknob was cold in his hand. It reminded him of that dreadful day when shrieks of pain and sounds of panic brought him to the door of the room, where Florence was in labour. A nurse, cradling a bundle of bloody sheets in her arms, burst out. He froze on the threshold. Before him was the bed, where he and Florence had made a second babe. Sudden silence surrounded him.

The doctor, in his morning coat, stood like a statue, his arms useless at his side. His haggard face announced what he lacked the voice and the courage to say. His patient was dead. The two men stood in silence, awed by the violence and the miracle of childbirth and the courage of women who endured its pains and sometimes did not survive. From a dark corner of the room came the sound of trickling water and a faint mewling cry.

Florence's first confinement had almost been the death of her. The doctors warned against another child. John did his best to avoid another pregnancy, but Florence wanted a son and was ruthless in pursuit of her ambition. She shed her stays and let down her hair. She kissed the angle of John's jaw and whispered in his ear as she opened his shirt buttons and ran her hands over his chest. She fondled the secret parts of him until he succumbed. He was not to know that giving birth to Tommy would the death of her. It was the boy that did it, the doctor explained, the size of the head.

John could not remember much afterwards. Florence's sister, Anna, arrived. Everyone comfortably assumed she would raise her sister's children. That's what families did. Someone must have arranged a funeral; it was all a blur to John. Anna took over her sister's role. Meals were prepared, the children supervised and the baby fed. She slept in the bed where her sister died. Somehow there must have been a new mattress.

Months later John climbed out of his pit of despair, to find he was sleeping in the small adjoining bedroom that Florence had planned to use as a nursery for the new baby. There was a door between the two rooms, which was now locked. At first, he found it disturbing to hear a woman in the next bedroom, the soft pad of her feet and the rustle of her clothing. Later he found it comforting to have a reminder of Florence close by, as if her shade watched over him.

Now both women were gone. John sat on the double bed, the emblem of his loss. He perched on the edge of the mattress and ran his hand over the rough ticking cover. The feather pillows were piled up in the centre like builders' rubble. With sudden resolution John took his candle and began to tour the rest of the room.

The small circle of light was too feeble for a thorough inspection but John could see there were no major problems. He went to the door that led into the small bedroom he used. Its lock was fitted with a brass key. He turned the handle. The door opened. Taking the key with its distinctive green tassel, he turned it in the lock and tested the door. It would not open.

Satisfied by his inspection he turned to leave by the door to the landing. A sudden tug of memory drew him back. He knelt and held his candle over the rug at the foot of the bed. There it was. A round brown mark where the wool pile had been scorched. A smile of reminiscence came over his face, as he ran his hand over it. He remembered the night Anna had dropped her candle. The rug smouldered. Her feet were bare; she could not stamp it out. She had called for help.

Memories of what followed flooded John's mind; the animal smell from the burning wool, the sudden powerful surge of desire, Anna's breast soft beneath his hand and her white throat half-hidden by her black hair but exposed to his kisses. Her arms enfolding him. Fate intervened. No doubt the vicar would see the hand of God in the sudden banging on the front door, the urgent shouts for it to be opened and the telegram with its urgent summons to her sick father's bedside. With an effort of the will John cleared the memory from his mind and went to his room. His body was less obedient to his will. That night it ached with longing as he lay in his single bed.

***

The town of Atherley was temporarily without a school. The Church of England school had burnt down in suspicious circumstances. Few regretted the destruction of the draughty old building, but replacing it was not a simple matter. A fierce debate raged between the ratepayers who were members of the Church of England and those who were adherents of the non-conformist churches. Their differences were not simply doctrinal. Money was at the heart of the problem. The Free Church members objected to subsidising a Church of England school their children could not attend.

Until a new school was built, the children of Atherley had to manage as best they could. The children of poor households simply spent more hours working at the little jobs they already had to contribute to the family income.

For the genteel class it was a different matter. In the Truesdale household, Margaret felt the imminence of her twelfth birthday qualified her to be the teacher. That morning she bustled about her task with enthusiasm.

'We are going to do letters,' she announced. Tommy groaned. Letters were not his strong point.

'Not A B C. Proper letters. We are going to write to Aunt Anna and ask her to come and live here.'

'Shouldn't Papa do that?' Jenny was growing tired of this bossy Margaret.

'He should. But he hasn't. I keep asking him. He just gets tetchy.'

Jenny did some counting on her fingers. 'It must be more than a week ago. Is that a decent interval?'

'Let's find out. Top right-hand corner for our address,' said Margaret.

'I know that,' snapped Jenny, 'but I think it looks better in the middle of the page.'

Margaret conceded defeat, but watched Jenny's efforts like a hawk. She could not resist warning, 'It's 'yours sincerely' at the end. With a comma.'

Jenny pulled a face and curled her arm round her piece of paper to hide it from Margaret's eyes.

'What's a comma?' asked Tommy who was drawing triangles on his slate.

The girls looked at each other and promptly dropped their squabbling to form a united front for the protection of Tommy.

'We can't let Papa see how dreadful his writing is,' hissed Jenny. 'He will send him away to school.' Their eyes grew round in horror at the thought of Tommy cast adrift without their protection.

'It's not his fault.'

'That dreadful Mr Cripps.' Both girls shuddered at the memory.

Tommy surrendered his slate and took the scrap of paper Margaret gave him. 'We'll have a practice run first,' she told him. 'It doesn't need to be a very long letter.'

There was silence while Tommy laboured at his task. Eventually he offered his letter for inspection. He did not look optimistic.

'You've got the right letters,' said Jenny, 'but they're in the wrong order.'

'They keep jiggling about.'

'They'll stop doing that one day,' said Margaret. 'I like how you say you miss her. Those Zeds are stylish.' She set out a fresh sheet of paper and told Tommy to sharpen his pencil. 'We'll keep your words but tidy up the spelling. I'll say the letters slowly. You write them down. We should get on all right. Ready? Dee, Eee, Ay, Are. New word. Ay, You, En, Tee.'

'You'd better put the odd mistake in,' said Jenny. 'Not too perfect. We want Aunt Anna to see we need her.'

'True. We'll keep the Zeds.'

After an hour of hard labour, Tommy's letter was ready.

Margaret felt it necessary to check Jenny's letter when it was finished. 'There are two spelling mistakes,' she said.

Jenny smirked. 'I know. I put them in on purpose. Like Tommy's so Aunt Anna could see how much we need her.' Margaret asked exactly which words Jenny had mis-spelt.

'Arithmetic and rabbit.' Jenny neatly side-stepped the trap Margaret had set.

'That's a nice touch. Reminding her about the blue rabbit.'

Tommy's ears pricked up at mention of the rabbit his aunt had given him; he felt her absence deeply. 'Why did Aunt Anna go? Were we naughty?'

'No.' Jenny's voice was emphatic. 'Papa was very strong about that. It was not our fault. He said it was her duty to go. She didn't want to leave. It was her duty. He kept saying that word 'duty'. You know what grown-ups are like about duty.'

They nodded glumly. They knew all about duty. Duty sent you to a cold church on winter Sundays, duty made you learn your tables and how to spell difficult words you never used. Sometimes it compelled teachers to punish you in painful ways: rulers whacked on outstretched palms, leather straps slapped against bare legs. They always claimed it gave them no pleasure; they were just doing their duty. You couldn't help wondering though.

'She had to go to nurse her own father. She left that blue rabbit she'd made in your bed.'

'It's not really blue any more but I still like it. Are lessons over? We're building a den in Moffat's Wood.' Tommy felt the need for his friends and fresh air; he'd had enough brain work.

'Ask Hannah,' said Margaret.

Hannah accepted that Tommy should go to join his friends. The girls were not allowed to wander freely. They had to help with the work of the house. They could run errands, but that was all.

'I've made scones,' said Hannah to sweeten the pill of housework.

John took the news that they had written to Anna with outward stoicism. He said he would look through their letters that evening. Margaret's was a flawless letter of formal condolence full of pious platitudes. Jenny hoped

Anna would not have to wear black for too long and bragged that she was managing the household accounts. Tommy's letter was a small masterpiece of childish longing and spelling mistakes.

Margaret folded the three letters and found an envelope. She put out a sheet of paper for John to write his letter of condolence to his sister-in-law.

'Later. I'll do it later. I need to think what to say.' He lit the paraffin lamp and they settled down to their usual occupations: John behind his newspaper, Margaret pretending to knit and Jenny mending the trousers Tommy had ripped while out climbing trees. Tommy himself, spent his customary half an hour on the hearthrug reliving the afternoon game of pirates and wishing he had a dog.

When the young ones had gone to their beds, the blank sheet of writing paper reproached John from the table as he wrestled with his thoughts. While he longed for the warmth of Anna's presence in his home and the comfort she brought to his children, he dreaded the torment he would endure from his desire to possess her.

He read her letter again. There might be some small nugget of information that would solve his dilemma. Seek and you will find. It appeared Anna's financial situation was precarious. The Post Office business she had inherited from her father had been transferred into the name of her late husband. George had inconsiderately died without making a will. His son, from his first marriage, would inherit two thirds of his father's estate and the Post Office franchise. John pictured Anna in poverty, cold, hungry and downtrodden by a stepson as avaricious as his father.

John's way was suddenly clear. Anna was in need of protection. Was it not his duty to support her? A man should support his female relations. Everyone knew that. Anna was family, his late wife's sister. It was his duty to invite her to live in his home. How wonderful that duty insisted he should do what he so longed to do; it was seldom so obliging.

He thought of the letter he would like to write to Anna. He wanted to say how he missed her– the full-throated laugh, the flashing smile, and her delight in small things from the sparrows pecking breadcrumbs on the windowsill to the scent of flowers in the hall. Anna always had flowers in the house; they never enjoyed their brief presence now. He longed to tell her that he loved her and wanted to marry her.

That was an impossible ambition. The law prevented him from marrying Anna. Parliament, no doubt with the best of intentions, prohibited such a marriage. Death in childbirth was not uncommon. It was accepted that the woman's sister, if single, would take over the role of the late mother, usually coming to live in the home of the widower. To protect her reputation, and no doubt, on occasions, her person, the Dead Wife's Sister Marriage Act was passed in 1835 declaring such a relationship to be forbidden by law. It would deter the widower from molesting the sister. No man wants to be accused of incest.

John knew he could not be Anna's husband, but he could be her brother. He could offer her the shelter of his home as a brother would. Could he keep to the narrow path of virtue? Could he be close to her without stretching out a hand to stroke her hair or leaning over to kiss her cheek? He pictured himself in his chaste bed in the little bedroom while lay Anna next door, naked between the sheets in the big double bed with nothing but a locked door between them. Was a key with a green tassel enough to keep them apart?

Monks manage to live celibate lives, John told himself. The world was full of single men who could not afford to marry. Many were wary of the risks that came with the prostitutes who thronged the city streets. They managed. If the price for having Anna close was celibacy, he decided he would pay it. She was worth it.

Accordingly, he wrote her a letter of formal condolence and offered her the protection of his home at this time of distress. He gave his word of honour that they would live as brother and sister and vowed she would be treated with the respect she deserved for looking after his motherless children. He regretted that he had on one occasion overstepped the bounds of proper behaviour. He vowed it would never happen again. The message was stiff, cold and deeply uninviting. He put the children's letters in with his, relying on them to tug her heartstrings and bring her to him.

****

Tommy's friends were not the kind of boys to ring the front doorbell. They naturally went to the back door. There, they clustered in the porch and draped themselves on the door frame. They would poke their heads into the kitchen in the hope that Hannah might have a spare scone or two. When the doorbell rang, that day it was Tommy who beat his sisters to the front door.

On the step was a gangly blonde lad with a bicycle. He was wearing the cap of a telegraph boy – and a wide grin. 'All right then,' he demanded of Tommy. It wasn't a question, so much as a statement. He defied you to disagree with him that all was well with the world.

'Aye.' Tommy's accent grew stronger to mirror the older boy. 'What you doin' with a bike, Edward Carter? You nicked it?'

'Nah'. A grin flashed across the older boy's face and he strengthened his grip on the handlebars as if threatened with its loss. Both boys looked down with approval and longing at the machine. 'T'aint mine. I'm just giving Johny Hodgson a hand. He's a telegraph boy. New to the job. S'been up this hill three times already this morning and he's knackered.'

They looked down the road to see a small figure in navy blue trudging up the slope. 'Said I'd get his bike up here then he can free wheel back down. Give him a break.' They watched the boy's slow progress. 'Not sure it's the right job for him,' said Edward. 'His chest's bad.'

Jenny arrived with her customary speed and silence. Margaret was close behind her. The girls did not leave Tommy unsupervised for long.

'Hey up, it's Spinning Jenny,' said Edward and doffed the telegraph boy's cap with an elegant bow. Jenny glared at him; her eyes dark with hostility; she was tired of all the reminders of Arkwright's invention that started the industrial revolution

Tommy took the cap from Edward to give it an experimental wearing. Could he be a telegraph boy? Would the letters stop jiggling about long enough to let him read the addresses? The sound of gasping breaths told them the official telegraph boy had arrived. He held out his hand for his cap.

'He only let me borrow the cap,' said Edward. 'He wouldn't trust me with the telegram.'

'More than my job's worth,' gasped the telegraph boy as he fished a buff envelope from the leather purse on the belt round his waist. 'It's for your father,' he said as he handed it to Tommy, by-passing Jenny's outstretched hand.

Edward handed back the bicycle. 'Let's hope that's your last trip up this hill. Gentry must've sorted out who's coming to tea and the Liverpool price of cotton by now.' He gestured to the top of the hill, the leafy heights, where the wealthy lived. The higher your income the further above the smoke and grime of the cotton mills and the coal mines you lived.

Tommy took the telegram to his father. The blonde boy took a discreet departure. 'Ter-rah then.' He waved in farewell.

As she saw the sweep of Edward's arm, Jenny felt a strange warm glow settle round her heart. It was a new sensation that only happened when she thought of Edward Carter, or his thick wavy hair or his disarming grin. She placed her hand where she thought her heart was. Another new sensation - two soft pads of flesh on her chest that had not been there before. She shivered. Strange things were happening; she would be glad if Anna came; she could ask her about them.

Tommy held the telegram by the corner as if it was a homemade bomb. First a black-bordered letter. Now a telegram.

John tore the buff envelope open and saw scrawled in green ink, 'Pleased to accept offer. Arrive tomorrow 6 pm.'

There was no time to speculate. Arrangements had to be made for Aunt Anna's accommodation. The fire in the big bedroom was lit and the pillows pummelled and plumped before the crisp white sheet was smoothed over the mattress. Jenny helped Hannah bake a cake and watched as she put a fat capon to roast.

Their father lined them up for inspection before they set off to the station. He tweaked their coats and scarves and checked their hands were clean.

'No rushing to hug your Aunt', he warned them. 'Remember she is newly widowed and will be in mourning. It would not be seemly for you to jump about with joy in public at this time.

They nodded, their faces serious. I am such a hypocrite, thought their father. It is me who wants to rush to Anna and hold her in my arms and devour her with kisses. He pictured the effect of such behaviour on the platform at Atherley railway station. The frisson of horror that would sweep through the passengers, the women reaching for their smelling salts, and hiding small children's faces against their skirts to conceal such debauchery from their innocent eyes. Men would brandish their umbrellas and mutter, 'Scoundrel.'

The youngsters' solemnity did not last long. The excitement of going to the railway station soon chased it away. They trooped down the hill while Tommy speculated on the colour of the engine. He hoped it would be a shiny red or green and not just one of those serviceable black ones.

When it arrived, the engine was a flashing scarlet with gleaming brass pistons. It breathed out smoke as it made its stately progress to the buffers. A few hisses of steam escaped and the brakes squealed when it reached its resting place. The porters rushed to open the doors and the passengers started to emerge from their separate compartments.

John was the first to spot Anna; he had concentrated his search on the second-class compartments. He guessed that she would be reluctant to endure the rigours of third class, but would find first class too expensive. As soon as he saw her at the open door of the compartment, he lunged through the crowd towards her. He could not stop himself. Tommy was hot on his heels.

Margaret was thoroughly confused. She had expected to see a widow, covered from head to foot in dense black, standing out like a crow on a lawn. What she saw was a flock of them. Safe behind their black veils, widows were scorning the convention of a male escort. Now in full control of their own money, they were grasping the opportunities for travel the railways offered them.

'Where is Papa going?' demanded Margaret in a sudden panic. He was rushing against the tide of travellers and heading down the platform.

Jenny laid a calming hand on her arm. 'It's Aunt Anna.'

Margaret wished she could see more clearly. She could only just make out her father. His right hand was held out to a slender figure with a stylish black hat. His other hand lay heavily on Tommy's shoulder, like a policeman with a suspect under arrest. Margaret was not to know that it was the only way John could restrain his arm from embracing the woman in front of him.

'It can't be her,' Margaret pronounced with unaccustomed conviction. 'That's not a widow.'

'She is in black. But it's not that dreadful sooty stuff.'

Their father still had an iron hand on Tommy's shoulder as he guided their aunt towards the girls. Although dressed entirely in black, Aunt Anna did not look like a widow, as even the short-sighted Margaret had noticed. It was Jenny who discerned that her aunt's dress had the dull sheen of silk and that her short cape swirled flirtatiously about her shoulders in a far from mournful manner. Mindful of their father's instructions both girls stood rooted to the spot like little soldiers.

Anna quickly took charge of the proceedings. 'John would you be so good as to see to my trunk. It's a navy blue one.'

Restored to sanity by having a specific task, John immediately set off to investigate the pile of trunks the porters were building on a trolley. Freed from his father's iron grip Tommy, staggered briefly. Anna took hold of his hand. 'Now my most favourite boy in the whole world must be my male escort.' Tommy stood upright and looked suitably serious. She kissed the cheeks of each girl in turn and took a moment to smile into their eyes. 'I have missed you both. We have much to talk about.'

Something that had been suppressed for too long rose up in each girl. It hovered in the air for a moment before departing upwards, like a plume of smoke. It took with it some of the tensions in their minds and left them with a promise of resolution. There had come into their lives something they had not been aware they lacked, female intimacy.

By this time John had found the trunk. The porter trundled it on his trolley to the cab stand. There the cab driver and the porter loaded it on the back of the cab. The girls climbed in and settled themselves either side of their aunt. John sat, smiling but thoughtful with Tommy next to him. A cab-runner set off behind them in the hope of being paid to help lift the trunk up the stairs.

It was a rare treat for the children to drive through the town and it was over too soon. At the foot of the steep hill they had to get out and walk. 'For the sake of th'orse,' as the cab driver put it. When the cabbie stopped at their modest home, he pulled the brake up tight to stop the cab rolling back down.

'You should call it halfway house,' the cabbie told them, as he went to unfasten the ropes that held the trunk. He gestured to the big mansions at the top of the hill and then turned towards the cramped and smoky town below. 'You is like the meat in the sandwich here. The tasty bit in the middle.'

John followed the unspoken agreement that those who are paid for reading and writing, don't do heavy lifting even when they are perfectly capable of doing so; they pay others to do it. He offered the cab-runner a coin. The man checked and found it acceptable. The two men took hold of the trunk.

'Upstairs, governor?'

John nodded.

Once in the house Aunt Anna hugged them all – except John - with greater freedom than she had shown at the railway station. Tommy threw his arms round her waist and buried his face against her bosom. To tell the truth he shed a few tears there; the others pretended not to notice. Hannah came from the kitchen and she too was hugged.

'Oh Miss Anna, it is good to have you back.' When she realised what she had said, the apologies started to pour out of her. First, she squirmed for ignoring the sad death of the husband and then for forgetting her married status by calling her Miss Anna.

'Mrs. Anna doesn't sound right.' They all agreed on that.

They ate the chicken with roast potatoes and afterwards had tea round the fire. When they could eat no more a silence fell that was difficult to break. Anna solved the problem by lifting the lid of the piano.

'We have run out of things to say so we shall have some music. Then perhaps you can sing.'

The youngsters stared in horror. They were too old for nursery rhymes. The only time they sang was in church. They didn't particularly enjoy it; the prospect of singing hymns at their own fireside mortified them. That was what chapel people did. They were Church of England.

'Fear not. I shall teach you a song that is not a hymn.'

John twitched as if in protest. 'Don't worry,' Anna said. 'It is perfectly respectable.' She pressed her fingers on the keys and listened to the result –a dreadful jangle of notes. They all started to giggle. She played on for a few moments relishing the cacophony produced by the neglected instrument. For a finale she played a huge clashing chord. The giggles turned into gales of laughter.

'When was this piano last tuned?' she demanded.

John looked sheepish as he confessed the instrument had not been touched since she left. His conscience pricked him; girls were supposed to learn to play the piano, weren't they?

'It will keep till later,' said Aunt Anna, smiling. The piano had served its purpose; it had broken the ice. Soon it was time for bed.

The girls lit their candles and wished their father and aunt goodnight. 'This has been an amazing day,' said Aunt Anna as she patted them fondly.

John took a candle and lit Tommy's way to bed. On his return he found Anna sitting alone on the couch by the fire. How it pleased him to have this woman at his hearth and in his home. He could hold her dear to his heart. That much was permitted to him. There was space to sit next to her on the sofa, but he chose an armchair some distance away.

He spoke across the room to her. 'I am so pleased you have agreed to come. I hope you will find a pleasant refuge here. There will be many practical matters for us to discuss. For tonight let us just enjoy sharing the same roof.' A strong emotion clawed its way onto his face. With an effort he controlled it. With a stern expression and a distant voice, he said, 'There will be no repetition of my dishonourable approach to you. I give you my word.'

She looked at him intently. For a moment he thought she would speak. She simply smiled and picked up her needlework. Being a man of his time, he took her silence for agreement.

Anna found the Truesdale house was eerily unchanged from the one she left in haste when her father was taken ill. Only the children had changed. As young things will, they had grown. The furniture, undisturbed for so long, had put down roots. The same ugly orange vase stood empty on the same crocheted mat on the sideboard. The net curtains skulked beneath three more years of grime and dust lay thick on the piano. The place definitely needed a woman's touch.

Like every new boss, keen to establish her authority, Anna decided to introduce some changes. She consulted Hannah who had done sterling work for many years, looking after the children and cooking their meals. They agreed a redistribution of work. Hannah swept old tea leaves into the carpets to clean them and polished the furniture with a mixture of linseed oil and vinegar while Anna mastered the vagaries of the kitchen range. The gleam soon returned to the house and appetising smells came from the kitchen.

Anna discovered John's dislike of their regular Friday fare of flabby white fish. Lancashire might be wet and grimy but it was the birthplace of the fish and chip shop. Atherley was proud of theirs. They cooked fish in great vats of oil heated by jets of gas.

'A job for Tommy,' said Anna and sent him down to the warm steamy shop. He scampered back with their supper wrapped in newspaper under his arm.

The household accounts were next to come under Anna's scrutiny. Jenny, who was quick at arithmetic, had noticed how much they spent on coal. 'We must keep an eye on it,' said Anna.

The next time the coal merchant's great horse heaved to a stop at their door they were quick to answer the bell. On the doorstep stood a humped-back black goblin that turned out to be a man with a hundredweight sack of coal slung on his back, ready to pour into their cellar. Where the wealthy kept their wine, the Truesdales stored their coal. It helped keep some of the insidious black dust out of the house and their lungs. Anna and Jenny ostentatiously counted the number of times the coalman wrestled a sack from his shoulders and tipped its contents into the open maw of the cellar.

'That's five hundredweights,' said Anna and made a note in her accounts book. 'I bet this lasts longer than the last lot. I'm sure he was short-changing us.'

After a couple of months of careful housekeeping Anna raised the tricky question of money with John. Was she spending too much? Should she economise? John agreed a generous amount for monthly expenditure. There would be enough to cover Anna's personal expenses - what a wife would call 'pin money'. He urged her to consult him about any major purchases that became necessary or desirable. Then he relaxed, sat back, and enjoyed all creature comforts a wife could provide – with one exception.

The rag and bone man took the ugly orange vase and Anna bought flowers to fill its place.

'John,' said Anna one evening after the children had gone to bed. Something in her voice made him prick his ears up. He laid his newspaper aside. He had a feeling this was going to be expensive.

'John,' she said again. It was definitely going to be expensive. 'The children need new clothes. It was easy when they were little. People handed on the clothes their children had outgrown. That doesn't happen so much anymore. There are always younger brothers and sisters waiting for the next size up. Tommy's trousers are a disgrace and the girls' dresses are tight. Jenny has let her bodice out as far as it will go.'

There was only one affordable way of providing the children with new clothes. Anna, with help from the girls, would have to make them.

'I have looked all over for Florence's sewing machine, but cannot find it. I cannot believe she did not have one.'

John squirmed uneasily in his chair. 'She didn't have one.' It was too painful to explain that he had wasted the money on a bicycle. He sought refuge behind his newspaper.

At breakfast Anna announced that they were to have new clothes. Margaret wailed with dismay. 'I can see what is coming. Hours and hours of hem stitching, back stitching and making buttonholes. My eyes will be too tired to read.'

'Well, Margaret,' said Anna, 'you'll be pleased to know that my sewing machine is on its way here. It is so heavy it had to come by the carrier. You will find it saves hours of work.'

They spent a happy time, and John's money, choosing fabric. The mills that pounded day and night ensured a variety of choice. Margaret dithered so long that Jenny lost patience and told her grey would suit her best. She knew Margaret liked to blend into the background. For herself she chose a deep blue that brought out the colour of her eyes.

The Singer sewing machine arrived in a wooden crate packed with straw and wood-shavings. The hefty little machine looked unexpectedly frivolous. It had rounded curves; its shiny black enamel was painted with green leaves and colourful flowers. In spite of its feminine appearance, it worked fast and tirelessly. Jenny watched entranced as the needle flew up and down, chugging its way along the seams. She quickly mastered the technique of feeding the fabric with one hand while turning the wheel with the other.

For two weeks the sewing machine took pride of place on the dining table. It was only moved to make way for their evening meal. The rest of the time they were busy unpicking old garments and pressing them flat to use as patterns for new dresses. Extra inches were added and carefully cut round in the new fabric. Margaret tried hard but was positively dangerous with a pair of scissors in her hand. In the end they decided her best contribution would be reading to them as they worked.

When their dresses were complete and their underwear had reached a quantity that Anna deemed adequate, she turned her attention to the men of the house. Tommy was still young enough to have his clothes made by women so they set about learning to make trousers and shirts. John's suits were made by a male tailor. It was not thought suitable for women to be involved in the measuring and fitting of men's clothes. They were confined to making waistcoats and buttonholes.

John was surprised one evening when Anna presented him with a brand-new linen shirt she had made from scratch. It was a long time since anyone had given him a present. He was on his feet with his arms out to embrace her before he remembered such contact was forbidden.

'I hope now you will look more kindly on new-fangled machinery,' she teased him. 'This particular machine has saved you a great deal of money and me and the girls a great deal of time.' A sheepish John had to admit the sewing machine had proved its worth.

In the absence of a functioning school the children had grown used to pleasing themselves during the many hours their father was away at work. Anna decided that had to stop. 'We will find out what is happening about the school in the town,' she told them. 'In the meantime, you have to keep in practice. When school starts again it will not be so hard for you.'

'If only,' Tommy muttered but would not elaborate when Anna cocked an enquiring eyebrow at him.

'So washed, dressed and breakfasted by nine o'clock and at the table ready to start work.'

'What will we learn?' asked Margaret, reluctant to lose her role of teacher. Much as she liked her aunt, she did not think of her as a teacher. She suspected there had been no schools in the olden days when her aunt was a child.

Anna was not flummoxed by the question. 'The next thing,' she announced with apparent confidence. 'You will learn the next thing.'

'She wants to learn Latin,' Jenny scoffed.

'That is not impossible. I do not know it, but I am sure we can find a good book on the subject.'

Margaret fell silent. At last, someone was taking her desire to learn Latin seriously.

'How long will lessons last?' asked Tommy. He looked anxious. All those letters that wriggled and jiggled about on the page. Anna told him to keep his friends from calling at the door until after their dinner at noon. 'You will be free to play with your friends in the afternoon,' she told him. 'Until it is dark. There will be jobs for you to do when you get back.'

'Such as?' he enquired suspiciously. Jenny and Margaret were shocked by his cheek. As girls they never questioned that there would be jobs to do around the house. Their friends were not free to come knocking at the door; they were too closely supervised and too busy helping their mothers.

Anna was prepared for this moment; she had an ace up her sleeve. 'Fires,' she told him crisply. 'You will be in charge of fires. You can build them and light them. And you will be responsible for poking them and keeping them going or damping them down as the case may be.'

'Do I get to use matches?'

'Obviously.'

Tommy swooned with joy.

'In fact, that will be one of our first lessons. The use of matches. You girls must learn as well. And all about the dangers of fire.' Anna had seen John's anxiety on the subject. She hoped to lessen his fear by tackling the subject head on.

Without more ado, they trooped off to build a fire in Anna's bedroom. She showed them how to fold pages of old newspaper into firelighters and to crisscross slender sticks to build a framework for small pieces of coal. They did not set light to it; you only had a fire in your bedroom if you were ill, very ill.

Next, they went downstairs to the kitchen where Tommy practised striking matches and lit a candle.

Jenny proved she could deal with matches. 'I've done it before. I lit the paraffin lamp when your letter with the black edges came. Papa's hand was shaking.'

'Is that so?' said Anna and gazed into space for a long moment. 'Now it's your turn, Margaret. You must strike a match and light a candle.' The girl was nervous so it took several goes before the match burst into flame. Mesmerised by watching the flame devour its little wooden stick she left it too late to blow it out. The flame touched her fingers. She squealed with pain and dropped the match on the stone floor. Tommy stamped his boot on it to squash the final flickers.

'You see now why I brought you into the kitchen where the floor is of stone,' Anna told them. 'There is nothing here for the fire to take hold of. Carpets and curtains are a different matter. And skirts. Now you are wearing longer skirts, you must remember to keep well back from the fire. It is so easy for skirts and petticoats to go up in flames.'

'That's all very well,' complained Margaret, 'but what would we do if we did catch fire and there was no Tommy here with his boots on to stamp it out?'

''Take good care it doesn't happen. Prevention is better than cure,' said Anna. As she well knew, bare feet cannot stamp out a fire and a man will come if he hears a woman shriek in fear. The brown mark on the bedroom rug was proof of that.

Anna quickly established a routine that was both humane and challenging. At regular intervals throughout the morning she sat and chanted spellings with Tommy. 'Tee Aitch Ee spells 'the', Em Ay Kay Ee spells 'make'. Saying the letters out loud helped him remember them. They stopped jiggling about so much.

Jenny mastered the imperial system of weights and measures and the complexities of pounds, shillings and pence; they were vital tools in a woman's ability to run a household. Anna alerted her to the tricks that tradesmen used to increase their profit and taught her to judge by sight when you received a fair measure. What does a pound of butter look like? Will a joint of topside serve six hungry people? How much is a hundredweight of coal? And more importantly, how long will it last?

The local bookshop provided a copy of Kennedy's Latin Primer which sent Margaret into a heaven of delight. While Tommy chanted spellings, she recited declensions and conjugated verbs. Amo, amas, amat, amamus, amate, amant. The lack of a teacher did not concern her. She had the right book. The girl was unaware that Mr. Kennedy's daughters had written much of the book. How it would have pleased them to see Margaret devour its contents

Anna raised concerns about how close to her nose, Margaret held her work. How she screwed up her eyes and suffered from headaches. Could the girl need glasses? The possessor of perfect eyesight himself, John was dismissive. He regarded spectacles as an accessory of old age, like ear trumpets and walking sticks. Anyway, ladies didn't wear glasses.

'You sound very confident of that fact,' said Anna gently.

Conscientiously John scoured his memory for a woman in spectacles. 'No,' he announced. 'Never seen one.'

'Have you ever seen a woman reading? Outside of your home that is.'

When John mixed in society the women were busy smiling, offering refreshments, listening attentively; and giving their attention to him, not the printed word. He conceded the point. They would see if Margaret would benefit from spectacles.

'They may help her to stop screwing her face up,' said Anna, 'but nothing is going to stop her reading.'

In the brief winter afternoons Anna and the youngsters would brave the cold and walk into town. Sometimes they would call on their father in his wood-panelled office in the Town Hall. It was not always possible to see him. His assistant would explain in a hushed voice that there was a grieving relative with him. They would tiptoe out again.

'Are you a grieving widow, Aunt Anna?' asked Tommy. The girls shushed him.

'Yes. Though to be honest I am more an aggrieved widow than a grieving one.'

'What does that mean?' For once there was a word that Margaret did not know.

'It means that I feel that I have been badly treated.'

'Fate was unkind,' said Jenny, 'taking your husband after such a short time.'

'Mmmm. You could think of it like that.' Anna did not encourage sentimentality in girls. There was too much of it about. 'My complaint is not against the laws of nature. My complaint is against the law of the land which has given the greater part of my husband's money to his son. Technically he is my stepson but I don't feel very motherly towards him.'

'Why should he have it? That sounds very unfair. Is there anything you can do about it?' asked Margaret.

'No,' said Anna. She sighed as she remembered George's whingeing complaints that he was not master in his own house. In a moment of weakness, she had signed the business over to him. It was the kind of thing her mother approved of.

Anna recovered herself and spoke briskly. 'The laws of inheritance favour sons over wives. There's a warning for you girls there. Take good notice of it.'

Anna still had a small inheritance from her father in her own name. A sliver of doubt had warned her to keep its existence secret from George. Although George was safely in his grave, Anna intended to keep that particular secret a little longer. Once bitten, twice shy.

John provided her with a comfortable home and the minor expenses of life; she felt she earned it by helping to bring up his children and running the household. It was an honourable exchange. She had not told John of her small store of money; given the way the world was organised, women needed every weapon they could lay their hands on.

'I hope to sort matters out without using lawyers. They cost so much,' she said cheerfully.

'You won't be an aggrieved widow then,' said Margaret to test out the new word she had learned.

'That's right,' said Anna. I've never really been a grieving one, she thought, but did not say. She looked at their young and cheerful faces. The sight drove away the memory of her half-hearted venture into matrimony.

Whilst Anna dealt with his children and his household, John was busy about his duties as the Registrar for Atherly. His day was full of the unexpected. The knock on his door gave him no warning of the caller's purpose. He kept his face expressionless until he knew whether to display discreet sympathy for the bereaved, a benign smile to a new father or cheery congratulations to an intending husband. On this afternoon, however, a hot needle of rage pierced his control. He could not stop the anger clouding his face.

'Not another one!' spat from his lips.

The Superintendent of the Workhouse flinched as from a blow. He recovered quickly and began reciting his excuses. 'Not my fault the babe died. T'were sickly from start. The cold finished it off.'

'This is the third child in four weeks. And it's only November.'

'Tell that t' Town Council. Tell 'em t'give us more coal.'

The authorities were not without fault, but John would not let the Superintendent shift all the blame onto them. He went for a different angle of attack – a stab at the man's heart. 'I'd like to have a word with the mother. Is she here?'

The Superintendent took a great gulp of breath before answering. 'She knows nowt about it. She's in a grand house over Tilton way. Wet nurse to some posh family.' He stopped, looked down at his cap as if for guidance, and folded it lengthwise in his hands. 'I'm on my way to tell her when I've finished here.'

The room went cold. The two men fell silent. John cleared his throat and asked, 'How long has she been there?'

'Best part offa fortnight.'

John looked at the date of the child's birth. 'The boy was barely a month old.'

'Aye. That's how it's done. Wean the child at fourteen days. Then mother goes where the money is.'

'And who looks after her child?'

'Oh. Wimmin do that. I know nowt about that.'

John leant over his mahogany desk and stared intently at the Superintendent. He spoke slowly and with menace. 'I suggest you find out about it very quickly. The good people of this town do not pay their rates to let the poor starve and their children die of cold.'

The Superintendent bit back his protest. John had been elected as a Guardian of the Poor by the townspeople to help supervise the running of the Workhouse; he had power over the Superintendent's livelihood.

John stroked his beard and gazed at the ceiling. He projected an image of a man gazing upwards for guidance as he weighed the pros and cons of a difficult decision. Which side would he come down on?

John came to his conclusion and turned to the Superintendent who twisted his cap in his hands as if to wring water out of it.

'If these deaths of infants continue,' said John, 'I shall call in the authorities. There will have to be a thorough investigation.'

The Superintendent gaped. He had a vision of the Board of Guardians sticking their bony noses into the nooks and crannies of his premises, asking questions and meddling in his accounts.

John took a moment to enjoy watching the Superintendent wriggle on the hook he had baited. 'Indeed,' he said, as if struck by a cheering thought, 'I could send a note to the doctor now. Ask him to pay a visit and check all the inmates. In case it is an infectious disease. We don't want an epidemic.'

The thought of the doctor's bill spurred the Superintendent into action. 'Whoa now, Mr Truesdale. Let's not be hasty. I dare say I could make a few – er – changes, get a bit more coal and such-like.'

'Shouldn't be too difficult. We do live in a coal-mining town.'

'As you, say, Mr Truesdale, as you say.'

'So, more coal.'

The Superintendent scowled but made no objection. 'And soap,' added John, while he was winning

The Superintendent looked puzzled.

'You must buy soap. The coal will heat water as well as the people. Use it to give the place a good scrub down. We all know that dirt breeds disease.' He had the man down so he kicked him for good measure. 'And soup. I think the inmates should have hot soup in cold weather.'

The Superintendent opened his mouth to protest at such extravagance. 'Cheaper than a doctor,' said John and picked up his pen as if about to write a note requesting some expensive medical expertise.

The Superintendent's shoulders sagged. 'As you say, Mr Truesdale. Coal and soap.' John dipped his pen in the ink and raised an enquiring eyebrow at the Superintendent.

'And soup,' muttered the man out of the corner of his mouth. He smoothed out his cap, ready to take his leave. 'Goodnight, Mr Truesdale.'

John nodded in dismissal. 'See to it. Take care you have no cause to visit my office again this side of Christmas.'

The Superintendent grunted and slunk away.

John did not envy the Superintendent his errand. He pictured telling a mother her baby was no more, while she held a stranger's child to her breast. He shook his head to rid himself of the distressing image. He picked up his coat and hat. As he locked the door behind him, he smiled with satisfaction; he was pleased he had asked the Superintendent for three things. It was a racing certainty he would provide only two of them. He'd wager a sovereign it would be the soap that was forgotten.

On Sunday John took the children and Anna to the morning service in their usual church, the Church of England. It was an essential step in establishing her presence in the neighbourhood. He introduced her to the vicar by her married name. Mrs. Mainwaring – pronounced Mannering. He emphasised her status as Florence's sister to strangle any romantic fantasies, sly speculations and vicious gossip at birth. Everyone knew a man could not marry his dead wife's sister. The act that prevented John from marrying the woman he loved, enabled her to live in his house without scandal.

The matrons of the town breathed a collective sigh of relief. This new widow was no threat; John could stay on their list of available bachelors for a sister or a niece in need of a husband.

Society followed its usual customs. John's office as Registrar entitled him to be a member of what used to be the gentry, but was now the middle-class. Like all new creations they were touchy about their status and followed the old ways of the aristocracy with anxious care. It was an iron-clad rule that new arrivals must wait for the locals to visit them. It was not long before established residents began to leave cards at the Truesdale house.

It was Anna's task to return these calls; she took the girls with her. Tommy was excused on the grounds of being male. Anna started with the families who were members of the Church of England. With the girls she climbed the hill to knock on the doors of the big villas. She presented her card to the maid who opened the door. The maid disappeared with the card, to see if the mistress of the house was at home or not.

'Some people may think we are not quite gentry enough for them,' Anna warned the girls. 'Although I feel I am gentry, we are definitely among the poorer ones. Some houses may feel we do not have sufficient means to be worthy of their acquaintance. They may just return my card. We will not know until we try. We are respectable and we know how to behave. What more can they ask?'

'And we have such smart new clothes,' added Jenny, looking down with approval at her new navy-blue dress.

If the maid returned to say that the mistress was indeed at home, they would make their way to the drawing room. Sometimes there was tea and cakes. Jenny took the opportunity to inspect the china and compare their sponge cakes with her own while Margaret examined the bookshelves.

On these days Anna took care to dress completely in black. 'Mrs. George Mainwaring,' the maid would say, pronouncing the name as it was spelt on the card. Anna's late husband had been very fussy about the pronunciation of his name. 'It is Mannering,' he would snap at some unfortunate domestic. Unlike George, Anna did not correct the maid.

From the snippets of information, she picked up on these jaunts it quickly became clear that the real power in the town did not lie with the Established Church. It was the adherents of the Free Churches who held the reins of government. A certain Mr Kenneth Woodward was at the top of that pecking order. He was the owner of several coal mines and cotton mills, a town councillor, a former mayor, and a lay preacher. A man of substantial means, he was generous to charities.

His wife, a lady from Southport, reigned as queen of Methodist society. While Mr Woodward was known for his charitable works, his wife was famous for her uncharitable opinions; she was a fearless critic in matters of manners and morality. From the styling of your hair to the state of your marriage, Mrs. Woodward had something to say. It was seldom flattering. Atherley was inevitably inferior to the elegant seaside town of her birth.

Anna took the precaution of writing to ask Mrs. Woodward if she might call. She explained that she was newly returned to the town and would be grateful for advice on schooling for her sister's children. Mrs. Woodward could not resist the appeal to her superior knowledge. Word came back that Mrs. Woodward was at home on the third Tuesday of the month. A well-written letter loaded with flattery can open many doors.

On that Tuesday Mrs. Woodward was having a difficult day. Her daughter, Dorothea, had announced a desire to wear her new dress with pink ruffles. Mrs. Woodward declared it too good for an at home when only very ordinary people would be coming.

'How ordinary?' demanded Dorothea.

'Very ordinary. Some aunt to the Truesdale girls. She will bring them with her; she wants to know about the school. Their father's not very important. Their only claim to fame is that one of the girls is a foundling.'

'What's a foundling?' demanded Dorothea.

'Oh. it's a child that's been abandoned by its mother.'

The idea of a child who escaped her parents' endless attention appealed to Dorothea. 'Left behind like an umbrella?' she asked.

Mrs. Woodward struggled to frame a charitable answer; she did not want the word 'bastard' to sully the ears of her innocent daughter. 'An unfortunate mother sometimes leaves a child where it will be found. On a doorstep. At an orphanage.' A vague memory floated at the back of her mind. 'This time it was different. It was the father who left the child.' She gazed at the ceiling as she struggled to recall an elusive detail. 'Something to do with a bicycle.'

'Do tell, Mama. Do tell.'

'Oh it must be ten years ago. You couldn't have been more than three at the time.' Mrs. Woodward dated all events by the age of her daughter. 'Mrs. Truesdale was alive then. She took the child in. Wouldn't hear of it going to the Workhouse. It was kind of her.'

Dorothea was not thinking about the kindness of the Truesdales. She was thinking about bicycles. She had seen boys and men on bicycles flashing past the carriage, when they had to stop to rest the horse. Perhaps one day she might be able to ride one.

'She died soon after, having a son. Mrs. Truesdale, that is.' Mrs. Woodward's eyes went misty as the shades of the sons who might have been hers fluttered past. The daughter, who most definitely existed, demanded, 'Which one's the foundling?'

Mrs. Woodward could not remember. She did not know their names. Though she grieved for the boys who had gone, in her heart she was pleased not to have added to her stock of daughters. One was enough.

The maid came in to dress the mother's hair. Dorothea was not diverted from her own ambitions for the day by the story of the foundling. 'Get my new dress out. The one with the pink ruffles,' she commanded. The maid, comb in hand, looked to Mrs. Woodward for confirmation.

'All right,' said the so-called mistress of the house. When the maid had gone, Mrs. Woodward turned to Dorothea. 'You can wear the dress but there is to be no singing. This is a ladies' tea party not a musical evening.' Dorothea pouted and went to put on the ruffled dress. She had won the first battle. She would tackle the problem of singing later.

When the maid returned to finish her hair, Mrs. Woodward sent her down to lock the piano and bring the key back. This left little time for finishing touches to her coiffure. When she went down to receive her guests, Mrs. Woodward was not completely happy with the arrangement of her hair.

At this moment Anna and the girls were presenting themselves on the front steps of Mr Woodward's mansion. As Anna rang the bell, she refused to let the impressive porch with its Doric columns and shining brass letter box daunt her. The steps glowed in the afternoon sun. A maid must have spent considerable time on her knees, scrubbing them clean before finishing them with a donkey stone. There was no other way to achieve such a perfect creamy finish.

The Truesdale contingent was ushered into a drawing room, stuffed with dark furniture that loomed menacingly over them. Between the mammoth of the grand piano and the grizzly bears of the china cabinets lurked spider-legged tables loaded with vases, ornaments and photographs. They lay in wait for some unsuspecting prey to blunder into them.

Anna was relieved when she arrived at her hostess without mishap; it did not last long. Mrs. Woodward was a stout little body of a woman with sharp black eyes buried in her round face like currants in a bun. Her penetrating gaze travelled slowly over Anna. It ignored her smile and concentrated on her clothing; Anna was clad entirely in the compulsory black.

Mrs. Woodward' gave a brisk 'Tsk' of annoyance. She pursed her lips and looked into the far corner of the room as if in search of divine consolation. It was clear some detail of mourning etiquette was missing. Perhaps it was the absence of a thick black veil, or mourning jewellery decorated with the deceased's hair. Perhaps it was the lustre of the fabric and the stylish cut of the garments.

Whatever it was Mrs. Woodward felt compelled to interrogate her guest. She questioned Anna with the rigour of a detective investigating a body found on the floor of the library with a knife through the heart. She wanted to know the place and time of Anna's marriage, the length of her husband's illness, the exact hour and cause of his death.

Anna decided to fight Mrs. Woodward with her own weapons – the conventions of mourning. 'My late husband,' she murmured. 'Dear George.' She produced a lace handkerchief she kept for this purpose. She dabbed her eyes, made her chest heave as if with suppressed sobs and declared that she could not talk about it. The wound was still too raw. Time was not the healer it was reputed to be. Gone to glory. Re-united in heaven. The clichés dropped smoothly from her lips like pearls on a necklace.

Satisfied now she had drawn blood, Mrs. Woodward relented enough to acknowledge the presence of Margaret and Jenny. A fond smile melted her face as she called her daughter over to introduce her. Dorothea was a strapping girl who looked as if she could wrestle a swan to the ground. Her lips and cheeks showed very red against her white skin. She had jet black hair and fierce eyebrows that snaked across her forehead like two slugs.

Anna accepted a cup of tea from the maid and subsided into a chair. She smiled and nodded at the other ladies as they arrived. They settled down to criticize a wedding they had attended recently. Mrs. Woodward led the charge with gusto. Anna gave an encouraging nod to the girls and looked pointedly at the cake on the tea table. Jenny took the hint. She was holding out her plate for a piece of cream-filled Victoria sponge when Dorothea came up behind.

Dorothea was in a bad temper. She had discovered the piano was locked. The key was missing. Quickly she considered possible lines of action. Sing unaccompanied and unannounced? Too humiliating. Stage a tantrum until her mother gave way and sent for the key? That would mean admitting in public that her control over her mother was not absolute. That was not going to happen in front of these ordinary girl visitors. Dorothea seethed. Someone had to pay.

She saw Jenny, the plate and the cream cake. A sudden elbow, hard in Jenny's back, the plate flew, the cream cake squelched and Jenny yelped with surprise. Her cry was lost in the stream of female disapproval pouring from the hostess and her companions.

The maid gave Jenny a sympathetic smile and offered a napkin to wipe the worst of the damage from her new blue dress.

Margaret wandered up. She had been looking for bookshelves and failed to find any.

'They're this way,' said Dorothea and led her to a window seat that lurked behind dense velvet curtains. 'There.' Dorothea pointed under the seat. Margaret sank to her knees and scrabbled out a few dusty volumes. Undeterred by their state of obvious neglect, she took her new spectacles from her pocket to read the titles.

At the sight of the spectacles Dorothea clapped her hand over her mouth as if, out of politeness, she was holding back a great gale of laughter. In mock obedience to the rule that children should be seen and not heard, she mimed intense amusement, pointing at Margaret's spectacles, pulling a face and shaking her head. Jenny was supposed to join in the wordless mockery. A glance at Jenny showed that, like Queen Victoria, she was not amused.

'Oh dear,' said the oblivious Margaret from the floor. 'These are just old sermons. Don't you have any Jane Austen? Or Thackeray? I just love Thackeray.'

'Put the books back,' said Jenny in a voice that Margaret knew to take seriously. Jenny gave her a hand to help her climb up from the floor. Dorothea stopped her pantomime laughter and moved swiftly to block their escape route. Stretching out her arms to fill the gap in the curtains, she held the two girls at bay.

'What I want to know,' said Dorothea, as she loomed over them, 'What I want to know,' she repeated for emphasis, 'is, which one of you was swapped for a bicycle?'

Jenny and Margaret stood side by side in the alcove and looked at each other. There was no need to exchange words; they had dealt with this question before. Together they said very loudly and firmly, 'I am.'

Dorothea's cheeks flushed scarlet, her eyebrows scrunched together, her eyes blazed and her vermilion lip curled into a snarl as she blocked the route out of the alcove. Margaret curled up like a small furry mammal and slipped quietly under Dorothea's outstretched arm. The lanky Jenny could not follow the compact Margaret's example. She stared at Dorothea, smiled to distract her, and poked her sharp elbow hard into Dorothea's stomach. The slender Jenny slipped through the gap she had made. Then as cool as if the tussle had not taken place, she asked the maid for another slice of Victoria sponge. The maid, who had seen it all, obliged her with a cheery smile. Dorothea was not popular with the servants. Jenny took her plate and went to sit near Anna. Anger boiled inside her.

Mrs. Woodward had almost finished her critical review of the wedding. It lay on the floor like an injured animal, waiting for the coup de grace. She lifted her teacup, extended her little finger, raised her chin and her voice, 'You can say what you like about the meringues, but they wouldn't do in Southport.'

At home, Jenny laughed, 'We've made an enemy there.'

'It doesn't matter,' said Margaret. 'It's not as though they've got any books I'd want to borrow. Imagine a house that big with no Jane Austen.'

51

Jenny's prophesy proved true. When they found themselves in the same room as Dorothea, she jostled their plates in passing, or crept up behind them to inflict a painful pinch. If they were asked to deliver tea to a grown-up it never arrived without spillage. Jenny and Margaret were always blamed for these minor infringements of society's rules. The hostess would stare pointedly at them and then at the crumbs on the carpet. Dorothea would stand close by, smiling.

EDUCATION

Anna soon realised that their manner of worship was not the only matter to divide the members of the Established Church and the Free Churches. The true source of friction between them was education. The draughty old barn of the Church of England school had burnt down to the ground. No-one lamented its passing. Everyone agreed it was too small and was totally inadequate for the needs of the growing town. Its only virtue was that it was free.

Chapelgoers had their own small National school but they resented paying rates for a Church of England School they did not attend. They certainly did not want to pick up the bill for replacing a school destroyed in suspicious circumstances. Local politicians tossed the problem from hand to hand until a solution was found. It was decided to build a new school, open and acceptable to all. Most importantly it would be free.

Anna quizzed John about it. 'You work in the Town Hall. You must know when it will open.'

'That's exactly why I know nothing at all on the subject. Do you know how hard it is to work in a place riddled with politics and keep yourself out of it? People come to me to tell me about the deaths of their children. I don't want them wondering whether I'm chapel or church, liberal or conservative.'

He had a point.

'Does it not concern you that your children have no school to go to?'

'Of course, it does. But not too much. The girls can read, write and add up. Once they're twelve no-one fusses if they never go to school again.'

Anna found it depressing that the doors to education closed so early to the girls. John agreed.

'If we can find somewhere reasonable and cheap, I'd keep them on for a couple of years. Tommy is a different matter though. Boys must learn to be able to work. That's why people send their boys to boarding school. To get a better education.' John looked thoughtful. Whenever he was reminded about Tommy's education, he gave boarding school serious consideration.

Anna panicked. She pictured Tommy in a strange place with his jumbled-up letters and without his two big sisters to protect him. A lamb to the slaughter. She shivered at the thought and promptly made it her mission to prevent it happening.

The opening shot in her campaign was to take the youngsters to see the new school which was in the process of construction. They showed no enthusiasm for the expedition but she wasn't going to let that deter her.

The black barn of an elementary school had squatted in the grounds of a fine mansion in the Palladian style. It belonged to a wealthy aristocrat with more taste than sense but a shrewd eye for horses. Fire destroyed his stables along with several of his finest animals. Heart-broken, the owner fled to Italy where he found consolation in a genuine Palladian palazzo.

The town council tried, and failed, to collect the tax on the property. Year by year the debt grew. No word – or money – came from Italy. When he became mayor, Mr Kenneth Woodward, decided to kill two birds with one stone. He would punish the nobleman's lofty indifference to the democratically elected council and provide the town with an urgently needed an elementary school. The ruined stables were the ideal site. A single large classroom with a row of outdoor privies was built in the once pleasant gardens of the elegant house. It was intended to be temporary, while the legalities were sorted out.

Time passed. A second fire consumed the barn of a school and brought the question of education to the top of the town's agenda. It was agreed to build a new elementary school on the same site and to claim the handsome mansion for a grammar school.

Jenny, Margaret, and Tommy stared at the building site in wonderment. The walls of the new elementary school were made of bright red brick. The roof was almost completed. Through the unglazed windows came the sounds of the sawing of wood and the hammering of nails.

A man in a top hat came to stand next to them as they gazed at the scene. He tipped his hat to Anna. 'A grand sight isn't it?'

'Indeed,' said Anna.

'A real step forward for the town.' The man gave a smile of satisfaction and waved his hat towards a wooden board in front of the mansion. It announced in large letters

Atherley Grammar School
For Boys.

As he read the last line Tommy's heart made a small leap of hope. He had heard of grammar schools. A boy from Sunday school went to one in Manchester. He travelled up on the train on Monday and stayed with his aunt until Friday. Tommy wondered if he had an aunt in Manchester.

The girls felt the familiar sensation of being ignored.

A woman in a grey dress emerged from the noise and clamour of the building site. 'Here she comes,' cried the man, 'the driving force behind the project. You must meet, Miss Hulme.'

Miss Hulme was a woman of indeterminate age. She was not twenty and she was not sixty but somewhere in between. She offered a firm handshake and a brisk smile. 'You are too kind, Mr Woodward,' she told the man. 'It could not have been done without you. The elementary school will be ready on the first day of term and the grammar school will be open for business. The finishing touches may take a little longer'.

Mr Woodward had no chance to reply. A clear girl's voice piped up. 'Do you think one day there will be a grammar school for girls in this town?' Margaret spoke directly to Miss Hulme.

Jenny sucked in her breath and braced herself. One, at least, of the adults was bound to give Margaret, usually the mouse of the family, the sharp side of their tongue.

Speaking uninvited to grown-ups was not allowed. Everyone knew that.

Mr Woodward waved his hat around and gazed at the sky. Miss Hulme leaned forward to examine Margaret closely. She took a breath.

'It's coming,' thought Jenny, 'she's going to slice Margaret like bacon.'

'Well, child, that's a very good question. Would you like there to be a grammar school for girls?'

'Oh yes,' breathed Margaret. 'Very much so.'

'So, would I,' said Miss Hulme.

Jenny both sighed with relief and gaped in amazement.

Miss Hulme continued, 'The boys' school is the first step. All being well I hope one day there will be one for girls. We had to start somewhere and naturally it was with the boys. That is the way the world works. Even Mr Woodward agrees, and he has a very good reason to want a girls' grammar school. He has a daughter.'

Mr Woodward nodded his agreement. 'Miss Hulme is right. Just the one chick and she's a treasure. But I am happy to pay for Dorothea's education.' He beamed proudly, filled with the sense of doing the right thing in difficult circumstances. He had so longed for a son.

'And where does your daughter go to school?' asked Anna.

'Here in the town. With Miss Fossil. We used to have a governess for her, of course.' Mr Woodward stopped for a moment and pursed his lips. By nature, an honest man he had understated the number of governesses who had passed through Dorothea's hands. 'Then Miss Hulme's friend, Miss Fossil, came to town.' His face cleared. He turned to Miss Hulme and bowed.

'She is a properly trained teacher,' explained Miss Hulme.

'Once I knew Miss Fossil was opening a school for girls, I gave the governess her cards. You should see the drawings our Dorothea does. She can play the piano and sing like a dream. She's learning to speak French. Mrs. Woodward didn't want Dorothea going away to boarding school.'

After a few more politenesses they went on their way and sauntered round the town. It seemed less dark and forbidding than previously. They saw boys running errands and girls out with their mothers and exchanged shy smiles with them. The presence of the adults prevented anything more exuberant. Jenny kept an eye out for Edward Carter but caught no glimpse of him. He was probably busy working somewhere. Employers paid well for strong lads who could follow instructions and who were good with their hands.

In the evening, in the quiet half hour after the children went to bed, with John at the other side of the fire gazing moodily at the newspaper, Anna considered the children's education – or lack of it. She did her best but unlike Miss Fossil she was not a trained teacher. Tommy's spelling was improving but with professional help he might make better progress.

As for the girls they were well beyond the standard the authorities demanded of them. Many people saw no purpose in educating girls beyond the point where they could read the Bible, an important way of keeping them on the straight and narrow path of virtue. The churches had always taken care of that in their schools and Sunday schools.

On the other hand, there were women, like Miss Hulme, who cared passionately about education for girls. They were going to university and founding colleges where women could study. Today Anna had met such a woman, living proof that women could be educated without turning into the kind of monsters portrayed in the newspaper cartoons.

It seemed to Anna that Margaret, who was teaching herself Latin, would benefit from the education that Miss Fossil offered. Jenny was a different matter. She could do calculations with enviable speed, wrote clearly and with ease and could read a novel from the circulating library in a day. Latin, she regarded with scorn. She would probably refuse the offer of more education with a firm No Thank You. On the other hand, what was she to do all day? Help around the house? Pay calls? She was too young for the serious business of husband hunting. Or was she? The girl was growing fast. Anna had caught her looking at boys in a way that Margaret never did. With interest. That was how Jenny looked at them.

Anna's mind did a complete turnaround. Perhaps the girl who wasn't keen on education was the one most in need of it. Jenny had an eye for colour. You could see it by the way she chose her outfits. It wouldn't do her any harm to study painting seriously. Better for her to exercise her brain in learning French verbs than for it to go soggy by wallowing in the sentimental novels she was addicted to.

Now it was Anna's brain that needed a rest. She sat back with a sense of satisfaction; she could see a way forward for the girls. She would investigate Miss Fossil's school, the one that Dorothea Woodward attended. She looked across at John who was deep in an article about Irish Nationalism. Could he afford the fees? A flea bite to the wealthy Mr Woodward might involve considerable sacrifice for him. Anna felt her resolution harden. For her sister's girls she would dip into her own resources if necessary. But only as a last resort.

Her attention turned to her embroidery. As she stabbed her needle through the linen stretched tight on its frame a nasty niggle pierced her smug sense of having just solved a problem. Tommy. She had forgotten about Tommy. Everyone agreed the education of boys was much more important than that of girls. She glanced across at John. The grand affairs of state in the newspaper had not stopped him falling into a peaceful doze. This was not the moment to tackle him about Tommy. Sufficient unto the day, she decided.

The next day Anna settled the children at their lessons. Tommy did his daily spelling chants while Margaret read about Julius Caesar. Jenny was busy with Gulliver's Travels. Anna thought it would be a good antidote to her usual reading matter. They always took a break halfway through the morning. The youngsters had milk and Anna drank coffee. She didn't believe in doing anything serious until she'd had her coffee.

'I'd like to know what you think about school,' she began. Her gentle approach to the subject was deliberate; she had seen boys sobbing on railway station platforms saying goodbye to their mothers.

The effect on the youngsters was electric. They froze. The temperature in the room dropped. The silence grew profound. A sudden clatter as Tommy's chair fell to the floor. The boy blundered across the room, his eyes tight shut. When he reached the couch, he hurled himself into its comforting softness. With his free arm he piled the cushions over his back until he was safely buried.

Anna looked enquiringly at the girls. Margaret looked round for escape and found none. Then she looked for the right word – and found it.

'Gruesome,' she said, 'it was simply gruesome.'

'And boring,' added Jenny. 'It wasn't too bad until Mr Cripps came. He didn't teach us. He had the boys. Not that Miss Rivers taught us anything we didn't know. We could already read and write. The afternoons were an escape for us girls. We had washing and mangling and ironing. Sometimes we had sewing. That wasn't too bad; we could have the odd chat.'

'It was worse for the boys. They just had to do the same thing they'd done in the morning. Mind you, some of them wouldn't remember if they did it a thousand times,' said Margaret who was blessed with a quick memory.

'It's the ones who go to work,' Jenny explained. 'They have to come to school for three hours a day. Some come in the morning and some in the afternoon. So, the boys have to keep doing things twice. There was no carpentry or mechanics or science.'

'It was worse for Tommy when Mr Cripps came. Mr Cripps got his knife into Tommy. Mr Cripps wasn't very good at arithmetic. Sometimes he got the answers wrong and Tommy always, but always, got them right. And he could do it quicker, much quicker. Mr Cripps didn't like that. He'd go very red and his eyes sort of bulged. Then he found out Tommy had trouble with his writing. He can read perfectly but, as you know, when he writes the letters go in the wrong order.'

'They get jumbled up,' sniffed Tommy who had emerged from his cushions.

'Mr Cripps started to torment Tommy. We could see him and hear him from our side of the room. It was awful. He'd say things like, 'Shall we ask the little professor how to spell this word?' Then he'd get him to write it on the blackboard. He knew he'd get it all wrong.'

'He wanted the others to laugh at him.'

'Did they?'

'Not the girls. We wouldn't let them. But the boys did.'

'At first. Then Edward Carter got them together and asked them what the hell they were doing.'

'Language!' Anna rebuked her automatically.

'Jenny was just quoting. She wasn't swearing.' Margaret liked to be precise.

'Edward Carter,' Jenny took every opportunity of naming her hero, 'told them that by laughing at Tommy they were doing Mr Cripps' dirty work for him. After that the boys stopped laughing. They just sat silent. We all sat silent and stared at Mr Cripps. We sent waves of hate at him.'

'That made Mr Cripps even angrier,' said Margaret, following the grisly logic of thwarted power. 'He started on the punishments. A rap on the knuckles for a spelling mistake. Poor Tommy had plenty of those. Pelted with chalk for not looking as if he was listening. The strap for coughing. The cane for cheek.'

'He got worse after Edward Carter turned fourteen and stopped coming to school. It was just luck he was there that last day. The truancy officer had brought some of his brothers in. Edward came to see fair play. Mr Cripps was arguing with them. We could hear them outside shouting. Margaret had gone over to the boys' side of the classroom to help Tommy with his letters.'

'When Mr Cripps came in, he was already furious, waving his cane and shouting. Then he saw Margaret on the boys' side.'

The wall of silence that Margaret, Jenny and Tommy had built to shield them from the events of that dreadful day, crumbled.

Memories of the chaos poured out of them. Margaret thrown across the classroom. Girls screaming. The red eyes of the teacher. Giant hands grabbing Tommy's jacket. His head banging on the ceiling. His feet dangling. Boys roaring. The man shrieking, spit spraying. Bodies bruising and fists flying.

Anna pieced together the patchwork of their words and saw a terrifying picture. It was clear Mr Cripps had lost all control and had picked up little Tommy, shaken him until his teeth rattled and flung him in the air, while spewing words of hate into his face.

'It was Edward Carter who saved us. He grabbed Mr Cripps and got a couple of his brothers to hold his arms. Told us to scarper. Told us to come home and tell Papa what'd happened.'

'And did you? Did you tell your Papa?'

There was an uneasy silence.

'We would have done,' said Margaret, 'but Papa wasn't here. Hannah put some ice in a cloth and Tommy's face went down quickly. The bruises on his arms were covered by his shirt. We didn't tell Hannah the teacher did it. We didn't think she'd believe us. We wouldn't lie to Hannah. But she didn't ask. She thought Tommy had been fighting other boys. She said she wouldn't tell Papa unless he asked.'

'And he didn't,' added Jenny cheerfully. 'We thought we'd get into the most awful trouble for being so naughty. Fighting with the teacher.'

'That evening Edward Carter came to the back door. Told Hannah there was no school until further notice. There was no teacher. Mr Cripps was sick. Miss Rivers was in hysterics. Said we could sleep easy in our beds that night.'

'And we did.'

'Then the school burned down. Everyone said Mr Cripps did it for spite before he left town.'

'Then you came.' Tommy was on his feet now. He put his arms round his aunt and buried his face on her shoulder. 'I think everything is going to be all right now.'

Anna toured the drawing rooms of Atherley to research how the local matrons educated their daughters. Their answers ranged from 'a governess, of course,' to 'don't bother. It's a waste of time and money'. Mrs. Woodward regarded the girls' school run by Miss Fossil as the only satisfactory school in the North of England. After all, Dorothea went there. Anna smiled politely but secretly vowed to look for further evidence. One Sunday she accosted Miss Hulme, the new headmistress, on her way out of church for her view of Miss Fossil's establishment.

'The government should provide better education for girls. Fourteen is much too young stop their education. Her school provides girls with an opportunity to study further. Better than spending their time gossiping and giggling.' Miss Hulme's face showed what she thought of such occupations.

'It's not perfect but it's the best opportunity for the girls of Atherley at this time,' said Miss Hulme. 'I am confident that it will become a proper grammar school for girls.' She halted and coughed. 'I must admit I am not a completely impartial judge. Miss Fossil is a close friend of mine. We studied together at Girton and we share a house in the town.'

'Is Latin taught in the school?'

Miss Hulme was surprised by the question. Deportment and sewing were the subjects most parents asked about. Anna explained that Margaret was teaching herself Latin.

'Amazing,' said Miss Hulme. 'Miss Fossil is herself a classicist and no doubt intends to introduce the subject one day. I would advise you to put the girl's name down immediately. There is a waiting list. Miss Fossil is going to set a stiff entrance examination. I don't think that will trouble your girl too much from the sound of it.'

Anna came to a decision. Next year it was Miss Fossil's or nothing. The iron entered her soul. All three children would spend a year at the town school when it opened. Then the girls were going to Miss Fossil's school.

Her one area of indecision was who to approach first. The girls or their father? She was sure Margaret would faint with delight at the prospect. Jenny might be a different story. In theory their father was in favour of more feminine company and influences for his girls, to make up for the absence of their mother. In practice he might jib at the investment of time and money involved. He was their father. His word was law. His permission - and his money- were essential for the project.

Anna waited until the evening of the following Sunday. The predictable monotony of the Lord's Day – church, roast dinner and an afternoon doze – always made her long for something new. She thought John might feel the same.

John, however, was not feeling open to new ideas as he sat by the fire for a quiet half hour with Anna after the children had gone to bed. He was luxuriating in comfort, a good meal, a warm fire, clean clothes in the wardrobe. What more could a man ask?

At first the evenings had been a torment to him. He wanted to stride across the room, grasp Anna in his arms like the hero in a novel, and carry her off to bed to ravish her very thoroughly. With practice it had grown easier to suppress this urge. Sometimes it died very quickly if he concentrated on the many real benefits Anna brought to his life, rather than on what could not be. Their relationship was, he concluded, like a mature marriage – not exciting but reliable. He had a well-run and happy home with problem-free children. There was just that one magic ingredient missing.

'You know the new school will be opening soon,' Anna began.

'About time too.'

Undeterred by his gruff response, Anna went on to explain her research into the problem of his children's education. She had chosen the wrong moment to open her campaign. John was deep in his newspaper. An item on riots in Bradford had caught his attention. Angry people had attacked some of the Poor Law Guardians. It was an office John held. He shivered at the thought of such violence in Atherley. He must remember to check that the Superintendent of the Workhouse had bought more coal.

'……so what do you think about the girls going to Miss Fossil's school.'

Anna was looking at him and expecting an answer. He had heard only the end of her speech. What to do?

It took him less than a second to prepare his defence. 'I'll think about that when I've got Tommy's schooling organised. I can't commit to further expense for the girls just at this moment…Tommy boarding school … toughen the lad …boy's education so much more important… prepare him for the world.' He floundered on.

A hot spurt of rage flashed through Anna. She took in a breath ready to launch an arrow of stinging complaint between his eyes. The words were on their way to her lips when she abruptly stopped them. Her antennae told her that John was not rejecting her suggestion; his words were the bluster of a masculine ego in self-defence mode. John was flannelling. Every cliché he had ever heard fell out of his lips.

Let it go, she told herself. Let him ramble on. A mixed bag of proverbs is better than an emphatic, serious and reasoned No. Withdraw discreetly. Fight this battle another day.

'Yes, of course,' she said when he ran out of steam. 'I'll start making enquiries. Tommy's education is so much more important.'

And so much more of a problem. But she didn't say that out loud.

'Edward Carter's got his own bike,' a breathless Tommy announced. 'He's helping deliver the meat and the butcher's paying him double.'

Anna looked up from her needlework. 'That's the boy who rescued you at school?'

'He's a hero,' said Tommy. Jenny just thought it.

'How could he afford a bike?' asked Anna. 'And no jokes about swapping a sister for one.'

The youngsters all laughed and smirked at her. 'The Carters don't do girls. They just have boys,' Jenny explained.

Tommy had all the details of Edward's bike at his fingertips. 'He saved up half the cost. The rest he's bought on tick. He gets much more for delivering now. He's so much faster and he can carry more.'

'I don't suppose he'll be going to school when it opens.' Jenny's voice was mournful.

'He will,' piped up Margaret. 'He's got a scholarship to the new grammar school. The lucky dog. You know, the school that is just for boys. Not that I am jealous or anything.'

Jenny was affronted. Margaret wasn't supposed to know more about Edward Carter than she did. If Edward Carter was going to school, she would study the book on geometry she had been ignoring; he liked to talk about triangles and things. The prospect of returning to school in town suddenly looked an inviting one.

Anna changed her mind about the menu for the next day. They would have shepherd's pie. Hannah could order the mutton on her way home. 'Tell the butcher I want it delivered by ten o'clock. And it must be fresh.'

The next day Anna put on her pinafore set about making scones. When Edward Carter arrived with the meat, she invited him into the kitchen. She sat the handsome blonde lad in a kitchen chair and offered him tea and a warm scone.

Then she propositioned him.

He was quick to understand her plan. Indeed, he improved on it. He had a brother the same age as Tommy. The chances were they would be in the same class. The brother could take a hint and the odd sixpence. He would keep an eye out for Tommy. Edward Carter left with a florin in his pocket.

Anna took off her pinafore, buttered two scones and set off in search of Tommy. His eyes popped with terror at the prospect of returning to school, but as Anna said, school in the town was much less frightening than a boarding school like Wackford Squeers in the Dickens novel. There would be no Edward Carter there to keep an eye on him.

'Because he saved you from Mr Cripps, he feels responsible for you,' she told him. 'And Edward has a brother. Might be in the same class. That would be nice.'

Tommy wondered which brother he was thinking of.

'Are there a lot of Carters?'

'Loads of them.'

Anna's insides went into a spasm. As if her womb had sprung into life. Imagine. A whole tribe of beautiful boys.

'I'm glad you think that will make it easier for you,' Anna told him. 'The thing that will help most is learning the spellings. We must stick at that.' She gave him a hug.

Tommy nodded, his face serious but free of tears.

By the evening it was all agreed. The three children would go to the school in the town when it re-opened. Tommy looked forward to it with anxiety rather than full-blown terror. The girls were happy to give their brother a helping hand. The new school might not be so boring, and they would not be there for long. Just until Tommy was settled. After that their father might let them go to Miss Fossil's school.

Margaret hugged the prospect of attending Miss Fossil's girls' school to her chest, although it was disappointing that they taught French, not Latin. Already she was fretting at the prospect of the waiting list and the entrance exam.

The chance of contact, however fleeting, with Edward Carter thrilled Jenny to her core. She was not so sure about Miss Fossil's. The fearful Dorothea Woodward would rule the roost there. Jenny knew Dorothea would make it her business to torment new arrivals.

John sat back with a satisfied smile on his face. 'I think that has all worked out very well, Anna,' he pronounced. 'As long as Tommy copes. Then if the girls pass the entrance examination, I could stand the fees for a year.'

Anna did not tell him she was confident that they would pass and that one year was most definitely not enough. For the second time in her life she omitted to tell a man that she still had the money she inherited from her father.

The three youngsters walked down the hill to school. Tommy with some trepidation, Margaret with glee and Jenny with every expectation of seeing Edward Carter. They found him on his bicycle riding lazy circles in the road outside the new school gates. He gave them his usual cheerful greeting.

'Hiya. All right then.' He grinned down at Tommy. 'If you get into a scrap with a teacher, send our Jimmy for me and I'll come and give you a hand.' He pointed to a scruffy boy with a shining pink face. 'That's our Jimmy. Our mam scrubbed him up special for today.'

They laughed. Jimmy did not take offence but beamed at being the centre of attention.

'We have to say goodbye to you ladies, here.' Edward dismounted from his bicycle. 'This is our gate. Yours is round the corner.' He pointed up at the sign above the gate that said, 'Boys' Entrance'.

Jenny and Margaret had not realised that there would be a separate entrance for girls. 'It's a bit like being a servant and having to use the back door,' Margaret complained.

'You girlies have your own playground. It's to keep you safe from our rough boys' games.'

Jenny glared at him.

'Don't worry,' he told her. 'We can talk through the railings.'

'You seem to know a lot about the place.'

'Been here several times,' he smirked at her. He ran his knuckles down his chest and flicked his chin up. 'Scholarship boy.'

It was Margaret who glared at him this time.

Anna spent an anxious day and hovered at the window watching for their return. It was a relief to see them strolling up the hill, swinging their bags of books and joshing and laughing at each other.

A closer inspection revealed that Tommy had grazed his knees, and Margaret had mislaid her scarf. Jenny was as neat and as clean as she started in the morning. When asked how the day had gone, they were monosyllabic. Margaret disappeared to her bedroom to catch up on her Latin while Tommy begged Hannah for bread and milk. Jenny came to whisper in her ear that Edward Carter had been there to welcome them, and Jimmy was in the same class as Tommy where there was a very nice lady teacher. Anna sighed with relief.

'It seems Edward Carter is a man of his word,' she said, thinking of the florin she had invested in him. There had been so many opportunities for it to go wrong. She had visions of Edward holding up the money and telling the world that Tommy was a sissy, that he'd been bribed to look after him. The perfect way to make Tommy a target for the bullies.

'Of course,' said Jenny. 'What did you expect?' She had complete confidence in her hero.

As school settled into a comfortable routine, Anna found she missed the lively company of the youngsters. Life was drearily domesticated without the challenge of the morning lessons when she had to rack her brains for something new to offer them. She kept up the regular drill of spelling with Tommy and was pleased when his letters settled down to something approaching the conventional order.

The obligatory afternoon calls were especially trying without the girls. But how else was she to spend her time? Her main function in life appeared to be cooking the evening meal.

For the first time since her return Anna felt underemployed. Her spare energy turned her thoughts to John. The years gave him an air of dignity and importance, without demanding his handsome head of hair in exchange. He behaved towards her in a most gentlemanly manner, keeping his distance when they were alone of an evening. In company he was meticulously polite, and had stopped watching with hungry eyes when she kissed the children goodnight.

Damn the man. Why couldn't he unlock the door that separated them? She would not turn him away now. She would welcome him into her bed, with warm arms and hot kisses. Marriage to George had not been particularly enjoyable or demanding, but give the old devil his due, he had cured her of the maidenly ignorance the Victorian world conspired to keep girls in. She knew now what it was that husbands and wives did together in the privacy of their bedroom. The thought of doing it with John frequently strayed into her head.

While Anna indulged in lustful daydreams there were two women in the town who were more purposefully occupied. Miss Hulme had helped to persuade the different branches of the same religion to forget their differences and replace the burnt ruin of the town's school. The new school, among other refinements, boasted separate classrooms for the different ages of children. The grammar school for boys was an instant success. Wealthy businessmen all agreed that a skilled labour force was vital for their continued success. They put their hands in their pockets to help finance technical education for boys beyond the official leaving age. Miss Hulme was busy persuading her benefactor, Mr Woodward, to help her friend Miss Fossil expand her school for girls.

These two shrewd ladies had found Mr Woodward's weak spot - his daughter, Dorothea. She might not be the son he longed for, but she was the apple of his eye. Unlike the boys, the girls would have to pay fees. The state was not ready to give girls an advanced education for nothing. However, there was already a waiting list of anxious parents eager and able to pay. He would be sure to get his money back with interest. Mr Woodward pursed his lips and nodded. He signed the document the two schoolmistresses gave him and wrote a cheque.

'His main concern is Dorothea. If he, or Mrs. Woodward, think she will get special treatment they are mistaken,' said Miss Fossil with grim determination in her voice. 'He may have helped to finance the school but that doesn't give him the right to interfere.'

'It will be easier when the blessed Dorothea leaves. I doubt she'll be with you long. She's one of those girls who matures early, if you know what I mean.

Miss Fossil looked sideways at her friend. They both knew exactly what she meant.

The entrance exam for Miss Fossil's school was a serious occasion. Margaret and Jenny, along with several other girls, were ushered into a classroom, seated at individual desks and given a question paper. Silence engulfed the room. In the corner a clock ticked ominously. Two hours later Miss Fossil collected the papers and told the girls, who were sighing with relief, 'We'll let you know within a week.'

'If parents think the only test for getting into this school is how wide their cheque books open, they have got another think coming,' said Miss Fossil to her friend as she sat down to mark the papers. 'They will not all pass.'

Suddenly Miss Fossil's pen red stopped and hovered over the sheet of paper in front of her. 'By Jove, we've got something here. The essay title is My Ambition. And here we have a little star. 'Atque inter silvas Accidemi quaerere verum.' My God, she's quoted Horace.'

'You forget I am not a classicist,' said Miss Hulme sourly. Why was it that she always felt inferior for not knowing Latin? Useless subject that it was. No one ever apologised for not knowing chemistry.

'I will seek truth in the groves of Academe.' Miss Fossil translated. 'Remember when we felt like that?'

Miss Hulme allowed herself a brief smile of reminiscence. 'We were young then.'

'Oh dear.' From a high pitch of excitement Miss Fossil fell into despair. 'She has a sister. Two girls from the same family. Their father is the Registrar here in the town. I do hope he can afford to send both of them.'

'Are they twins? That is unusual.'

Miss Fossil scrabbled through the application forms. 'No.'

'Is your little classicist the older one? Then you could delay the younger one till next year.'

Miss Fossil rattled through the application forms. 'Here we are. How strange.' She held up the two pieces of paper, her head swivelling from side to side as she checked the information.

'Well?' Miss Hulme was growing impatient.

'No. I am not mistaken. One was born in November and the other in July. The sixth to be precise. The following year.' Miss Fossil paused, frowned and looked again at the form. 'And it claims they are the same age. And they have the same surname.'

'So, it's either a miraculously brief pregnancy or a stepchild of some kind.' They pondered possible explanations and found none. They had not heard the story of the girl swapped for a bicycle. Formidable women are always last in the queue when the gossip is passed around.

In the end Miss Fossil stopped speculating. 'Well if Mr Truesdale has to choose one of his two girls to send us, I know what I would advise him.'

'Perhaps you could persuade Mr Woodward to endow a bursary for the first girl to quote Horace,' suggested Miss Hulme. 'He is generous man. And he does so like his good works to be recognised in public.'

Miss Fossil laughed. 'Not such a bad idea.' She picked up the exam papers and tapped her friend playfully on the shoulder with them. 'Time for tea.'

John had endured a trying morning. A woman had come to register the death of her husband, a miner who had been fatally injured in an accident underground. She wanted his death recorded as a murder. In vain had John told her that the coroner had ruled that the death was an accident; no-one was going to arrest the people who ran the mine. Her best help would be the union who would deal with the insurance company and the medical experts for her. He felt bad as he saw the panic and incomprehension on her careworn face. Her son was with her. A white-faced boy barely a year older than Tommy. In the end it was the lad who coped best. He put his hand on her arm. 'Come on, Mam. Time to go home.'

The letter that awaited him at home was a welcome contrast to the grim realities of the morning. Both his girls had passed the entrance examination and, for a consideration, would be welcome to attend Miss Fossil's school at the beginning of the school year. In the case of Margaret, the school was pleased to offer her the position of monitor in recognition of the high standard of work she had demonstrated. As a monitor she would pay no fees. If she proved satisfactory, she would be a candidate for pupil-teacher status. If Mr Truesdale wished to know more, he should arrange an appointment at the school.

John did wish to know more. For moral support he took Anna with him in her position of honorary mother.

'Mrs. Mainwaring,' he said to introduce her. 'My late wife's sister.'

Miss Fossil needed no further explanation. The situation was not uncommon. Briefly she explained the position of monitor. It was the first step in the process of qualifying as a teacher in an elementary school. Later small amounts of money were paid to the student and the training was free. Some girls went on to college where they could qualify as a certificated teacher.

'That is looking a long way ahead. The next step is whether you agree for Margaret to be a monitor. She would be working with me mostly. Running errands and doing a few necessary tasks. She would attend all the lessons just like the other pupils.'

There was something about Miss Fossil that inspired confidence. John considered agreeing immediately, but the habits of a lifetime prevented him from doing so. Men didn't just accept what women said straightaway. They always had to scrutinise it, find some minor flaw and make a suggestion for improvement. Unfortunately, at that moment, he could not think of a single one. Mostly he was thinking that they would have to economise. He played for time and asked about Jenny's test results.

'Her arithmetic is faultless. But she does not have that academic spark that her sister has. Nonetheless I am sure she would benefit from the classes here.'

John had still not found a flaw in Miss Fossil's plan, but he was not going to give way easily. He played his last card, the card of power. He was their father; his word was law. He would consider the matter and let Miss Fossil know his decision by the end of the week. He picked up his hat and made his farewell. Anna followed in his footsteps. Her lips had been sealed tight shut for so long she could scarcely prise them apart to murmur a polite goodbye.

As they walked home up the hill, Anna wanted to clatter John about the ears for not welcoming such an opportunity with open arms. Fortunately, the climb did not leave her with enough breath to give him the ear-whacking she thought he deserved. The words narrow-minded, short-sighted, mean-spirited and downright rude were going through her mind.

Such thoughts had been going through John's mind too. The climb gave him time to reflect. He realised he had been grumpy and negative. When they reached the house, he had his defence ready. As he helped Anna remove her shawl he said, 'We must tell the girls first and ask them what they think. That is why I did not want to agree with Miss Fossil straightaway.'

Anna felt such a burst of joy that she wrapped her arms round him and kissed him. The brief contact was electric in its effect. They leapt apart and stared at each other, suddenly frozen with horror at the force they had unleashed. The sound of footsteps on the stairs returned them to reality. John hung up Anna's shawl and set his hat on the table.

Margaret was first, desperate to know what Miss Fossil had said. The light-footed Jenny followed. Both girls jumped up and down desperate for news. John could not speak. His capacity for thought was obliterated by the sensation of Anna's lips on his.

Anna took over. She shooed the girls off to make tea. 'We cannot have a proper family conference without tea,' she told them, smiling and nodding to show the news was good. Reassured they bustled off into the kitchen.

Margaret was ecstatic at the thought of being Miss Fossil's monitor. 'What will I have to do?'

'Mix the ink and fill the ink wells,' suggested Jenny. The task always left you with vivid blue hands.

'I'd do that. I'd clean her shoes if necessary.'

'I expect her maid does that for her,' said Anna. 'She is a certificated teacher. She can afford a maid. She must earn nearly a hundred pounds a year.'

'I think you'll find she has private means as well.' John brought a note of realism into the conversation.

'Well you can save some money,' said Jenny to her father. 'I think it's best if I stay on at the elementary school. We don't want to leave Tommy on his own there.'

'Why not? I don't need a sister looking after me.' Tommy was a picture of indignation. His voice rang out with the confidence of having truth on his side. School held no fear for him now. His letters were not so jumbly and he was popular with both his teacher and his classmates.

'That's not the point,' Jenny began and stopped. The point was that she wanted to go to the railings at playtime and talk with Edward Carter. Their conversations had strayed way beyond the protection of Tommy. Edward looked out to the world of engineering and technology; it held an allure for him that Jenny was beginning to share.

Under Edward's influence she had come to appreciate the wonders of machinery, like the sewing machine that saved her so many hours of tiresome labour. With Tommy as chaperon, Edward had given her a guided tour of the mangle that supplied the Carter family's modest income. When his mother had been left on her own with several small boys to rear, the parish had provided her with a mangle. The massive contraption had given her both an income and a social life. Women brought their wet washing and for a small fee watched it transform from a flapping monster to a manageable sheet that would dry on the rack in the kitchen.

Edward made her see the marvel of the cog wheels that enabled her to turn the heavy machine with little effort. She wondered at the precision and balance of the rollers that squeezed out the water and would flatten her fingers if she were so careless as to let them be caught. Edward promised, that when she was older, they would go to the Mechanics Institute where there were talks and classes on manufacturing. The prospect of such an outing made Jenny quiver with delight.

John's voice interrupted this happy train of thought. 'The point is, Jenny that you are too advanced for the elementary school.' Her father stared hard at her, challenging her to deny it.

She looked away in search of a fresh argument and found one. 'This Miss Fossil's place is very expensive.'

'True.' John grew cunning. 'There's plenty to do around the house. Your aunt would be glad of some help.'

The prospect of dreary domesticity sent Jenny desperate. She played her last card. 'I could get a job.' She waved her hands in front of her father. 'Everyone says they'd be glad of me in the mill. My hands are so quick. Both of them.'

John went white round the lips. 'Are you deliberately trying to disgrace me in public? As if I would let my daughter go to work in the mill.'

'There's no disgrace,' Jenny began to say. The look on her father's face made her quail. He raised a finger.

'Stop now, Jenny. Stop before I really get angry. I will write to Miss What's Her Name tonight and accept for both of you.'

'That's not fair.'

'That is exactly what it is. It is fair,' said John. 'I will not deny one of my girls an opportunity that I give the other. Your Aunt Anna agrees with me. This is one of those many occasions where parents know best.'

Words bubbled up to Jenny's lips. She bit them back.

That night Anna unlocked the door that separated her room from John's. She took out the key and hoped that the light from her candle might shine through the empty keyhole. A tiny glow-worm of a hint. Would he see it? Would he act on it?

Family life is seldom perfect; there is always one member of the family who is not happy with his or her lot. Adults grow accustomed to living with less than perfection; the young find it more difficult. John and Anna contrived to ignore the gnawing of their sexual appetites and concentrate on their good fortune. They were both healthy and, with care, their income was sufficient. The raising of the children gave them both pleasure and satisfaction. Tommy went to school without fear and had ceased to be tormented by nightmares where capital letters chased him with angry sticks and raised voices. Margaret was in a seventh heaven of joy. She saw herself reading Virgil in a book-lined room under the approving eye of Miss Fossil.

It was Jenny who had fallen into the pit of despair. Her nickname of Spinning Jenny was no longer justified. The girl, who flitted through the house on quick light feet, had sunk into a slothful and resentful silence. She spent more time in her bedroom and emerged with tear stains on her face.

Anna ran through a mental list of possible causes. Margaret's success in the entrance exam? Jenny was jealous? Very unlikely. She was nervous of starting at the new school. Jenny nervous! Even less likely. It was her birthday soon. Could her age be the cause of her distress? The girl was growing up. Anna's heart sank. The first thing Anna had known about menstruation was when it happened. Women didn't talk about such things. She remembered her shock - and horror.

History must not repeat itself, Anna decided. It was time to have a little talk. She did not look forward to performing this duty and she definitely wasn't going to do it twice. She summoned both girls to her bedroom where she had taken the precaution of locking the adjoining door and leaving the key with its green tassel ostentatiously on the dressing table.

First, she would eliminate all other possible causes of Jenny's distress. 'I can't help noticing that you are not very happy, Jenny,' she began.

Margaret looked surprised. She was so enfolded in her bubble of happiness she had not noticed Jenny's low spirits.

'I know you do not want to leave the town school,' said Anna.

'I don't mind so much now. I've got used to the idea. The things we do are babyish. There's no higher class for us girls. Like there is for the boys.' Really, she wanted to go to the grammar school with Edward Carter and study trigonometry and chemistry. She knew it wasn't going to happen.

'Is it Miss Fossil's school that is the problem?'

'It will be better than baking scones and making calls every afternoon.'

'True,' said Anna who saw that was exactly how she would spend her days.

'Anyway, it's important that I go there,' said Jenny, suddenly her usual brisk self.

'Why?' asked Margaret who could not understand this change of mind. It wasn't Jenny who wanted to learn Latin and quote Horace. She would not be a monitor.

Jenny pulled a face at Margaret's naivety. 'I've got to be there to look after you, stupid.'

Margaret protested that the work held no terror for her.

'It's not the work, you silly missy. It's the other girls. Dorothea Woodward is going to make your life a misery.'

Anna and Margaret looked puzzled by this prophesy. Jenny saw their incomprehension. 'Dorothea likes hurting people,' she explained. 'She does not want to be monitor but she won't want Margaret to be one; it makes her special. As far as Dorothea is concerned there is only one person who is special. And that is Dorothea.' Jenny remembered the nudges that sent her plate flying and the pinches that left bruises on her arm. 'She punishes you for having something that she hasn't.' She looked to Margaret for corroboration.

Margaret nodded. 'She's very clever at not being seen. Sometimes I think her mother sees but she does nothing about it.'

'So, you are frightened of Dorothea?'

'No!' The denial was emphatic. 'I can deal with Dorothea Woodward.' Jenny spat out the loathsome name. At the same time tears welled up in her eyes. 'She's not the problem.'

'Can you tell me what is?'

The words came out in a wail. 'I'm growing fur. Like a rabbit.'

It took some time and many blushes and much pointing at body parts that women normally kept covered. To make matters worse, they did not know the names for these areas of their bodies. Anna did her best to explain a few of the basic facts of life to both girls.

'Will the same happen to me?' a worried Margaret asked.

'I expect so. It happens to all girls at about this age.'

'You'd think I'd be first. Being the eldest.'

'It's different times for different girls. It happens when your body says it does. And of course, we cannot be sure which of you is the oldest.'

'And it happens every month?'

'Usually. When you get old it stops.' Anna paused and did a small calculation. It would be some years before she would be free of that monthly business. Hope flickered in her heart. Perhaps then she could persuade John to be less of an honourable man. 'And it stops when you're having a baby. That's a long way off and you'll be married before that.'

'Will I get that fur?' asked Margaret.

'I expect so.'

Margaret pulled a face to show her distaste at the prospect.

Suddenly they had all had enough of the topic. Anna clapped her hands and shooed the girls out of her bedroom. They ran up the stairs to their own rooms. Before she disappeared into hers Margaret stood at the door and turned to Jenny.

'I don't care what Aunt Anna says.' Her voice was choked with distress. 'I am not having that bleeding business happen to me.'

Anna sat at her dressing table and looked at the framed photograph of her sister. The rigid pose and the sepia colouring didn't do Florence justice, but it was all Anna had to remind her of the once vibrant girl. 'I'm glad that is over. I hope you appreciate what I have done for your girls today, Florence. It's a lot more than our mother did for us.'

In the evening Anna crept close to John and whispered a reminder in his ear. It would be Jenny's birthday soon. 'Our girls are growing up,' she added. She did not elaborate but blushed prettily.

Women's matters, he thought and blinked rapidly in embarrassment.

What is it about eyelashes? Anna wondered, when she returned to her chair. Everyone has them but some are just so beautiful it melts your heart. John's were dark brown and thick and they curled up deliciously at the tips. Anna spent a few moments in happy contemplation of them until it was time for bed.

She sat at her dressing table brushing her long black hair and looking at the photograph of Florence. Her sister's ghostly presence was all the comfort she had. There was no-one else she could confide in. She could not share her deepest concern with John. He was her deepest concern. The women she met across the teacups in the afternoons were no use. One hint of her feelings would precipitate a major scandal.

The sweeping strokes of the hairbrush came to a halt as Anna thought about John and his eyelashes and his wavy brown hair. Drat it. I'm in love with him, Florence. I want to feel his strong hands on my body and his man's voice in my ear. I cannot believe it is wrong to love him. I don't care what those busy bodying bishops in London say. It's not in the ten commandments. It didn't come down the mountain with Moses. We nearly did *it*, you know Florence. The night I dropped my candle. I shrieked. John was doing his rounds. Locking the house up to keep us safe.

He came and stamped out the candle as it smouldered on the rug. The only light was the moon through the window. I must have put my arms round him for comfort. Then he was kissing me properly. None of those brotherly pecks and I was wrestling with his shirt buttons, my body on fire, begging him to do to me whatever it was that men did to women.

'You can guess, Florence, what stopped me. The sudden paralysing fear. The total ignorance. Mother's brainwashing won. I wasn't exactly sure what virginity was but I knew the consequences of losing it were dire. I just froze.

'Then there was the banging on the door. The telegram. Our father ill. As if God was sending a warning. I had to leave.'

Anna put down the brush and began to plait her hair.

'Well I am older now. I know now what it is that men and women do together. And I'd still like John to do it to me. After all I was married to George for six months and there was no baby.'

She sighed. John promised to behave with honour. And, drat the man, he is doing so. The sepia photograph in its silver frame had no words of comfort for her.

The plait was finished. Anna spent a few moments plucking the stray hairs from the bristles of her brush. Absent-mindedly she twisted them into a knot. As her fingers tied the hairs even tighter, she felt the knot in her mind unravel. An expression of great serenity came over her face. She had found the answer to the question that troubled her most.

'Thank you, Florence. You have been a great help. I can see my way now.'

'You look very smart,' Anna told the girls as they lined up for inspection. 'The white blouses look right.'

'Papa goes to work in a white shirt. Lots of men do. But not many ladies wear them,' said Jenny.

'Some people think you can't be a lady and go to work,' said Anna. 'It is women who go to work. Usually they get their hands dirty and wear pinafores.'

'But you went to work. You're still a lady. Did you wear a white blouse?'

'Yes. A post office is a cross between an office and a shop. That's quite genteel. Especially as it was my father's post office.'

'A white blouse looks clean and efficient. A monitor should look efficient.' Margaret loved saying the word 'monitor' and beamed every time she managed to shoe-horn it into the conversation.

'These collars and cuffs will save an awful lot of washing.' Jenny checked her cuffs with proprietorial pride; she had spent hours making the tiny buttonholes and sewing on the buttons that held the detachable collar in place.

'You can wash the blouses on Saturday. They will dry overnight.'

'That means ironing on a Sunday,' Margaret looked doubtful. The Lord's Day was sacred in Atherley. The act of hanging out washing on a Sunday sent scandalised neighbours round to the culprit to complain.

''No-one will see a bit of ironing.' Jenny's expression was scornful. A wicked gleam came into her eye. Margaret saw where she was heading and together, they chanted Mrs.Woodward's mantra. 'It wouldn't do in Southport.'

Even Anna joined in the laughter. It was against the rules to encourage children to mock adults, but for Mrs. Woodward's favourite phrase of condemnation, she made an exception.

With Tommy in tow they set off down the hill. Lofty thoughts and high ideals swirled through Margaret's mind. A bride on her way to the altar, a nun about to take her vows was not more fervent than Margaret on her way to start her life as a monitor.

Jenny saw the faraway look in her eyes and realised Margaret was daydreaming. She tugged her sleeve. 'Remember don't say anything unless you have to. I'll do the talking,' she urged her.

'I won't,' Margaret promised.

Jenny eyed her doubtfully. The role of monitor made Margaret a target. It was as good as a bull's eye painted on her back. Then Jenny's attention was distracted by the familiar sight of Edward Carter weaving about the town square on his bicycle. Her heart melted at the sight and she smiled. It wouldn't be so bad going to Miss Fossil's school if she could still bump into Edward in town. Her spirits lifted.

'Hiya, Tommy.' Edward, as custom dictated, greeted the other male first. Only then could he turn his attention to the girls. He told them he was in the first class of the new Grammar School; he had a bursary.

'A what?' Jenny thought it sounded painful, like a whitlow.

'It's money. To pay for my schooling. So, I don't have to go down pit just yet.'

Jenny made a face at the thought of coal dust in his blonde hair.

'No chance,' he told her. 'I like being in the fresh air too much.' He paused and glanced at Tommy. 'Better be on your way, Tommy. You don't want to be late on the first day back.' Obedient as a dog to his master's voice Tommy set off. Edward gave a satisfied smile. That was one inconvenient witness out of the way. He looked towards Margaret and saw no danger there. Her head was in the clouds.

He leant close to Jenny. 'As I said, I'm very fond of fresh air.' He winked, thrilling her to her very bones. 'I sometimes go in the churchyard here in the dinner hour, or after school. Have a walk. It backs onto Miss Fossil's. Trust the Church of England to have the only green place in the town.'

'I know the place. We often go there. Visit our mother's grave.' Understanding passed between them.

He glanced up at the church clock. 'I'd best be on my way. Don't let those posh girls push you about.' He grinned and was gone.

Jenny and Margaret turned the corner beyond the church and presented themselves at Miss Fossil's school. There was no noticeboard proclaiming it to be a grammar school or an academy, simply a white painted door and a bell pull. The girls exchanged glances to see which of them would be brave enough to ring the bell. As they dithered, three chattering girls arrived and solved the problem for them. A maid flung open the door. They followed the other girls in.

'Just do what they do,' Jenny muttered to Margaret, 'and we won't go far wrong.'

What 'they' did was to hang their bonnets and capes on pegs and join the other pupils in a large airy room. A group of five or six girls with brightly coloured clothes, loud voices and extravagant gestures were busy getting themselves noticed in the centre of the room.

'It's worse than Mr Cripps' class,' Margaret gasped.

'I might have guessed,' muttered Jenny as she watched Dorothea Woodward queening it for the benefit of the new girls. Dorothea's dramatic colouring, the white skin and the raven black hair was always going to make her stand out. Today it was emphasised by her silk dress in that most expensive of colours - violet. A small coterie of elaborately dressed girls vied for her attention with strident voices and extravagant gestures. Whilst the group preened and paraded centre stage, the other girls, oppressed by a sudden loss of confidence, took shelter against the walls where they felt drab and undeserving of notice.

'They're always like that. Today it's worse. They haven't seen each other over the holiday,' said a girl, standing alone on the fringes of the room. 'They've got a lot to talk about, especially her.' She nodded across the room.

'Oh her,' said Jenny. 'We know her. Who are the others?'

The girl reeled off some names. 'They're her mice.'

'Mice?'

'They're her creatures. They do her bidding.'

The two white blouses caught Dorothea's eye. She straightened up and headed towards them. The mice trooped after her, their faces gleeful. They sensed sport. Silence fell.

Dorothea took her time as she inspected them. 'White blouses. Huh. I know you.' Contempt dripped from her. You're the Truesdale girls. You look as if you are going to work in the post office.'

There was an insult there, but Jenny was not exactly sure what it was. She felt the expression on her face harden.

Previous encounters with Dorothea had taught her to show no sign of weakness.

Dorothea waved a lace-trimmed arm. 'This establishment is for the daughters of gentlemen. We don't sell stamps and weigh parcels. Here we learn to draw and to play the piano.' She drew herself up to her full height and in an excllent accent announced. 'Ici nous apprendrons le Francais.' She paused for effect. 'That means that here we learn French.' She looked round in triumph. The new girls gaped at her; they were impressed - and apprehensive. Just as she intended.

Dorothea smirked and turned again to Jenny and Margaret. She put her hands on her hips and stuck her elbows out. The light of battle glinted in her eyes.

Jenny saw that Dorothea was looking for a fight and chose to thwart her. Tempting though it was, she did not let rip with a stinging reply. She arranged her face into a benign smile and turned away from Dorothea and her cohort of admirers. There is no point in preaching to the converted. Jenny wanted a different audience; she wanted the eyes and ears of the silent girls who stood uneasily round the edges of the room.

'As Dorothea says,' she began silkily, 'we are the Truesdale girls. I'm Jenny and this is my sister Margaret.' She gestured to Margaret who gallantly stuck to her instructions and remained silent.

Jenny's eyes swept the room. She was rewarded with a few glances and shy smiles, potential allies. That gave her confidence. Her chin went up and her voice came out clear and loud. 'I don't know anything about French, but my sister here already knows Latin.'

Even the most ignorant girl knew that Latin trumped French. It was the language their brothers were sent away to learn. It had a mysterious power to open doors that otherwise remained closed. A few of the new girls, who did not yet know how dangerous it was to cross Dorothea Woodward, tittered quietly.

Jenny's use of the word 'sister' shrieked through Dorothea's head. How dare that girl claim to have a sister when one of them was a foundling bastard? A light went on in Dorothea's mind. Did the other girls know? They might not have the same opportunity to sit in their in their mother's drawing room and listen to gossip. Dorothea saw it as her duty to inform her fellow pupils.

'You're dressed like twins, but you're not twins, are you?' she demanded and did not wait for an answer. Oozing menace, she circled the two girls. 'You don't look alike. A tiny little brown mouse and a long lanky thing that looks like a floor mop.'

Jenny's cheeks flushed, almost a match for Dorothea's scarlet patches. Margaret, mindful of Jenny's instructions, screwed up her eyes and pursed her lips.

Dorothea had the stage now. She prowled round Jenny and Margaret, stabbing them with insults. 'You're not twins. You're not even sisters.' She was a tiger stalking its prey, jabbing at them with a sharp paw. 'One of you is a bastard.'

A murmur ran through the girls. They exchanged puzzled glances. Few knew the meaning of that word or had heard the story of the bicycle. Dorothea prepared to enlighten them. A glance told her that the audience was hooked, waiting for the victims to buckle and burst into tears. She threw her head back, her plait of black hair swinging behind her like a tail.

'It was in the newspaper. A huge headline. Child abandoned on Sunday. The Lord's Day!' Dorothea arranged her face to show dismay. 'How wicked was that? To abandon a helpless child. On the Sabbath. And to steal a bicycle to make your escape.' More in sorrow than in anger Dorothea looked round the room and found heads nodding in agreement. No-one dared speak.

She turned to Margaret and Jenny and pointed dramatically. 'What I want to know,' she said, 'what I want to know,' she repeated for effect, 'is which one of you was left behind in exchange for a bicycle.'

Suppressed giggles escaped from unkind lips.

Jenny and Margaret stared straight at their tormentor while many pairs of female eyes watched. Some hoped that this time Dorothea would be bested.

'Now.' said Jenny.

In perfect unison she and Margaret turned to each other and pointed.

'She is.' Their voices came out loud and clear.

The room held its breath. Dorothea swallowed a great gulp of air. Then the laughter started.

Jenny smiled at Margaret as if she had been doing nothing more serious than playing pat a cake.

Dorothea was in luck; she was saved, literally, by the bell.

Miss Fossil arrived swinging a hand bell with the vigour of a miner with a pickaxe. Silence fell upon the room. The headmistress strode through her pupils, mounted the platform and announced the number of the morning hymn. Miss Fossil was too experienced a teacher to think the girls' sudden silence was a mark of respect for her. Something had been going on. There was always a certain amount of jockeying for position at the beginning of a school year.

As the first rousing chords of Onward Christian Soldiers filled the air Dorothea's voice rose clear and sweet above the others. Dorothea had many faults in her character but she had one great talent. She could sing.

The hymn came to an end. Dorothea set about thinking of ways to get her own back on those Truesdale girls. It had to be something major. They had twice outmanoeuvred her. Spilt tea and jammy smears on dresses were not enough. It had to be something that really hurt.

Miss Fossil recited a short prayer and then came to the business of the day. She welcomed the new students and announced that Margaret Truesdale was to be a monitor. She asked Margaret to step forward so that everyone could recognise her in future. Margaret stepped forward, her face pink with embarrassment.

'This is a new position. To be appointed monitor is the first step in training to be a teacher. The new colleges and universities are opening their doors to girls. There you can study and take degrees just as men can. It is important for girls to have highly trained teachers to help them make their way in the new century that awaits us. Gone are the days when girls only learnt how to embroider their names and make flowers from wax. Here we offer academic subjects and demanding courses of study. I am proud that we in Atherley are in the vanguard of progress.'

Dorothea was not listening. Nothing more strenuous than a little light needlework was her idea of an education. She looked at her inner circle of supporters. The mouse she called Ship had started to clap. Dorothea's glare made her realise it was a mistake. Ship's hands fluttered down to her sides.

Margaret with her head down and her spectacles slipping from her nose crept out of the limelight and back into the anonymity she preferred. Dorothea watched as she disappeared among the other pupils. Goofy goggle-eyed creature, she thought. Not worth bothering about. Tormenting Margaret would be no more satisfying than taking the wings off a butterfly. Yet this flimsy girl had been picked out for special notice while she, Dorothea Woodward, only child of the man who ran this town and all who lived in it, had been foiled by that wretched bookworm and her so-called sister. That ridiculously loud bell had saved them. Otherwise she'd have had one of them in tears. She could guarantee it.

The little pantomime of, 'I am,' and 'She is', was scorched into Dorothea's brain. Those mocking words and that cheerful pointing needed two actors. Something started to whir in Dorothea's mind. Margaret was a monitor – whatever that was. She would have a different status from Jenny. Dorothea saw straightaway the opportunity to play divide and conquer. It was the girls' unity that gave them power. She would not waste her energy on the nondescript Margaret. All her malice would be concentrated on Jenny. She would make that lanky red head suffer.

Miss Fossil's vision of the ideal school was a microcosm of a just society where the love of learning, truth and fairness prevailed. She dreamed of opening girls' eyes so they might see beyond the narrow futures that society ordained for them. She wanted to show them that the world held possibilities other than marriage.

To bring such a school into existence she had been forced to compromise. The ladylike subjects of French, Music and Drawings dominated the timetable. Even that most frivolous of activities – Deportment- was included. These were the subjects parents valued. Wealthy factory owners wanted their daughters to have the accomplishments and refinements previously confined to the aristocracy. They knew it improved their daughters' opportunities in the marriage market.

Miss Fossil consoled herself by giving Margaret extra tuition in Latin. A good gallop through Cicero or Virgil cheered her up enormously and reminded her why she wanted to run a school. Not only had Miss Fossil been forced to compromise on the timetable, but she had also to tolerate a high rate of truancy. Mothers regularly took their daughters out of school to accompany them on afternoon calls. Dorothea's mother was the worst offender.

After a few weeks of term Mrs. Woodward came in person to inform Miss Fossil that this year Dorothea was to come home every afternoon. They received many invitations and wished Dorothea to take advantage of the opportunities they presented to meet new people. For 'people' read 'eligible men' thought Miss Fossil. Accordingly, the carriage would come at 1 pm. to take Dorothea home every day, regular as clockwork.

Miss Fossil tried pointing out that if Dorothea only came part time, Mr Woodward would not be getting good value for his money. Mr Woodward was a businessman and knew how many beans made five. Mrs. Woodward was not impressed by this argument; she came from Southport where money was not regarded as a suitable subject for conversation among ladies. Dorothea had taken the precaution of persuading her father to sanction the plan. She knew exactly how to manage her parents.

There was nothing more Miss Fossil could do. Dorothea's schooling was not compulsory; it was an optional extra. If her parents wanted her to make an early start on the marriage market, she could not stop them. She gave a half-hearted smile to Mrs. Woodward and watched as she swept out, her bustle bouncing merrily on her substantial derriere.

Miss Fossil was rewarded for her forbearance. In the afternoon, the whole atmosphere in the school improved; it hummed with concentrated study. Staff and pupils grew more business-like and cheerful while free of Dorothea's unpredictable and tyrannical presence. Only the members of Dorothea's little coterie suffered from her absence. They hung about like lost planets with no sun to circle. They soon discovered it was much more comfortable to blend in with their classmates. Some found they actually enjoyed the obscure delights of Mathematics and History.

The tutor of mathematics was in the process of introducing the girls to the principles of geometry; they were busy drawing triangles with their rulers and measuring angles with protractors. Jenny's neighbour was one of Dorothea's mice. At first, they did not speak. The other girl's ruler slipped and her pencil shot across the page leaving a jagged line. She tutted with annoyance. Jenny passed her an eraser. The ice was broken. The girls started to converse quietly, their heads bent over their work.

'I like geometry. Though I'm not sure what it's for.'

'It's very useful for measuring distances.' This gem of knowledge had come to Jenny courtesy of Edward Carter. She still managed to catch a few words with him.

Jenny introduced herself. The other girl said nothing. 'You are supposed to tell me your name,' she told the other girl. 'I'm not sure what to call you. I hear Dorothea call you 'Ship'. That's not your name really is it? When she says it fast it sounds like a very rude word.'

The girl grinned. 'That's one of Dorothea's jokes.' She stopped smiling and looked thoughtful. 'Well it started as a joke. It doesn't feel like one now.'

'I don't really like jokes about names. It's not as though we can choose them.'

'It's not my name. It's my title.'

Jenny frowned; she did not understand.

'It's short for 'Your Ladyship. Sometimes people call me that but my family call me Ella. I'd be pleased if you would call me Ella.'

Jenny agreed to oblige her.

'What's a hypotenuse?' Ella asked. Jenny pointed at the diagram. 'Ah,' said Ella. 'I see now.'

One by one the other girls started to call her Ella. It was not long before Dorothea added it to her list of crimes to be punished.

Anna found the afternoons long and dreary as the girls stayed later at school. Margaret blamed her tasks as a monitor. Jenny had to stay behind with her; a girl could not walk home on her own. Both girls carefully avoided mentioning that Jenny spent this free time with Edward Carter in the vicinity of the school.

The thought of filling the empty hours by making duty calls on other women depressed Anna. Then she recalled how she had toured the drawing rooms of the town in search of information about schools. When she had a purpose, her visits seemed less tiresome. Sieving the gems of information from the dross of gossip gave her mind some exercise. Perhaps she could fulfil her social duties while pursuing the mission that was closest to her heart.

With her second-best hat crammed on and her stays laced tight she set off with her card case. The matrons of the town gave her an unexpectedly warm welcome. At first, they had been wary of Anna. The newly widowed are automatically suspected of wanting a replacement husband.

Anna started her quest with Mrs. Woodward. It was best to pay her the respect she was convinced she deserved. The necessary obeisance to Mrs. Woodward did not yield the information Anna was looking for; she was foiled by the presence of Dorothea. An unmarried girl in the room prevented the kind of conversation Anna hoped for. Who was about to give birth? Who had been married six months with no obvious sign of pregnancy? Who was having hot flushes? Who had a false alarm?

On other afternoons, untrammelled by the presence of a teenager, confessions and speculations swarmed in the air as thick as autumn leaves. Still the vital nugget of information that Anna sought remained resolutely hidden. After a tedious afternoon devoted to varicose veins Anna came home, and threw her hat across the room in despair. The only way she was going to find out was by asking some very direct questions. She could not do that in Atherley. She would be branded as a scarlet woman and John reviled as a monster. He would lose his position and his income. His children would not dare to show their faces at school and the whole family would be forced to flee the town in shame.

Margaret and Jenny came bustling in, their cheeks pink with the cold. Margaret glowed with delight. Miss Fossil had given her an extra half hour of Cicero. Jenny was careful to point out that she had occupied the time practising her French. Anna marvelled that in such a short time the girls had learned so much. That's what could be achieved when you had a good teacher. Margaret unpacked her bag and laid her precious copy of Kennedy's Latin Primer on the table.

'You wouldn't think, that was how it all started,' said Margaret looking down at the modest volume in its khaki cover with gilt lettering. 'And now I'm reading Caesar's Gallic Wars!'

Anna remembered that book. The man in the bookshop had guided them to the right book and then ordered a copy. Margaret had not looked back since. Now it was Anna who needed a teacher. The right book might be the answer to her problem. She laughed out loud.

'What's so amusing?' asked Jenny.

'Nothing. I just remembered something.' What had amused Anna was the thought of asking the bookseller in the town to supply the book she needed. She pictured his amazement. He would show her the door and probably chase her up the street, while shouting his disapproval.

There are other bookshops in this world, she told herself. And libraries. They are good places to get information. Manchester, that thriving modern city is only a train ride away. The information is sure to be there. It will be embarrassing- very embarrassing. No worse than explaining those monthly things to the girls. She had survived that conversation. Afterwards she had communed with the ghost of her sister, Florence, asking for her approval. What, she wondered, did Florence think of her plan? The answer was as clear as crystal. Poor Florence, dead in childbirth, would thoroughly approve.

At breakfast, Anna announced that she was going to take the train to Manchester.

John looked up from his porridge, his brown eyes wide with surprise.

'Why?'

'Because I have things to do there. Just occasionally I like to escape this grim little town. I want to walk up Deansgate, see the Free Trade Hall. Be in a bustling and vibrant city.'

'If you wait till Saturday, we could all go. Make a day of it. Take the girls.'

'Thank you. But I want to go on my own.'

John frowned and turned over several thoughts in his mind. None of them particularly pleasant. Jealousy and suspicion were the first to arrive. Next was fear for her safety. She would be in an unfamiliar city without a male escort.

Anna saw his turmoil. If only he knew her purpose. That would bring a smile to his face - when he'd recovered from the shock. She decided to put him out of his misery. 'To be honest I'm going shopping. I want to visit the fabric shops. The ladies here have recommended one. They have told me how to get there. There's a horse-drawn tram from Victoria Station.'

John gave a little gasp of relief. Shopping. Women's stuff. She was not going to meet a potential suitor. She would be in the world of wide streets and big department stores, one of those rare parts of the world that worked to women's rules. She would be perfectly safe there.

'Let me know what train you're getting back. I'll come and meet you at the station. It'll be dark by then.'

When Anna's business was completed, she sent a telegram to John's office to tell him the time her train from Manchester would arrive. She felt the extravagance was justified; her mission had been successful. Excruciating but successful. As the train pulled out of Victoria station she wanted to leap up and down and shout, 'I did it', to the other passengers sitting in neat rows in the compartment. She did no such thing, of course. The years of patient training by family and society won.

Anna sat upright in the rattling carriage. The whalebones in her stays dug into the soft flesh of her stomach. Her neck ached from the weight of her hat with its stiff brim wreathed in artificial flowers and foliage. Her many petticoats were entangled round her legs. The rigours of the day had swollen her feet and her bosom was fighting to get out of her tight bodice. For several minutes she envied the way the mill girls dressed in their comfortable clogs and loose dresses. Then she remembered their long hours and the man paid to knock on the bedroom window to wake them for the early shift in the winter darkness.

John was waiting for her at the station in Atherley. Her heart turned over when she saw his figure in the light from the gas lamp. There was something so reassuring about his height and his broad shoulders. In his overcoat and his felt hat, he radiated warmth and solidity. Here was someone you could lean on, who would shelter you from the cold winds of the world. Anna longed to run to him and lay her head on his chest. As a wife would with her husband. If only. If only.

They greeted each other formally. He raised his hat. Just the slightest touch of their fingers as if they had been going to shake hands but decided not to. He asked if she would like to take a cab home. Tired though she was, she shook her head. She was mindful of the school fees he was paying. He took her parcels from her and offered his arm. She took it gratefully. The day had been a solitary ordeal. She was glad of this token of male support.

Their pace was leisurely as they walked up the hill. It was seldom that they were out together, as a man and a woman, without an escort of children. By an unspoken agreement they wanted to make this sensation of being a couple, illusory though it was, last as long as possible. The night was bitter cold but still and clear. The ugly town was bathed in the magic of moonlight. Anna's stays no longer stabbed unkindly, her feet and shoulders no longer ached. The alchemy of love melded her heart, her mind and her body into a state of harmonious bliss. She knew, in her bones and to the very centre of her being, that John felt the same.

'Did you manage to buy everything you wanted?' he asked.

'I did. I did indeed.' Anna smiled. She tried to picture his face if he knew what her parcels contained. She kept her left hand on John's arm. She did not want to let it go for fear the spell would be broken. They did not talk more. There was no need. They sauntered on up the hill.

At the door of the house they had to break the fragile connection that had bound them. In the dim light of the hall they looked at each other in a serious and solemn silence.

John's hand went to smooth back a hair that had strayed across her forehead. 'You must be tired, my dear.' He paused. Tommy clattered into the hall to hug his aunt. Margaret and Jenny arrived hot on Tommy's heels. They were pleased to see her. It was an unusual event for them to come home from school and find that their aunt was not there. They'd had a moment of panic; they knew what it was like to lose a mother. Being young, they recovered quickly. Now all they wanted was for her to describe Manchester, that great metropolis that was so often spoken of but seldom seen.

Anna assured them she had seen Albert Square. And the Free Trade Hall. She did not mention her visit to the Library in King Street. And now she was very tired and would like some tea if there was anyone who was capable of making it.

That night Anna locked the door that led to John's bedroom. The heady delight of the walk home had gone. Absurd though it might be, she felt confident that their love would one day be fulfilled. There was no need for haste and this night was not the moment for it. The ordeals of the day were fading: the librarian who kept asking her to speak more loudly when she enquired for information on how married couples could limit their family. His eyes had immediately leapt to her left hand in search of a wedding ring. George would have turned in his grave if he'd known how she had abused his ring that day.

Then, in contrast, there was the sensible woman assistant librarian who took over from her bad-tempered and evil-minded boss. She produced a booklet and found Anna a quiet table to sit at. 'Best to buy your own copy,' the woman told her. 'So, you can read it at your leisure. I guess you've come in from out of town and will want to buy the er... necessaries here.'

The woman flicked through the pages. 'Amazing isn't it? A young American doctor wrote this over seventy years ago. Thirty years ago, they reprinted it in this country. They got taken to court for doing so. They did all us women a favour though. The publicity helped.' The librarian indicated a page. 'Start here,' she said. 'This is the bit that'll tell you what to buy. Read the rest of it when you get home.

By the light of the candle in her bedroom, Anna unwrapped the parcels and spread out their contents on her dressing table. There was the book, and some small sponges and a syringe. She ran a test run of the syringe, filling it with water from the jug and pressing the plunger with vigour. A jet of water plumed into the air and landed on the rug, close to the brown scorch mark.

She settled down to read the booklet with its misleading title. The Fruits of Philosophy. By the light of her candle she read the pages she had skipped in the library. They were a revelation to her. The author described the reproductive organs and conception with clarity and elegance. He used scientific language to describe parts of the body Anna had not known existed.

How she wished she'd had access to this booklet before she'd married. It would've helped her to know what was going on. Even better if she'd read it in her adolescence. So much more helpful than her mother's dark warnings of immediate damnation and public disgrace. She was embarrassed now by her floundering attempt to tell Margaret and Jenny the so-called facts of life. For a moment she contemplated showing them the leaflet. A sense of self-preservation changed her mind.

In the rest of the leaflet there was good news and bad news. The author assured her pregnancy was not an inevitable result of intercourse. He calculated the odds as one in fifty. That might satisfy most women but Anna was looking for one hundred per cent certainty. She was sure it was fear of pregnancy that restrained John. His wife, her sister, had died in childbirth.

'I hope you won't mind Florence if I borrow your husband.' Anna kissed the photograph of her sister and set it back on the dressing table. She hid the items she had bought in Manchester in the second drawer of the chest. Then she climbed into bed and blew out the candle. As she settled back on the pillows, she felt that she had done as much as she could. Telling John of her precautions was not part of her plan. If – or when - the moment came she would be prepared. She lay back and smiled. It was up to John now.

***

Dorothea was having second thoughts about her afternoons off school. The jolly parties and the many conquests she'd imagined had not materialised. Instead there were endless at homes with gallons of tea and dowdy matrons who shushed each other and pointed to Dorothea whenever a juicy bit of gossip raised its head. The ladies all played by the rule of not talking about anything exciting in front of children and servants. Dorothea did not regard herself as a child. And she was certainly not a servant.

She considered returning to school for the afternoons. The gossip was better and there was more scope to exercise her talent for bending people to her will. Her mama was too easy and the servants most unsatisfactory. They did as she told them but there was no skill in that. That was their job. If she pushed them too far, they gave in their notice and went to work in the mills. The wages were better. Even worse, they did not scruple to give her father their reasons - in minute detail. The last chambermaid to depart had listed Dorothea's shortcomings in no uncertain terms.

Like Alexander, Dorothea was looking for a new world to conquer. It did not take her long to find one. Her mother's blanket term of disapproval – it wouldn't do in Southport – proved to be a double-edged sword. Dorothea put it to her mother that it was her duty to give her only daughter the opportunity to experience those high standards of taste and behaviour. What better way than to visit the town that was the source of all that was excellent? Mother and daughter should make a trip to Southport.

Mrs. Woodward was not as enthusiastic as Dorothea expected. Her mother's origins were not as high on the social scale as she would have people believe. There were no elegant homes or refined family members to visit; she had no grand acquaintances to renew.

Dorothea sensed her mother's discomfort and found a way round it. Could they stay in a hotel? Dorothea had never stayed in one. It would be good experience for her.

One day she might go to France. What was the point of all those French lessons if there was no chance of visiting the country? There was a whole world out there just waiting for her. Mrs. Woodward realised she was out of her depth; she referred the matter to a higher authority.

After due consideration Mr Woodward agreed to the enterprise. Let the girl have a practice run at the world. Soon she would be launched into society with every expectation that she would make a 'good' marriage. By 'good' Mr Woodward, chapelgoer though he was, meant someone with a pedigree, a family with a long- established position in society, perhaps even a modest title. A baronet, or an honourable would do nicely.

Mr Woodward even expressed the wish to accompany them to Southport. Dorothea held her breath. His presence would cramp her style. His ostentatious checking of bills was just the start. She intended to meet young men and form their acquaintance. Her father's dominant presence would put paid to that.

Mr Woodward had doubts about leaving his business at that moment. A contract he was negotiating was at a critical point. His presence was needed; Mr Woodward was never happy unless he had a deal coming to the boil. He might manage to join them for a day.

A great deal of packing was involved. Dorothea looked at the trunks her mother's maid was filling. Even she was surprised at the number of clothes needed for five days away. 'You cannot manage with less,' said the maid and started to count on her fingers. 'Five days, that's five evening dresses for dinner in the hotel, five morning outfits and five for the afternoons. Then there's the hats, and the shoes. Not counting the nightclothes and the underwear.'

'I expect we'll do some shopping while we're there.'

'I should hope so, Miss Dorothea. You'd be silly not to. Lord Street is famous for its shops.

It took two porters to load the Woodward luggage on the train for Southport. Once there they marvelled at the flatness of the landscape. The horizon encircled them; such a contrast to Atherley hidden its valley. The horses clip-clopped sedately along Lord Street instead of straining their bulging muscles to master steep slopes. The weather was kind to the Woodward women. They drove in an open landau down streets, fringed with wrought iron pergolas and elegantly curled lampposts. They strolled on the promenade and they looked out to the sea.

Dorothea at last received her rightful quota of masculine attention. The men tipped their hats to her as she passed in the landau. They ran to offer an arm to her mother as she negotiated some tricky steps, but it was on the daughter they lavished their gaze. In the hotel they found excuses to start conversations, recommending sights, walks and shops.

In the evenings a pianist came to the hotel to play for the guests as they drank their after-dinner coffee. He asked Dorothea to assist him by turning the pages of the music. Her help was not necessary; he knew all the songs by heart, but audiences like to have a pretty girl to look at and sometimes she can be persuaded to sing. Dorothea did not need much persuasion. What she needed was material. Her repertoire consisted mainly of hymns. The pianist, an Irishman, taught her a song his grandmother had taught him, 'Down by the Salley Gardens.' She mastered the lyrics in minutes. He gave her half an hour's rehearsal and sat back in admiration at the result.

Her debut was a stunning success. The sweet simple sadness of the song, the purity of her voice and the innocence of her youth combined to melt the hearts of the audience. The following day she was congratulated by the other guests, both male and female.

Mr Woodward paid a flying visit that interrupted Dorothea's singing, shopping and flirting. That evening the pianist played nothing but Chopin and turned the pages himself. The men in smart suits who strolled the streets and filled the hotel lobby disappeared when her father arrived. The minute he boarded the train for home, they popped up again.

When the time came to depart Dorothea looked with satisfaction as the maid struggled to close the trunks. There were several dress boxes, their contents carefully wrapped in tissue paper. In her mind's eye Dorothea gloated over her purchases one by one. The green silk tea dress, the pink cotton for summer, the teal evening dress. She had so wanted a black one; it would look amazing with her black hair and her white skin. Her mother had, for once, put her foot down. Black was for mourning. She would not have the bereaved mocked. Since then Dorothea lived with the hope that a distant relative might conveniently die and so allow her to wear black – as long as it was low cut. She didn't want to be muffled up to the neck in the stuff.

As Dorothea looked at the fourth and final box, she pictured its contents, a grey alpaca dress with a high collar and discreet cuffs of white lace. She would wear it to school on her first day back. The girls would go green. The thought of their jealousy almost consoled her for the pain of leaving Southport and its many pleasures.

'Are you not sad to leave?' Dorothea asked her mother as they sat in the pony trap on the way to the station. 'Southport is so clean and fresh. The people are not rushing off to work in grubby clothes. They have leisure to enjoy themselves. You are right, mama, about Southport being so much better than Atherley.'

For once in her life Mrs. Woodward rebuked her precious Dorothea; she was a little nervous at the size of the final bill for this jaunt. 'Just remember, Dorothea, Southport is where people come to spend their money. It's in Atherley and places like it that they make their money.'

On Monday morning Dorothea stood before the mirror and smoothed the bodice of the grey alpaca dress. She sighed with satisfaction. It was perfect. A sober design in a luxurious fabric. Her 'mice' would gnash their teeth with envy. If she couldn't be queening it in Southport, the next best thing would be reasserting her hold on her followers. They may have grown a little lax in her absence. Without her whipping they may have missed opportunities for tormenting those Truesdale girls.

'I think, mama, that it would be better not to send the carriage for me at one o'clock.'

Mrs. Woodward looked up in surprise. 'Why? I thought you would come to visit Mrs. James with me. What has made you change your mind, Dorothea?'

Exactly that, thought Dorothea. The prospect of visiting dreary Mrs. James. The only pleasure to be found would be in bragging about her new clothes. How much more satisfactory to do that with people of her own age. She knew better than to say that to her mother. What she said was, 'Papa is paying the full fees for school. If I only go in the morning it is a waste of his money.'

Mrs. Woodward's jaw dropped at this volte face by Dorothea. Her surprise was followed by an unpleasant shock. The bill from the dress shop in Southport arrived in the morning post. It exceeded her gloomiest prediction. She began to think it might be sensible to have Dorothea handy to shield her from Mr Woodward's wrath. That girl could wrap her father round her little finger.

While her mother struggled for words, Dorothea made a speedy escape. She told the maid there was one less for lunch, summoned the coachman, put on her hat and set off to school.

She was, as so often, the last to arrive at Miss Fossil's premises. She rang the familiar doorbell, ignored the maid and strode inside. As she hung up her hat and her coat, she heard the chatter coming from the hall. Good. Miss Fossil had not started the morning assembly. She could make a grand entrance. She smoothed her dress in anticipation of receiving a great deal of attention and opened the door into the hall.

What she saw took her breath away.

A sea of white blouses confronted Dorothea. Wherever she looked she saw girls wearing white blouses. Marie

Antoinette faced with a mob of *sans culottes* could not have been more devastated. Her girls, her mice had deserted her. They were following the Truesdales, not her, Dorothea Woodward, daughter of the wealthiest and most powerful man in town. She searched the sea of bobbing white foam for the culprits; they no longer stood out from the crowd like daisies on a lawn. She spotted the lanky red head deep in conversation with the girl Dorothea called Ship, to punish her for having a title. And Ship was wearing a white blouse!

Dorothea felt she would faint – or explode. The treachery of her mouse, Ship, was a knife plunged deep into her heart. Where were her other mice? Surely, they would be loyal to her and her dress code of elaborate, showy and expensive clothes. Desperately Dorothea scanned the room and found three dabs of colour. O the relief. Her mice were loyal to her. Only Ship had gone over to the other side. Dorothea frowned as she struggled to recall Ship's given name. Ella that was it. From now on she was Ella. Only loyal mice had the privilege of a nickname.

Once again Dorothea was saved by the bell. Miss Fossil arrived and started the assembly.

'Please, God, don't let her welcome me back from my holiday,' prayed Dorothea with unaccustomed fervency. It was just the sort of sarcastic remark Miss Fossil would make to embarrass her in front of the others. God must have heard Dorothea's plea as Miss Fossil moved straight on to the Lord's Prayer.

Dorothea's mind began to function as the great storm of emotion settled down. She did some quick calculations; only three allies left. That was not enough to fight the tide of white blouses. Like a good general she knew when to admit defeat.

The assembly came to an end. The girls scattered about the hall as they waited for the first lesson of the day. It was Deportment. Dorothea placed herself next to Ella. She looked with disapproval at the white blouse.

'I see you're wearing the latest fashion,' she said.

Ella quailed at this frontal attack but took courage from being in the majority. 'Yes. A lot of us are doing it. We think it looks efficient and business-like.'

'I'll probably wear one tomorrow. It will save me going through my wardrobe deciding what to wear.' Dorothea could not resist flicking the lace of her cuffs and running her hands over the soft grey alpaca. Ella ignored her. Dorothea raised her voice a decibel to be sure all the girls could hear her. 'I got so many new clothes in Southport, choosing one is quite a problem for me.'

No-one rose to take the bait. No-one commented on the grey alpaca or asked about the other new clothes. Dorothea bit her lip. How quickly her subjects had deserted her. Five days away and they behaved as if she never existed. Ruthlessly Dorothea cut her losses. The minute she got home she would tell her maid to have a white blouse starched and ironed for the next day. It was the first thing she must do when she got home. When she got home. Her heart sank as she remembered. Afternoon school. She'd arranged to stay for the afternoon. How could she bear it? Two whole hours surrounded by treacherous swots in white blouses doing mathematics and history.

That would be a humiliation too far. Dorothea decided she would leave school at one o'clock as usual. There was only one snag to her plan, but it was a formidable one. The carriage would not be there. Now that was a problem. Then she remembered one of her father's favourite sayings. 'There are more ways of killing a cat than skinning it alive.

As she walked round the room with a book balanced on her head Dorothea contemplated the different ways she could get home. A telegram asking for the carriage to come? It would take time. Where could she wait? She remembered her empty pockets. There was no thin silver sixpence lurking there, ready to pay for a telegram. Dorothea Woodward had no need to carry money; she had servants. If her father was in his office, he would arrange a cab for her. Her heart sank at the explanations that would be necessary. If the worst came to the worst, she would walk up the hill to her home. Dorothea had a sinking feeling that the worst was coming. Also, it looked like rain.

At one o'clock Dorothea put on her hat and coat and walked out of the front door of the school as she usually did. This time no glossy carriage with a well-groomed horse awaited her. She walked round the corner and the next corner until she was in a street where she could not be seen from the windows of the school. There she stopped and looked around her. No matter which direction she looked there were identical double-fronted houses with white front doors. The names of the streets had no meaning for her.

She scanned the sky for a glimpse of the church tower to help her get her bearings. She looked in vain. It was hidden behind the roofs. To return to school was impossible. She had to find the road home. Panic was beginning to squeeze her chest so her breath came in gasps. Dorothea Woodward, treasured daughter of a wealthy man had never stood alone on a street before and she had no plan of action, just a vague hope that something would turn up.

It did. The something that turned up was the Truesdale girls. They pattered round the corner deep in conversation. Both parties were surprised at their meeting. Margaret, the monitor, was on an errand for a teacher. Jenny was the indispensable chaperon. This left the question of why Dorothea was out of school and alone on the pavement. A desperate Dorothea improvised.

'Something must have happened to the carriage. You know what horses are like. Always losing their shoes or breaking their fetlocks.' The lies dropped smoothly from her lips.

Margaret and Jenny did not argue; they knew about horses and how those fortunate enough to own one, complained long and loud about them.

'You can't stay here. You'll have to come back to school with us.' It was Margaret, the monitor speaking, not the mousey girl with spectacles. Her voice was firm, her expression confident. As a monitor she represented the authority of the school. Dorothea gave a faint squeal of despair. She was close to tears.

'I can't go back,' she wailed.

'You cannot stay here,' said Margaret, emphasising her words with a fierce glare.

'I know. I know. I can't go back and I can't go home.'

'Good afternoon ladies.' The voice was Edward Carter's. He gave them a sweeping bow, worthy of an eighteenth-century dandy. 'I think you are in need of a male escort.' His grin took the sting out of the remark.

'Not us,' said Margaret firmly. 'We have an errand.' She looked to Jenny for confirmation. Jenny said nothing but her cheeks glowed pink.

'Then it must be you,' said Edward turning to Dorothea. 'I recognise you from Chapel.' She looked blank. Edward Carter was too far down the social scale to be noticed by her family. One of nature's gentlemen, the lad introduced himself. 'Edward Carter. I hold the scholarship your father founded.'

Margaret, in her innocence, explained that Dorothea's carriage had failed to arrive.

Edward Carter saw a chance of bringing himself to the attention of the town's biggest employer. 'It's quite a hike up the hill to your house,' he said. 'Why not go to your father's office; it's nearer.'

Dorothea chewed her lip as she weighed the pros and cons of involving her father. Her lies would quickly unravel under close investigation. On the other hand, the hill was steep and it looked like rain. The presence of Edward might discourage her father from questioning her closely. She gave in. 'I was going to Papa's office but...to tell the truth I'm a bit lost.' Amazement showed on the other youngsters' faces. 'It's all right for you,' she told them. 'You're used to walking to places. I'm always taken in a carriage.'

'Like a baby in a pram.' Jenny's lip curled as she spoke. Edward glanced at her; she was seldom ill-natured.

'Yes. Like a baby. I don't know my way because there's no point in learning it. I never get to choose where I'm going. I just get taken where other people want me to go.'

Her audience fell silent. She had turned upside down all their assumptions about wealth and privilege. They were temporarily stunned, as if a firework had exploded.

The gallant Edward took charge. 'You go on with your errands,' he told the other girls. Margaret was squirming with impatience. 'I'll show Dorothea the way. I might have to miss a bit of Chemistry, but that's all.'

Jenny watched anxiously as Edward disappeared round the corner with the dreaded Dorothea.

Margaret tugged her sister's elbow to set off back to school. 'Stop looking back,' she snapped. 'You know the rules. You've got to stop going all pink and smiley when you see him,' she told Jenny. 'He's not supposed to know you really like him. You'd know that if you read some proper books. In Jane Austen, the proposal is always a pleasant surprise to everyone except the gentleman concerned.'

As luck would have it, Mr Woodward was leaving his office when Edward and Dorothea arrived. Edward removed his cap. 'You won't know me, Mr Woodward. But I've seen you at chapel.'

Mr Woodward looked closely at Edward who suddenly remembered he was not exactly a regular attender. Hastily he added his scholarship at the grammar school to his credentials. 'I did not think it right to leave Miss Dorothea to walk through the town alone.'

A smile spread over Mr Woodward's face. Edward had hit his soft spot.

Dorothea played her part. A muddle over ordering the carriage, she explained. She was supposed to accompany her mother on a visit. She had lost her way. She was so grateful to Edward. A few tears of female weakness rose to her eyes. Not too many. They were only a down payment on the gallons of tears she would need if the full scope of her misdeeds came to be known.

Mr Woodward arranged a vehicle to carry Dorothea home. As the cab rocked on its way, she reviewed her untruths and misdeeds of the day. The list was too long and complicated for comfort. If her mother and father compared notes, what she called muddles would be revealed as downright lies. It was fortunate her mother was too much under her thumb to volunteer more information than strictly necessary. If her parents put their heads together and pooled their resources, they had enough to build a water-tight case for the prosecution.

There were the fibs at school to be counted, as well as going out without a chaperon and being seen alone in public with a boy. She had better delay telling her father that the expensive dresses from Southport were temporarily redundant and that a white blouse was now the fashion of the day.

On his way back to school Edward weighed up his gains and losses from this adventure. There was no disputing that the shilling in his pocket from a grateful Mr Woodward was pure profit. Edward calculated that the greater prize was catching the favourable attention of Dorothea's father.

The chemistry teacher was in the middle of a tricky demonstration when Edward arrived in the class. He demanded to know the reason for what he called Carter's tardiness, but his heart wasn't in it. His attention was elsewhere.

'Damsel in distress,' said Edward and slid onto the nearest stool.

Miss Hulme and Miss Fossil sat at their elegant little dining table eating their early evening meal and compared notes on their day at work. The flow of their conversation was constantly interrupted by their maid, in her black dress and white cap, as she delivered the dishes of food. When she was in the room they did not talk about their pupils; they preserved their privacy very strictly.

'I don't want to sound smug, Frances, but I am really very pleased with the progress we are making. The truancy officer is complaining that he'll be out of job soon,' said Miss Hulme.

'Something to do with the free school meal you provide?' queried Miss Fossil with a sly smile. 'Parents send their children to school to be fed; it's cheaper.'

Miss Hulme did not deny the charge. 'It's Mr Woodward I have to thank for that. He's footing the bill.' Miss Hulme fell silent as the maid delivered the main course. She waited until the domestic had left the room. 'Mr Woodward called round this afternoon. Wanted to know about one of my pupils, Edward Carter.'

'He has one of Mr Woodward's bursaries, hasn't he?'

'It wasn't the boy's work he was asking about. His behaviour. His character.'

'Could you give him a glowing report?'

'Absolutely. He is my brightest star. A golden boy.'

'I wish I could say the same of Mr Woodward's daughter. The blessed Dorothea returned from her week of absence at Southport today. I wanted to make a spectacle of her in assembly. Ask how her she'd enjoyed her week at the seaside while the rest of us were toiling away here. Watch her go red in the face and splutter. But I decided against it.'

'Quite right. Sarcasm doesn't work.' Miss Hulme put the last piece of Irish stew in her mouth.

'She still left before lunch,' lamented Miss Fossil.

Miss Hulme finished chewing. 'Is there nothing the wretched girl really likes doing, apart from dressing up and showing off?'

'French. She likes French,' Miss Fossil stopped speaking as the maid came to pour water into their glasses and collect the plates. 'She is actually quite good at French. It's a pity our teacher of French isn't better qualified. Poor Miss Hughes. Her accent is more Yorkshire than Paris.' Miss Fossil went over a few possibilities in her mind, but Miss Hulme beat her to the solution she was groping towards.

'French conversation,' she pronounced. 'We have on our staff a native French speaker who is underemployed. More boys want to take Technical Drawing than French. We could arrange a special session of conversation for my boys and your girls.'

Miss Fossil gasped at the effrontery of the idea. 'You mean boys and girls in the same class?'

'That's how the world works. Men and women do talk to each other. Well at least they do in France.'

Miss Fossil's lips remained pursed in disapproval.

'Why not. They sit in the same classroom at elementary school. After that we pretend that the opposite sex does not exist. How sensible is that?'

'I think you exaggerate a little,' Miss Fossil reproved her friend.

'Well there's nothing like a little exaggeration to improve your case in an argument. Some of my boys could do with teaching some manners. Your girls could show them how to behave. Madam Tours is pretty sharp in that respect.'

'My little monitor could give her a hand. I want to promote her to pupil teacher next year. She's a wizard with languages. Prefers Latin. Obviously.' Miss Fossil stirred cream into her apple crumble. 'My premises or yours?'

'Mine. The rooms are bigger. You could bring the girls across one afternoon. Madam Tours and your little monitor can chaperon them while we retreat to my office and have a civilised cup of tea together.'

'I'd need parents' agreement.'

'And I will have to put it to the governors. I think Mr Woodward will agree. His horizons are not limited to this little town.'

'I will wager you five shillings that when Dorothea finds out that there will be boys, she will be very keen to improve her French conversation. There'll be no more leaving at one o'clock then.'

Miss Hulme chuckled. 'I accept.' She thought for a moment. 'Of course, I could find you some exceptionally

111

unalluring boys. Boys with scabies, boys with rickets or boys with ringworm. Take your pick.'

Miss Fossil waved her spoon. 'I still think I'd win.' She fell silent while the maid cleared the bowls away and brought in coffee. As she poured sugar into her tiny coffee cup, she leant across the table to tell her friend the best news of the day.

'The white blouse revolution is almost complete. White blouses outnumber dresses by twenty-one to four. It is virtually a uniform. I can thank the Truesdale girls for that.'

Miss Hulme congratulated her. She looked wistful. 'It would be nice if all my pupils could have a uniform. Most of them are in hand me downs and rags. All credit to their mothers. They are usually clean rags.'

Her father summoned Dorothea to his study. She passed her mother on the stairs, her face streaming with tears and her chest heaving with sobs. 'Go, child,' she managed to gasp. 'I cannot help you now.'

At the door Dorothea removed the smile of greeting from her face and replaced it with one of contrition. She had a handkerchief ready in her pocket. Tears were an essential ingredient of the case for the defence. When she opened the door, she found her father was standing with his back to her, looking out of the window. As he turned, she saw how tired he looked.

Mr Woodward sighed when he saw his daughter looking woebegone. What is it about the female of the species? he wondered. He could start work at five in the morning, ride thirty miles, argue prices with the coal merchants, inspect his cotton mills, and settle a strike, all before dinner, without a whiff of tiredness. Let him have a disagreement with a woman and he was ready to throw in the towel after five minutes.

'I think I've been a very silly girl, papa. I'm sorry.' Dorothea saw her father had exhausted all his anger on her mother. It was time to play the penitent child. As she worked on the tears, she wondered which of her misdeeds her mother had revealed. Was it the leaving school early? The flirting in Southport? The exact cost of the clothes bought there? Lying about the carriage? The encounter with Edward Carter? These were murky waters. Better to steer clear of the details. Instead of raking over her past misdeeds, she would turn her father's attention to the future. The tears were ready. She sent one trickling down each cheek.

'Tell me how I can behave better in the future, please, papa. I so want you to be proud of me.'

Mr Woodward's heart melted. He put his arms round her. 'There, there, darling girl.'

Three days later Miss Hulme put the proposal for a French conversation class to Mr Woodward. He approved. As an afterthought he added the proviso that the class should continue for half an hour after the usual end of lessons. By giving up their free time, pupils would demonstrate genuine interest in the subject. He found it easy to act the stern disciplinarian when Dorothea and her tears were not in the room.

Miss Fossil wrote a cunning letter to the parents of her girls. Some, she claimed to know, were considering sending their daughters abroad to finishing school. A highly qualified teacher at the grammar school was available to provide extra tuition in French; she was a native speaker of the language. Such conversation classes could help prepare those girls fortunate enough to have the opportunity of continuing their education abroad. There would be no extra charge for this valuable addition to the curriculum. The class would be open to a select few of the grammar school pupils. The girls would be carefully chaperoned. Parents with social ambitions immediately signed their daughters up for the class.

At school Miss Fossil briefed Margaret about the conversation classes. She should not be concerned about the presence of boys. The choice of venue was for Madam

Tours' convenience. Margaret was pleased to be considered a responsible chaperon. It was another step on her way to becoming a pupil teacher.

'You will have to stay for that class, Jenny,' warned their father. 'Margaret cannot walk home on her own.'

Jenny pulled a face. French was not her favourite subject. If there was a spare half hour after school, she spent it drifting about the grounds and the churchyard for the chance of bumping into Edward Carter. It was surprising how often it happened. When it was cold, they took refuge in the public library, sitting at separate tables to avoid being rebuked by the librarian. They could exchange a few words while wandering the shelves in search of fresh reading matter. French conversation would put an end to this brief pleasure.

'Cheer up,' said Margaret, 'it might not be as bad as you think.' She winked at Jenny who misunderstood the message and glared at her. On the day of the first class five girls assembled in the hall and waited for instructions. Dorothea joined them.

'Don't look so surprised,' she told them. 'French is my best subject.' The statement was true but had nothing to do with the reason for her being there. A full day at school, and extra study. That was the arrangement laid down by her father.

Miss Fossil appeared. 'This is one of those occasions where the mountain will not come to us. Therefore, we must go to the mountain. Follow me.'

Walking to the boys' school was the most exciting event in the girls' limited lives. Their hearts fluttered beneath their bodices as they ventured into male territory. Margaret sniffed the air with disapproval; it smelt defiantly masculine. Miss Fossil led them to a classroom where the seats were arranged in a circle in the hope of encouraging conversation. Madam Tours greeted them in French, told them to sit down and wait quietly. She then disappeared with Miss Fossil on a mysterious errand.

'This isn't going to be much fun,' complained Dorothea. 'There are so many empty chairs.'

'Not anymore.' The voice was Edward Carter's. He was followed by Madam Tours and three other boys who looked distinctly apprehensive. Edward Carter took charge. 'Bon jour, Mesdemoiselles. We have come for a bit of French polish.'

Jenny's heart turned over. A whole hour in a room with Edward Carter.

That night Miss Hulme and Miss Fossil had liver for dinner; it was their least favourite food.

'What a pity such nourishing food looks so unpleasant,' said Miss Hulme as she looked at the grey slab on her plate.

When they had the room to themselves Miss Fossil held out her hand. 'You owe me five shillings.'

Miss Hulme laughed. 'I sent you my best boys. They are irresistible.' She went to look for two half crowns to pay her debt. 'Trouble is, everyone wants them. Mr Woodward wants Edward Carter to go to work for him. Promised him training, qualifications, a genuine future. The lad can't say no. I persuaded him to wait till the end of term. That's the best I can do. There's some important maths in the last couple of weeks.'

She smiled. 'I hate to say goodbye to him.'

Miss Fossil leaned across to pick up her winnings. 'Don't fret. Bright youngsters are like hansom cabs in Piccadilly. There's always another one behind.

NEW YEAR'S EVE 1898

'A dark-haired stranger with a piece of coal. That's the proper way to welcome a New Year,' John told his family as he rose to his feet. 'You'll have to settle for me. I'm not a stranger but I've still got my hair.'

Just a sprinkling of grey, thought Anna, but did not say. No-one likes to be reminded they are growing older. She followed him into the hall and watched as he put on his overcoat.

John went to join his neighbours, temporarily ejected from their homes. Holding lumps of coal, packets of salt or chunks of bread, they congregated in the middle of the road waiting for the church bells.

In the sitting room Anna was explaining the tradition of first footing. It was the first time the girls had been allowed to stay up.

'It's a way to ensure good luck for the coming year. The first person to cross the threshold shows what kind of year is ahead.' Anna's ambition for the New Year was for John to cross her threshold.

'The Romans had Saturnalia,' said Margaret whose thoughts seldom strayed far from the Roman Empire.' '

'What do you hope for in the coming year?' Anna asked her.

'To be accepted as a student teacher.' Margaret had no doubts as to her ambition.

'And you, Jenny?'

Jenny pantomimed giving thought to the question. 'Perhaps not hearing quite so much about the Romans.' She ducked as Margaret threw a cushion at her. They could have pulled out her fingernails before she revealed the ambitions she nursed in her heart.

The church bells pealed midnight. Anna went to open the door.

'Happy New Year,' cried John and went to give her the traditional kiss. The urge to enfold her in his arms swept through his body. He cursed his vow to behave honourably. Years of restraint lay before him. Awkwardly he shuffled past her to greet the girls and Tommy who had woken from a brief nap on the sofa. He poured two celebratory glasses of Madeira and watched the youngsters take an experimental sip. They screwed up their faces in disgust and settled for ginger ale.

Their bedtime ritual followed its familiar pattern but was tinged by the glamour of being at the beginning of a whole new year. It lay spread out before them, waiting for them to put their mark upon it. They went to their beds and dreamt of glory.

When they were alone, John raised his glass to Anna. 'Happy new year, my dear...' His voice fell away as he remembered his most recent and frequently repeated resolve to be chaste. How quickly temptation had come and how close to breaking his vow with endearments he had been. 'My dear sister,' he corrected himself.

Anna felt as if she had been kicked. Was it for this she had lain in her bed with the door unlocked? Had she endured the brutal questioning of a librarian and faced sly smiles and conspiratorial winks from a pharmacist for this? The dreadful crushing of her dreams of love showed on her face. Even John, not the most observant of men, could see that she had undergone some kind of cataclysm of the spirit.

With a shaking hand, Anna set her glass of Madera on a table and rose to her feet in what she hoped was a dignified manner. Her body moved of its own volition, following instructions issued by a deep and primitive part of her.

'I am not your sister.' she corrected him. 'I am your sister-in-law.' Her voice was cracked ice. She moved to the door, intent on climbing the stairs and seeking refuge in her bedroom.

John moved with the speed of a cat to bar her way. His arm outstretched between her and the door. 'Anna, Anna, Anna,' he beseeched her. His face begged what he could not say.

'Do you want me to call you "brother"?' she asked.

'No.' It was more of a wail than a word. 'Husband. I want you to call me husband.'

Anna shuddered as a great wave of emotion shot through her. How she had longed to hear such words. She placed her hand on his outstretched arm and looked into his face. 'In spite of that law.'

'Love beats the law,' he said and kissed her. It was not a brother's kiss. Anna reeled. His fingers found the buttons on her bodice and with unexpected dexterity reached her breasts. Between kisses he asked, 'Does this feel wrong? Is this a sin?' His breath was hot on the thin skin of her bosom.

'No,' she murmured. It was more a moan than a word.

John placed his firm hands on her breasts and raised his head to look into her face. 'Every year I register births to girls admitted to the Workhouse; they have been impregnated by their fathers and brothers. You know what crowded conditions they live in. Some of them are not fourteen years old.' His voice shook. 'That is incest.'

'And this?' said Anna, stroking his hair back.

'In the opinion of some foul-minded people, what I feel for you, is tainted with sin. I do not believe them. This is love. I can't help it. You have captured my heart. You make me glad to be alive. I haven't always felt like that. I cannot live by other people's opinions. I love you. What I feel for you is strong and good.'

Anna leant back to summon all her courage. 'I know we cannot be married publicly, but I do not see why we cannot have an unofficial marriage. I know it must be secret, but it could be a marriage,' she groped for words, 'in every other respect.'

'How I wish that could be so. It is my heart's desire but you run too great a risk. As I know to my peril love makes babies. I will not have the world pour its scorn upon you.'

Anna put her finger to his lips. She hesitated, fearing she might shock him. 'I have learnt how to take precautions.' She looked at him anxiously.

'You mean there would be no consequences?'

She nodded. He could find no words but his face flooded with joy. He grasped her shoulders. She backed away and raised a warning hand. 'Give me a moment to warm some water. Then come to the bedroom.' She slid away to the kitchen.

John went through his habitual bedtime routine of locking doors and damping down the fires with a spring in his step. He pictured Anna, her hair loose on the pillow, her body naked beneath the sheets, waiting for him. He ached for the bliss of body and soul that satisfied desire brings.

As first love-makings go, it was a success. There were some moments of fumbling when they feared failure. The conclusion was satisfactory to both parties. It took all Anna's will power to lever herself from the bed to do the necessary business with the syringe. She was glad she had practised using the metal equipment and the water was warm.

'I'll get better with practice,' said John as he welcomed her back to bed. 'If I'm allowed to,' he added humbly.

Anna remembered her wedding night with George. The scratchy hair, the laboured breathing, her anxiety. 'I'll be very happy to repeat the experience,' she told him.

They lay together warm and comfortable with each other. 'Did that feel like a sin?' Anna teased him.

'No. This is heavenly bliss.

'The law does not think so.'

'The law is an ass.'

'That is true, but not very original. Mr Dickens said it first.'

When dawn cracked the night sky, John returned to his single bed.

The Truesdale family sat at their breakfast on the first of January 1899 just as they had done the previous year. Their habits and rituals appeared unchanged, but beneath the placid surface, strong emotions seethed. The senior members of the Truesdale family exchanged their habitual nods and polite good mornings at the breakfast table. Nothing more. John wanted to kiss Anna and stroke her hair. She wanted to embrace him and rest her heart close to his.

They knew such intimate gestures were not allowed. Their happy musings shivered to a halt. There is a difference between being private and hiding a secret. John and Anna began to realise that they were condemned to a life of deception.

Anna would be anxious every month until, as lovers put it, 'the redcoats landed'. She foresaw the frustration she would feel as other women made wifely gestures to their husbands, bidding them to bring a shawl or touching their hand as they shed their coats in the hall. These tokens of affection were denied her.

John had found it hard to restrain his passion during the evenings they had spent alone together. Now he must restrain himself all the time they spent in public. He must not tuck back a lock that had strayed from her hair or steal a discreet kiss to the nape of her neck. Such gestures were forbidden while his children were present, even though he had explored the secrets of Anna's body with his searching hands and lips.

The younger members of the family, unaware of the change in John and Anna's relationship, had their own thoughts for the future. Margaret, the monitor, looked forward to becoming a student teacher and spending as much time as possible in the company of Latin authors. Tommy wondered if this might prove be the year that he at last got a dog to lie beside him on the hearthrug.

Jenny's plans were more immediate and specific. She knew exactly what she wanted to do and where she wanted to be. She was determined that the coming year would bring her plans closer to fruition. All she needed was time and a little luck.

While John and Anna were reconciling themselves to a certain amount of concealment from their family, Mr Woodward sat at the breakfast table and urged more honesty on his. The trip to Southport and Dorothea's escapade in the town had caused him concern. He intended to insist on a higher standard of behaviour from his wife and daughter.

He started by cutting the housekeeping and limiting his wife's use of the carriage to three days a week. The horse was showing his age and he was not prepared to spend the money on a new one just yet. Furthermore, Mrs. Woodward was to make her calls alone. Dorothea was to stop leaving school in the afternoon. She was to attend all the lessons and to complete the tasks the teachers set her. He urged her to use the start of the year to take stock of her behaviour and consider how to improve her conduct.

For once in her life Dorothea did as her father told her. She sat at her dressing table and watched her eyebrows meet in a frown of concentration as she trawled through the past year in search of those moments of triumph that made her feel life was worth living. There were not many. Southport was one, but there was a heavy price to pay. Her father had cut her clothing allowance and her mother had begun to ask awkward questions instead of doing as she was told.

Her record at school was no comfort. Those Truesdale girls with their white blouses had taken all the fun out of showing off her clothes and bullying the younger girls. And as for her mice! They were beyond contempt. Disloyal cowards the lot of them.

Dorothea scowled as she sought someone to blame. The Truesdales were the obvious candidates. From there it was a short step to planning her revenge. Dorothea had not studied military history but she instinctively understood about divide and conquer. Together the two girls had proved impregnable. She would have to pick one to target. That mousy Margaret was safe behind her books and her role as monitor. That skinny Jenny, that beanpole with a mop on its head was a different matter. Dorothea remembered the day she had left school early and got lost. She had spotted the change in Jenny's manner when Edward Carter arrived on the scene. A few meandering threads of clues wandered through Dorothea's mind. She gathered them together, ready to plait into a rope for Jenny's neck.

On Monday 3rd January 1899 Mr Woodward finished eating, rose from the breakfast table and announced he was setting off for his office. When he had gone Dorothea tested the rope she had woven for Jenny with her fingers.

'You know, Mama, the start of a year makes you think about the future. What would we do if anything happened to Papa?' Dorothea took careful aim with her next question. 'Where would our money come from?'

Mrs Woodward, suffering from the hefty cut in her housekeeping allowance, was painfully aware of the power and necessity of money. She narrowed her beady black eyes but had no ready answer.

Dorothea aimed a knife at her mother's heart. 'We could not manage the business. That's not women's work.'

Mrs Woodward braced herself against the pain that was to come. Dorothea turned the knife. 'If only I had a brother. He would take over the business and look after us.'

When spring arrived Miss Fossil surveyed the assembled girls with pleasure: their white blouses, their happy faces and their cheerful voices. There is nothing like the sight of youth contemplating a sunny future to lift the spirits. It even consoled her for the headache the timetable had caused her. The limitations of space and the comings and goings of part-time staff had turned the timetable into a jigsaw puzzle with several pieces missing.

One of the missing pieces was Miss Hughes, the teacher of French with a Yorkshire accent. Miss Fossil judged her to be more a failed governess than a qualified teacher but she was better than nothing. And nothing was exactly what Miss Fossil was left with. To make matters worse the unsatisfactory teacher of French had eloped with the elderly widower who taught piano and singing. Rumour had it that the pair were on their way to Gretna Green.

'How unoriginal,' remarked Miss Hulme sourly.

The gallant Mr Woodward came to the rescue. He agreed to allow Madam Tours to teach French at Miss Fossil's school. Few boys in the grammar school were keen on the subject; they preferred Science. Mr Woodward would continue to pay Madam Tours' salary until the end of the school year. He knew how much Dorothea loved her French lessons.

Then a new music teacher arrived in town. He talked his way into Miss Fossil's study and planted his chunky figure opposite her, resting his stomach on the edge of her desk. He claimed to have come from Naples.

'It's in Italy,' he informed Miss Fossil, as if she did not know. She suspected his Italian accent was fake and that he had been born within a few miles of the River Thames. She swallowed her doubts. Professional teachers of music prepared to cope with a room full of privileged girls were not exactly thick on the ground in Atherley.

Signor Martelli's exuberant personality and knowledge of music were impressive. He produced letters of recommendation on thick paper stamped with gold coronets. As Miss Fossil shuffled through them, he demonstrated his credentials by singing *La Donna e Mobile*. The strength of his voice made the glass lampshade quiver. Even Miss Fossil, who took pride in silencing forty babbling maidens with one bellowed word, was impressed.

It was with relish that Miss Fossil offered the assembled girls a greater choice of subjects. They could continue to have more mathematics or, if they preferred, they could have French conversation with Madam Tours or singing with Signor Martelli. Miss Fossil hid her crossed fingers in the folds of her skirt and prayed that the numbers would work out.

Margaret, the monitor, already knew her fate. She was to sit in the singing lessons. The news appalled her. Quiet, biddable Margaret stood before Miss Fossil and protested loudly and eloquently. She could not sing. It was well known she was tone deaf and did not have a musical bone in her body. 'Please, please', she begged Miss Fossil, 'don't make me do it.'

Miss Fossil did not show the anger Margaret expected. Instead she smiled approvingly. 'I am pleased to see,

Margaret that you can speak out and stick up for yourself. So many girls have been trained for so long to be obedient they have forgotten that they have rights as well as duties. It is not my intention to make you learn to sing. I need you to sit in any individual lessons as a chaperon. I do not anticipate there will be many such lessons as I intend to charge parents an exorbitant amount for private tuition.'

Margaret almost whooped with relief.

'You will not be idle. I am conscious that you are first and foremost a pupil. I will set you some Latin translation to do. We shall move on to Livy this term. Signor Martelli will be teaching some Italian songs. You might find it of interest to spot the similarities between the two languages.'

'Poor you,' said Jenny when she heard Margaret's fate. 'You know who'll be having expensive singing lessons.'

Margaret pulled a face. There was no need to spell out Dorothea's name. 'At least I won't have to trudge across to the grammar school with her flouncing about. Madam Tours is joining the staff here.' She glanced across at Jenny to watch her reaction. ''Course it's not the same since Edward Carter went to work.'

Jenny flicked a careless hand. 'I'm sticking to mathematics. You know when you've got the answer right. I got the right word in French but got told off for the way I said it. And as for Singing'. She rolled her eyes in horror.

Jenny was confident Edward would find ways to cross her path. They never specified a place or a time but, within the narrow bounds that Jenny could wander, they simply found each other. As an apprentice he was regularly sent on errands, though being a bright and likeable lad, he avoided the ignominy of being sent by the older men for a bucket of air or a long stand.

The news of lessons with Signor Martelli sent Dorothea into ecstasies. Her punishment afternoons of dreary mathematics were commuted into French and singing, the two activities she most loved. She decided that God did exist after all and

He had answered her prayers. Her mind raced ahead. Her father had said there were to be no extras but she would find a way to persuade him to pay for the private lessons.

'I'm for singing lessons,' she announced. She looked round the other girls to see who would join her. 'What about you, Ship?' she asked, momentarily forgetting that traitor mice lose their nicknames. 'You've got a nice voice. Don't you want to improve?''

'Actually,' said Ella, 'I am going to stick with mathematics. They say music and mathematics have a lot in common' she explained.' Ella was a kind girl. What she did not say was that Signor Martelli had briefly tutored her at home. Her father, the baronet, had given him a polite reference and his notice. He had found the maestro's technique too showy and theatrical for his refined English taste.

Margaret relished her role of monitor. Extra Latin almost compensated her for chaperoning the flamboyant Signor Martelli. Miss Fossil hinted that next year she would be promoted to pupil-teacher and would receive a small salary.

***

Easter was late that year, and the summer term was short. Madam Tours, irritated by Signor Martelli, as he liked to be called, wanted to end her time in England with a flourish rather than the vague sense of failure that oppressed her. Her one real success in passing on her native language was Dorothea. The girl's accent was excellent and she soaked up new vocabulary like a sponge. Unfortunately, Madam Tours was the only witness of this triumph; no-one else appreciated the progress the girl had made.

It came into Madam Tours' mind, to create an opportunity to display her prize pupil and her country's culture to the rough northerners. She arranged an interview with Miss Fossil who agreed the school should hold an end of term concert to display the pupils' talents. Dorothea could sing in French. 'Mr Woodward would like that', said Madam Tours and looked meaningfully at the headmistress. Miss Fossil could take a hint.

Mr Woodward, impressed by Dorothea's recent good behaviour, agreed to her having private tuition with Signor Martelli. He did not want his darling daughter to be less than perfect in a public performance. Dorothea could think only of singing in the concert, being the centre of attention and basking in the applause. Beyond it lay the future. There was no need to concern herself about that. Her looks, her talent and her father's wealth would take care of that. As far as Dorothea was concerned the future was a fluffy white cloud in a blue sky.

Unlike Dorothea, Jenny was thinking about the future. She took advantage of the doubt about her birthday to convince herself she was fifteen and she had learnt all that school could teach her. What she wanted was a job. Like most men of his class, her father regarded it as his duty to keep her until a husband claimed that privilege from him. She would have to find a respectable way of earning her living to have any chance of persuading him to agree.

Atherley offered factory work which was most definitely not genteel enough for her father. Governess or teacher might just be acceptable to him. Jenny grimaced at the thought. She pictured spending hours locked up with some frightful child, like Dorothea Woodward. The big department stores in Manchester were alluring, but the distance daunted her. She let her mind wander the shops of Atherley. The haberdasher, the milliner, the fabric shop. They might not be too bad. Her father would draw the line at the grocery shop where she'd have to weigh butter and slice bacon.

Her mental eye came to rest on the Post Office, a handsome brick building with an impressive stone portico. It was always the centre of a bustle of activity: horses and carts piled with sacks of mail and telegraph boys on bikes.

The red letterboxes with their gold crests of royal approval gave it an aura of respectability.

Her aunt Anna had worked in a post office. It all clicked neatly into place. Her father could not claim that working in a Post Office was not respectable when Aunt Anna had worked in one. The family knew how carefully he guarded Anna's reputation. Jenny worked out that her best chance of success demanded both her father's co-operation and the active support of Miss Fossil.

'Absolutely not. It's not respectable,' said John. Jenny took a deep breath and was about to launch into a defence of her plan when a voice interrupted her.

'I did it. And I'm respectable.' Anna put down her sewing. She kept her voice light and her expression determinedly neutral but John saw the challenge in her eyes. He opened and closed his mouth like a chub feeding in the stream. No words came out. Anna was respectable until he climbed into her bed. It was only their determined secrecy that kept her reputation intact.

'The Post Office is an excellent employer,' continued Anna. 'You won't find a better one, Jenny.' The girl's announcement that she wanted to find work had taken both her and John by surprise.

Jenny set her lip and looked stubbornly into the distance.

'There will be tough competition. At least thirty people apply for every position,' Anna warned her.

'You could tell me about the work, so I won't make stupid mistakes at the interview.'

'You would be joining something that touches everybody's life. People trust the Post Office with their news, good and bad. The broken engagement, the birth of a child, even the plans of the burglar. From the cheapest postcard to the £20 money order. We treat them all same.'

'One day, I'd like to train for the telegraph. That's even harder to get into.'

A strange sound came from John – half groan, half guffaw. 'The electric telegraph! You must be mad. Ghastly dangerous stuff.'

In spite of the entreaties of the female members of the household, John still refused to have gas light. Jenny realised mentioning the electric telegraph was a mistake. She took a breath and played her ace. 'Miss Fossil says she will write me a reference.'

That made him think. Miss Fossil was no fool; she was a woman of sound judgement. She would not give a reference if she thought it would damage the reputation of her school. John decided on a strategic retreat.

'Well I am not going to say No but I want time to think about it. And talk to your aunt. But remember, I am more than willing to pay for another year at school for you.' He raised his newspaper to prevent any more discussion.

Jenny smiled and said nothing; she would rely on Anna to talk him round.

Margaret chose this moment to make her contribution to the proceedings. 'I just don't understand how you could give up a whole year of school by choice.'

'Speak for yourself,' said Jenny and left the room in case Margaret's enthusiasm for learning changed her father's mind.

Just as Jenny had taken the precaution of consulting Miss Fossil about her employment prospects, Mr Woodward sought advice from her friend Miss Hulme on a different matter.

'That Carter boy is doing well. Good reports on him from all quarters.'

'No surprise to me. I hope you're not planning to cream off any more of my best boys.'

'The way business is going I'll take a dozen if they're as good as him'

Miss Hulme pursed her lips and considered suggesting he go round to Miss Fossil and ask for the pick of her girls. She refrained from saying it. Mr Woodward was a good and generous friend of the school. She ordered tea and settled down to wait until he could unburden himself of the problem on his mind.

Training and qualifications were on Mr Woodward's mind. It was all new and foreign territory to him.

Miss Hulme was able to reassure him. There were excellent part-time courses at John Owen's College in Manchester and the local Mechanics' Institute was breaking new ground all the time. Was there a particular position he had in mind? Would it be in the mine or the mills?

Mr Woodward mopped his brow. 'To be honest, Miss Hulme, I am looking for somebody to take over from me one day. I don't intend to keel over next week, but I'd be a great deal easier in my mind, if there was a safe pair of hands to help with the management of the business. Mrs Woodward is worrying herself about it. She's getting into quite a state.'

'O Dear!' Miss Hulme did not know that it was Dorothea who lit, and stoked, the fire of Mrs Woodward's concern. 'So, you are looking for someone with real potential.'

'I'd like to train somebody for the task. It's taken me years. There's a lot of detail. I need someone with a brain, who can do sums in his head and measure things with his eye and can judge cloth by running it through his fingers. Someone not scared to go down the mine and tell if the wood on the props has rotted and is not safe.'

Miss Hulme had not heard him string so many words together before. She fought her almost maternal desire to keep her best boy out of his hands. This was a great opportunity for the lad. 'There is no doubt in my mind that Edward Carter is the ideal candidate.'

Mr Woodward sat back with a smile of satisfaction on his face. 'I thought as much,' he said.

'You were just testing me?' asked Miss Hulme.

'No. Oh no. I value your opinion. I am glad we think the same. It's an important decision. You see, I have no son. My Dorothea,' his face softened at her name, 'she won't be marrying a man of business. We've brought her up to be gentry. It's a little lordling for her, not a man who gets his hands dirty.'

When he reached home, Mr Woodward reassured his wife that he had made plans in case the worst should happen. 'I know it worries you,' he told her. Mrs Woodward said nothing; the failure of a son and heir to appear caused her intense pain. Dorothea showed warm approval for her father's choice and smiled with secret and malicious satisfaction. It would peeve that skinny red-headed bitch to see Edward move closer into the Woodwards' sphere of influence.

Mr Woodward leant back in his armchair and contemplated the future. The fact that he had not yet asked Edward Carter for his agreement did not trouble him. The boy would accept. No doubt about it. Mr Woodward had too much power in the town and Edward had too few resources and too many brothers who would need jobs one day. For once Mr Woodward did not feel outnumbered by his womenfolk. This, he reflected, must be what it feels like to have a son.

The planning of the end of term concert at Miss Fossil's school was fraught with rivalry. Inevitably the programme included the singing of *Three Little Maids from School* from *The Mikado*. Then the whole school had to show their paces by singing in a choir. All the girls squashed onto the stage with Jenny and Margaret at the back, under orders to keep their voices down. In spite of Anna's efforts, their musical talents were non-existent.

Signor Martelli and Madam Tours fought viciously for the honour of closing the concert. Unable to reach an agreement they cornered Miss Fossil into giving a ruling. She decreed the concert should finish with the girls singing the French songs Madam Tours had taught them. It would demonstrate the school's values so much better than the solo by Dorothea that Signor Martelli lobbied for. Madam Tours gave a complacent smile. Miss Fossil hid her chagrin; she had planned to give Ella, the baronet's daughter, the final spot on the programme. A title is always a winning card.

Dorothea set her lips when Signor Martelli gave her the bad news. 'Do not fret, signorina,' he told her. 'The dress rehearsal runs smoothly but who knows what will happen on the day? These are not professionals.' He shrugged his shoulders, flicked a dismissive finger and crumpled up one side of his face. Dorothea was not sure if it was a wink or a leer; it was certainly a secret message of some kind.

No school concert is complete without a scene from Shakespeare's *As You Like it*. In a moment of great daring the girl, playing Orlando was persuaded to wear a doublet and hose. Her mother, courageously, gave permission for her daughter to wear this male disguise, even though it revealed to the world that the girl had two legs. The existence of these limbs on women was normally concealed under long skirts.

On the day of the concert, Signor Martelli seized his opportunity. 'Be missing for fifteen minutes,' he told Dorothea. She went to hide in the little library. As Orlando stood in the wings of the makeshift stage, waiting to make her entrance, Signor Martelli sent his gaze travelling up and down the girl's legs until he attracted her startled attention. Then he did his trick of crumpling up one side of his face. There was no mistaking his expression this time; it was not a friendly wink to wish her 'Good Luck'. It was most definitely a leer. The girl fled in panic and tears. The stage remained empty for a long time. Signor Martelli took charge. He went on stage to announce a change in the programme.

Madam Tours came to protest. Dorothea was next on the programme. Where was the wretched girl? Signor Martelli ordered Margaret, the monitor, to look for her. It did not occur to Margaret to look for such a determined non-reader, in the book cupboard they glorified with the name of library. She soon returned breathless and alone. Madam Tours had no option but to order her choir onto the stage.

They did their best, but without Dorothea's soaring voice, their act lacked lustre.

A stony-faced Madam Tours washed her hands of the proceedings and went to sit at the back of the hall. There she begged the Bon Dieu to send her back to France.

Signor Martelli's plan to re-arrange the acts to give the best build-up for Dorothea worked perfectly. Ella calmed everyone down with an aria by Mozart while Margaret found a handkerchief for Orlando's tears and a long cloak to hide her embarrassment. 'You cannot let your mother down,' she told the girl. 'She's on the front row. She won't mind about the cloak.' The white-faced girl braced herself to go on stage. Margaret thought of gladiators going into the arena and certain death.

After the mangled Shakespeare the audience was ready for anything that was not blank verse. What they got was Dorothea, singing *Where e're you walk*. Signor Martelli had concealed the lascivious nature of the oratorio from Miss Fossil. 'It's by Handel,' he had informed her. Miss Fossil had been in the north long enough to know the reverence Handel commanded. She asked no more questions.

As Dorothea sang Miss Fossil wished she had quizzed Signor Martelli more thoroughly about his choice of song. Where Ella was sweet and pure, Dorothea, with her dramatic colouring, was sensuous and seductive; her figure was voluptuous. The eyebrows, so alarming at close quarters, gave her features definition on stage. She demanded the attention of the audience – and she got it. Especially the men. Thoughts of a lustful nature strayed into their minds. A man, who would have felled the next man with a blow for having such thoughts about his daughters, found himself wondering about that firm young flesh and the breasts concealed beneath that straining bodice.

The audience paid Dorothea the compliment of a moment of perfect silence after the dying away of the final note before starting to applaud.

Mr Woodward was in tears.

When the concert was over, the girls demonstrated how school had prepared them for the adult world by circulating among the guests and offering fruit cup. Ella found herself with her father and Mr Woodward. They both complimented her on her singing.

'Oh! I am quite feeble compared with Dorothea,' she said. Mr Woodward did not deny it.

'Your daughter should continue to work at her singing,' said the baronet. 'Ella is going to a finishing school which specialises in music,' he explained to Mr Woodward. Ella's face lit up.

'I plan to learn a great deal there. Also to learn German.'

'Shame they don't offer German here,' remarked the baronet, flicking his cuffs. 'With the royal family and everything.' He turned to Mr Woodward. 'No doubt your girl will be going abroad to finishing school.'

'Absolutely,' said Mr Woodward and quickly moved away.

When the fruit cup was finished and the girls and parents had gone, Mr Woodward sought Miss Fossil. She had retreated to her study where she hoped to have a reviving cigarette to celebrate a fairly successful end to the school year. The concert had been patchy but not a total disaster.

'What's a finishing school?' asked Mr Woodward coming straight to the point.

Miss Fossil briskly outlined the facts as she knew them. 'I have friends who went to be finished. Usually in France or Switzerland for some reason. Girls study French and usually acquire a good accent. They learn about food, which knife and fork to use at dinner in a grand house or restaurant. Etiquette. How to address a duke or a member of the royal family. That sort of thing. I don't know much more. I went to university.'

'Would Dorothea benefit from going?'

'To university!' Miss Fossil could not keep the dismay out of her voice.

'No of course not.' Mr Woodward could not keep the contempt out of his. 'To finishing school.'

'Well yes. I suppose so. There's nothing here for her.'
Except idleness and troublemaking, thought Miss Fossil.

'She could do more singing. She sings like a bird.' Mr Woodward shook his head in wonderment at the talent he had fathered.

'Mrs Woodward wasn't too keen on her leaving home, I remember. She was clear that boarding school was out of the question.'

Silence.

Miss Fossil tried again to discourage Mr Woodward. She feared he was going out of his depth. 'It will be very expensive.'

'Bah. You find me a good one of these finishing schools and I'll look after the rest,' said Mr Woodward, getting up and buttoning his coat.

'I shall write to some friends and make enquiries,' said Miss Fossil.

The Post Master will see you now,' said the tall woman with the severe hair as she held the door open and led Jenny into a bright room with a coal fire. Behind a desk sat a man who resembled a beached walrus. He wore a brown suit. His domed head was as smooth as an egg; its surface shone with an oily lustre. The flesh of his chin and neck fell down in rolling folds until it met the stiff resistance of his collar. A drooping moustache and large liquid brown eyes completed the resemblance to a giant sea mammal.

'Miss Truesdale,' said the tall woman and pointed Jenny to a chair opposite the desk.

'Ah. Yes,' said the walrus and looked to the tall woman for guidance.

'Miss Truesdale is here about the position of counter clerk.'

'You'd better stay then, Miss er…. We must observe the proprieties.'

'You won't need to keep her long, sir. She had a very high score in the entrance test.'

'That is impressive. I hope we have a vacancy for her.'

'That's not a problem, sir. Two of our female clerks have left so we have two vacancies to fill.'

The Post Master fixed his moist eyes on Jenny. 'I expect they left to get married. After six years we pay them a dowry. So, what do they do? They go and get married.' The walrus flopped back in his chair. He waved a flipper at the tall woman.

'Miss ..er.'

The tall woman grasped his meaning and went to poke the fire that had fallen asleep.

A flipper wafted again. Jenny was dismissed.

In the corridor the tall woman introduced herself as Miss Titterington. 'If you want to laugh at my name do so now, and get it over with. You will address me as Miss Titterington here at work. I know you are Jenny, but in the office, you will be Miss Truesdale. The Post Master will not remember your name. I have worked here for 12 years and he still cannot remember mine. He is a man of numbers, not names.

Jenny nodded as she filed the information away.

Miss Titterington went on. 'The Post Master leaves me free to make all the decisions about the women's work. And just so you know, you have been accepted. Consider yourself as employed by the post office. I marked your test papers.'

Jenny let out the breath she did not know she had been holding in.

Miss Titterington led her behind the counter where the public bought their stamps and money orders. She gestured to three high stools. 'This is where we ladies work. Our work is always separate from the men. I don't suppose you are much used to working with men.'

Jenny could not deny it.

Miss Titterington continued. 'Most of them are very gentlemanly but it is best to keep your distance.' She led Jenny down a corridor to a solid wood door with a brass handle. 'This is the cloakroom for the ladies who work here. The Post Master had it built specially.' She waited while a man walked past. Then with a flourish she flung the door open to reveal a small room with a row of pegs and a further wooden door with a round window of frosted glass. Miss Titterington opened it with a flourish.

Jenny gazed open-mouthed. 'Is that what I think it is? I've never been so close to one before.'

'I'll show you how it works,' said Miss Titterington.

Afterwards Jenny washed her hands at the tiny sink. There was a slice of pink soap and a fluffy towel.

'As I said the Post Master is a man of numbers. He had this cloakroom installed to attract and keep female workers. It worked. There are five of us now. He gets away with paying us 40% less than a man for doing the same work.'

'Still more money than I've ever had before,' said Jenny.

Miss Titterington explained her duties to Jenny and led her to the side entrance. 'I want you here tomorrow, bright and early.'

Jenny felt giddy as she walked out of the side entrance to the Post Office. A horse and cart swept by, delivering a pile of mail sacks. A gang of men emerged to start unloading. Shrill whistles and cheerful shouts split the air. Jenny jumped.

'Ignore it,' said Miss Titterington. 'It's a compliment,' she explained. 'They do it because you're young and pretty. Enjoy it. It doesn't last long.'

The white blouse of the schoolgirl became the uniform of Jenny, the working girl with a wage packet at the end of the week. To celebrate her £65 a year, she bought a pair of high heels. Her skirts kept her ankles concealed as the rules of society insisted. The extra inches on the heels kept her skirt from contact with the pavement. With relief, she consigned to history the tiresome nightly task of brushing the mud from the hem of her skirt.

Each morning Jenny felt a thrill as she joined the queue – mainly of men – at the clocking-on machine. It made a satisfying thump as it stamped her card. From behind her polished wooden counter she dealt smoothly with requests for stamps and postal orders. It was easier than dealing with the devious Dorothea. Occasionally, very occasionally, Edward Carter appeared. He did not buy many stamps but contrived to mention a time and place when they might just pass each other.

While Jenny settled into her new job and Margaret revelled in her role of pupil teacher, things were not going well for Dorothea. Though the prospect of going abroad to finishing school for six months thrilled her, it sent her mother into hysterics. Mrs Woodward took to her bed and stayed there. Her only comfort came in spoonsful from a bottle the doctor prescribed, and in visits from Anna who was always kind, always understanding.

It was Anna who kept Jenny and Margaret up-to-date with events in the Woodward household. Miss Hulme and Miss Fossil had called on their friends and colleagues for addresses of possible finishing schools. Letters went backwards and forwards to France. Dorothea, in an agony of impatience, translated the letters, inspected the brochures and chose an establishment run by a Madam Flet.

Mr Woodward might be a besotted father, but he was also a cautious businessman. Caught between the opposing views of his wife and daughter, Mr Woodward sought a third party. He called in Madam Tours to reassure the fearful Mrs Woodward that 'abroad' was not a den of vice and the presence of wine on the dinner table was not an infallible sign of moral decay. As Madam Tours set about her mission, she looked through the letters from Madam Flet and discovered a potential fly in the ointment. She said nothing to Mrs Woodward but made a casual enquiry about Dorothea's birthday.

The diplomatic skill of the French is legendary; it enabled Madam Tours to bring to Mr Woodward's attention, what she tactfully described as a discrepancy. A red-faced Mr Woodward thought fast and hard. Best not to tell Mrs Woodward, just yet. He quickly set about persuading Madam Tours to stay until the end of the autumn term. and delay returning to her native country. She agreed that, for a consideration, she would escort Dorothea to France when the time came.

When the time came. Those four short words contained the explosive force of six sticks of dynamite. Mr Woodward said a brief prayer as he knocked on the door of Dorothea's bedroom. He had his escape route planned. After all, he was only telling her what she knew already. Madam Tours had revealed to him what Dorothea had concealed.

He stood awkwardly in the doorway, his hand on the doorknob, and spoke across the room to her. 'You will have to wait to go to the school in France. They won't take you until you are seventeen.'

He backed out, closed the door and went to tell his wife the good news. She leapt from her sick bed. She arrived in time to find Dorothea lying on her bed, drumming her heels and screaming, 'It's not fair. It'll be the next century before I get there.' She had started throwing things when the cheery maid arrived with a jug of cold water from a handy washstand. Afterwards the maid regretted she had not taken the time to find a chamber pot. A full one.

An uneasy calm followed. The broken ornaments were quickly swept away as thoroughly as Dorothea's *mistaking* sixteen for seventeen in French. Even Mr Woodward found it hard to believe she had confused seize with dix-sept. He buried his suspicions and turned his mind to his work. Distracted as he was by domestic matters, he found he was coming to rely more and more on Edward Carter. The lad had the figures at his fingertips, could remember names and was quick to respond in emergencies.

Dorothea's complaint that it would be the next century before she could go to France was not adolescent exaggeration; it was literally true. The twentieth century would arrive before Dorothea turned seventeen. With gritted teeth, she returned to Miss Fossil's school and endured the autumn term in a semi-detached way. She put some effort into French and persuaded Signor Martelli to teach her a little Italian. The rest of the time she managed to steer clear of Mathematics, History and trouble.

The months plodded past her on leaden feet. Winter arrived and Christmas appeared on the horizon. Dorothea extracted a promise from her parents that Madam Tours would accompany her to France in the New Year that heralded a new century.

'Good riddance,' said Margaret when she heard. 'She has been a perfect pain at school.' Now enjoying the status of pupil-teacher at Miss Fossil's school. Margaret received a miniscule salary for her work. She cheerfully coached bemused pupils, marked exercise books, and delivered messages while soaking up every scrap of information she came across.

One morning Miss Fossil had summoned her to her office to discuss what she cautiously described as 'possibilities'. Had Margaret thought of going to a teacher training college? Had she considered studying classics at university?

In the evening as the Truesdales sat close to their fire, Margaret told them of Miss Fossil's ideas. The word 'university' stunned them; it had never passed their lips before.

'Well I never,' said Anna. 'Who'd have thought to hear the word university in the same sentence as our Margaret?'

John felt a dismissive Huh coming to his lips but quickly swallowed it. Living with three growing girls had taught him to be more cautious in his disapproval of new ideas.

'Why not?' asked Jenny, although she could think of plenty of reasons not to spend three years in stuffy classrooms.

'Well,' said Anna that's certainly worth thinking about. It looks as if this new century will open more and more doors for women.'

A NEW CENTURY DAWNS

The men gathered on the street with their lumps of coal and flasks of whisky. A mood of melancholy hung over them as they waited for the church bells that would welcome the new century.

'It'll be very strange.'

'All my life when I've written the date it's started with 18.'

'Might not be the only change.'

'Queen Victoria can't last forever.'

They fell silent, sensing the end of an era. Presided over by a tiny woman, the British Empire, was at its zenith. Their age had been one of amazing progress, and growing prosperity. It couldn't last much longer.

'Our Samuel is thinking of going as a soldier. This to-do in South Africa. Reckons it's sunny there.'

'Best of luck to him', said John pulling his collar up.

'Why is it the twentieth century when it begins with 19?' asked Tommy. Several explanations were offered. None of them convinced him so they sent him to bed. He went off cheerfully to the privacy of his tiny room. From being a boy with a mother-shaped hole in his life, Tommy was drowning in female advice and exhortation. Aunt Anna, Margaret and Jenny took turns to tell him to wash his hands, put his coat on and stop kicking that ball about. The only terror school held for Tommy now was the fear of not passing the entrance exam for the grammar school. Failure to do so would cut him off from the Carter tribe. Their spelling, unlike Tommy's was effortlessly precise; his still had moments of originality.

He dreamed, as he always did, of having a dog

The girls went to their beds and dreamed of glory. This was to be their century. Margaret's heart beat with the certainty that, it would hold out opportunities beyond her imagining. There would be events so startling and revolutionary that her mind could not begin to give shape to them. Yet she was sure there was a part for her to play. It troubled her that she saw no role for her beloved Latin in the shiny new future; she had a feeling that the language and civilisation she so loved would not be an essential part of the age that lay ahead.

Jenny dreamed of exploring the world she lived in. The mines, the cotton mills and all the other places she couldn't go. She pictured walking through the mahogany doors of offices, without knocking as she saw the men do. Many girls dream of weddings. Jenny dreamed of taking a seat at the table where the men made all the decisions. Somehow or other, Edward would be there with her.

Dorothea did not need to dream; she was living it. There was snow on the distant hills when she arrived at the finishing school. The Maîtresse, Madam Flet came to welcome the English girl and thanked the Bon Dieu that she spoke good French. Dorothea's abundant dark hair and porcelain complexion passed Madam's scrutiny; they were pronounced exquisite. Dorothea was asked to sing; her father was paying for extra lessons. Madam Flet suggested Dorothea could improve her breath control; a tutor would help.

Ballet lessons were compulsory for all girls. They would make Dorothea move elegantly and give her gestures more expression and grace. The French woman poured scorn on the English method of walking about with a book on your head. She refrained from telling Dorothea that she walked like a duck; the word waddle was not in her English vocabulary.

That was the good news. Madam Flet quickly moved on to the bad. She nodded at Dorothea's abundant breasts. Too much embonpoint. She would have to join the girls who were served small portions at mealtimes. Madam Flet's girls had tiny waists. Men liked to put their arms round them. When it came to Dorothea's eyebrows the French woman abandoned any pretence at tact. Mon Dieu they had to go! She plonked Dorothea in a chair; produced a pair of tweezers and the black slugs were expertly plucked into two fine arcs.

Her experience at Miss Fossil's school had taught Dorothea to be cautious with her fellow pupils. She quickly realised that any attempt to impress the French girls was doomed to failure. They were newly returned from the Christmas holidays and talked of the parties, balls and dinners they had attended. They described the dresses they had worn and the men they had met. All Dorothea had to offer was a trip to the Messiah at the Free Trade Hall in Manchester and a teetotal evening of readings from Dickens' Christmas Carol.

Dorothea shared a room with Hortense, a petite French girl who moved like a ballet dancer and had the effortless chic of a Parisian. She could recite Racine by the yard, understood restaurant menus and knew about wine. Dorothea believed every word that fell from her neat pink lips.

The desire to be like Hortense motivated Dorothea to pay serious attention in lessons. A tutor demonstrated the different shapes of wine glasses and explained which were for red wine and which for white. Dorothea made notes and nodded to show she understood how the design of the glass could affect the temperature of the wine. The uselessness of this information in her father's Methodist household did not dampen her enthusiasm.

As they were in France, food was an important subject. Madam talked them through the complexities of creating an appropriate menu for different occasions in the different seasons of the year. Dorothea who had never eaten anything more elaborate than a roast dinner was introduced to banquets which included such exotic dishes as quenelles, souffles and steak tartare. These discussions of food were particularly difficult for her. The prescribed small portions left her permanently hungry.

Once the menu for the fictional dinner had been decided, the table had to be correctly laid for the imaginary guests. Dorothea was amazed at the great array of knives and forks. 'If in doubt, start at the outside and work in,' commanded Madam. She then gave them place cards and told them to seat their guests. They argued earnestly over the problem. Which is the place of honour? Does a count take precedence over a bishop? Or a wealthy businessman? Who should sit to the left of the hostess?

'My mother saves that place for her lover,' whispered Hortense behind her gloved hand.

A thrill beyond imagining ran through Dorothea. One day she might sit at a long table, laid with sparkling glasses and silver cutlery, and entertain her guests. She did not bother her head with the compulsory husband at the far end of the table. Her mind was on the place at her left hand.

The ballet lessons were an ordeal for Dorothea. The spindly old teacher flicked her legs with his cane, if her feet were not in exactly the right position. When she squealed in protest, he hit her again. In Atherley, Dorothea would have stormed out and gone home to her father. There was no such escape route for her in France. She bit her lip and kept going. The exercises improved her arm gestures and the carriage of her head. She endured because deep down she knew it would help with her singing.

The snow melted, spring came, and travellers took to the roads again. The girls' brothers called in on their way to Italy and the Grand Tour. Madam Flet took the view that learning to converse with the opposite sex was part of a girl's education. Suitably chaperoned, girls were free to talk with gentlemen in the public rooms and stroll about the grounds with them. A brother was officially deemed to be an impeccable chaperon. The only problem was that brothers were seldom alone; the young men tended to travel in packs.

Hortense seemed to have a great many brothers. Dorothea relished their visits as opportunities to practise her flirting. One day in the spring a brother's friend suddenly grasped her hand, twirled her behind a handy tree and pressed his lips on hers.

A tsunami of sensations engulfed Dorothea. She had never felt such consuming joy in her life before. It lasted for hours. Later she was disturbed by another totally new sensation; it was the voice of her conscience. She thought of her father, far away in grimy Lancashire. He had not sent her to finishing school to practise kissing. But he had sent her to improve her marriage prospects. She sought advice from Hortense.

Her roommate gave the matter careful thought. 'You are not promised to someone, are you?' Dorothea shook her head. 'Then I don't suppose it matters,' she said. 'As long as nobody finds out,' she added. 'I doubt gossip can cross the Channel.' Hortense was busy smoothing on her white gloves. No lady left the house without gloves and a hat; the rule was iron-clad.

'As long as you don't get caught,' she warned Dorothea. 'If you like that sort of thing, you can kiss to your heart's content.' Hortense picked up her parasol and set off on her afternoon stroll. She had no concept of the power of the tiger she had unleashed.

Dorothea found she did like that sort of thing; she liked it very much. But her heart was very far from content. The stolen kisses left her restless and peevish. The stirrings of her body told her there were further pleasures to come from a man's hands. Although she had no idea what they were, she longed for the chance to find out.

Madam Flet always arranged to finish the term with a social event. This time it was to be a ball. There is little point in going to a ball if you cannot dance. Ballet is good for your posture but it is no help when the band is playing a waltz or a polka. At their next dance lesson, the wizened old ballet master with the wispy hair, propped his cane against the wall and went to sit at the piano. Madam Flet came to introduce the new dancing master. The girls gaped. What a contrast! This dancing master was tall, lithe and young. 'Count Aleksy,' said Madam and wafted a hand in the direction of the young man.

Count Aleksy, in a hussar's jacket, stepped forward, clicked his heels and bowed elegantly. All the girls promptly fell in love with him. Except Hortense who

146

reserved judgement. 'There are more counts in Poland than leaves on a tree,' she said scornfully and wondered why he was not with his regiment. 'But he can dance,' she admitted.

First, he demonstrated the steps, striding them out on the wooden floor, all long legs and slim hips, calling out, 'Un, deux, trois,' in his accented French. When the girls had mastered the moves, he clicked his fingers to make the pianist play and the girls whirled about the floor. He swooped on them one by one, held them in his arms and twirled them across the room. It was all very thrilling.

The newly slimmed down Dorothea enjoyed feeling Aleksy's arm round her waist and the scratchy gold braid of his jacket against her breasts. As a teacher he was careful to spread his favours equally among the girls. At the end of the lesson he would find a reason to keep one of his pupils back for a few minutes to correct some minor error. As the ballet master played, he would manoeuvre the girl out of sight and whisper compliments in her ear. Those who melted under his attentions, might find the treat repeated. Then the kisses would start.

Dorothea was the first but not the last to be kissed. As the weeks flew by, she was convinced she was chosen more than any other girl. As he spun her round the floor, he murmured compliments into her ear. 'You are a natural dancer. You have rhythm. Your skin, your hair…. '

The girls were busy learning how to fold napkins when Madam Flet came to warn them to write to their parents to make arrangements for their departure. The end of term was the Thursday after the ball.

Reality hit Dorothea between the eyes. Her time of fun and frivolity was coming to an end. How could she face going back to that house where no-one flirted or drank wine, in that dingy town where men wore tweed and thought only of the price of coal, in that country where the skies were grey and it rained all the time? There had to be a way to stop it happening. Or at least delay it.

It did not help that her roommate was looking forward to joining her family for the holiday. Hortense spent happy hours, speculating which of her brothers' handsome friends might visit at the seaside and which of her many gowns to take. How she looked forward to strolling on the beach and spending evenings in restaurants with the writers and lawyers who formed her father's social circle.

Jealousy grabbed Dorothea by the throat so hard that it choked her. She should be at those parties, the centre of attention in a low-cut gown. She saw herself surrounded by admiring men, conversing with them in her faultless French and modestly obliging when they begged her to sing.

To Dorothea the solution was obvious; Hortense must invite her to stay during the holiday. She dropped hints. How well they got on. What fun they had together. Such a shame it had to stop. When that didn't work, she pleaded injustice. Hortense had all the pleasures of Paris with brothers to escort her, while she, Dorothea, was the only child of teetotal parents in a grimy town on the outskirts of Manchester.

Hortense took this complaint to heart. She wrote secretly to her brother asking him to bring some of his fellow officers to the ball, so Dorothea would not lack for partners. On the subject of inviting Dorothea to stay with her family, she stayed resolutely silent.

In the end, Dorothea lay on her bed and drummed her heels in childish rage. Hot tears spilled from her eyes and sobs of despair from her throat. The technique always worked with her parents. Hortense was different matter; she had been raised in a disciplined home. She ignored Dorothea's toddler tantrum.

Then Dorothea made a big mistake. 'You're jealous,' she spat across the bedroom. 'You're scared, I'll get more attention than you. You know I will be the belle of the ball.' She smoothed her hand across her breasts still sumptuous in spite of the small portions and smirked down at the flat-chested French girl.

Hortense folded her lips and went for a walk in the garden. Twirling her parasol, she thought how she had coaxed her brother to supply Dorothea with partners. The wretched girl's ingratitude for her secret diplomacy was too much. Hortense came to a decision. The next time Dorothea pressed her for an invitation, Hortense smiled, looked her straight in the eyes, and lied.

'I have sent a note to mama to ask her to write to your family for their permission to visit for the holiday. Obviously, you will need your father's permission.'

'Obviously,' said Dorothea who still took for granted her father's agreement to all her schemes. Not the most conscientious writer of letters home, on this occasion, she rushed to find pen and paper.

In reply, Mr Woodward wrote that she was not to go gallivanting off to the seaside with foreigners. She had been away six months; he wanted her home. Surely, she had learned all that the mesdames and mesdemoiselles had to teach her? To put it bluntly he'd had his money's worth. Dorothea was to let him know the date of the end of term.

Dorothea ignored him.

Mr Woodward clenched his teeth and wrote to the school. They sent him the bill with the date in French. They used the continental way of writing the number seven. The slash across the stem confused him. Was it a badly written nine or a four? And what the dickens was jeudi?

Once again Mr Woodward wrote to his daughter. Nothing had arrived from the French lady and anyway the answer was No. Dorothea was to return home at the end of term. She was needed; her mother was not well. The postman trudged up the hill three times a day to the Woodward mansion. He brought many letters with him but nothing from France.

Although he was not an imaginative man Mr Woodward pictured in vivid detail all the calamities that might befall his daughter alone in foreign parts. Doting father though he was, he was not blind to Dorothea's nature. He knew her to be wilful and impulsive. Panic hit him. He sent a telegram.

It arrived on the evening of the ball. Dorothea left it unopened. She was too busy putting on her magenta gown.

She stood alone in front of the mirror smoothed her bodice and adjusted her breasts to show some cleavage. She smiled with satisfaction; she was ready to make her entrance.

Hortense introduced her brother and his fellow officers; they queued up to ask Dorothea to dance. Count Aleksy asked only for the last dance.

'I have to look after all my pupils,' he said as she wrote his name in her programme. 'I want you for the waltz,' he whispered in her ear. 'All eyes will be on you. You dance so beautifully. You have music in your soul.'

To her intense satisfaction he escorted her to supper, a mark of special favour. How jealous the other girls would be. Afterwards he excused himself. She would understand; he had responsibilities. But first he must speak to his fellow officers. He waved vaguely in the direction of Hortense's brother and his friends. They greeted him with slaps on the shoulder. It was not long before he left amidst loud guffaws. As he danced with all the girls in turn, he flashed past Dorothea and warned her, 'Beware of those cavalry officers. They are wearing their spurs. They will rip your gown to shreds.'

The last waltz went exactly as Dorothea hoped. The candles glimmered in the summer twilight, the musicians, sensing a release from their labour, made the violins soar. The other couples, aware they were outclassed, drifted to the fringes of the floor leaving the centre to the graceful figures of Dorothea and Count Aleksy

When the music stopped, they strolled about in the warm summer night, enjoying being young and having their lives before them. Madam Flet kept a watchful eye on them and after half an hour of freedom shooed her girls off to their beds. Dorothea did not expect to sleep, she planned to stay awake to savour the feeling of triumph that enveloped her. It didn't work like that. She slept deep and long.

In the morning Hortense had gone. She left a note, explaining she was leaving early to travel home with her brother. Her conscience must have bothered her; she added a postscript. Her brother thought their mother may have forgotten to write to Dorothea's father. 'You had better make arrangements to travel home', she wrote and placed the note on top of the unopened telegram.

In the absence of someone to berate, Dorothea vented her rage by throwing things. Her hairbrush travelled through the open window in a graceful arc. A shoe followed. Its landfall was accompanied by a shout of protest – a male shout. With the other shoe in her hand, Dorothea went to the window, in the hope of finding somebody to hit. Count Aleksy stood in the garden waving her hairbrush. She let the hand with the shoe drop to her side.

Count Aleksy gestured to warn her he was going to climb up to her window; her room was on the first floor. The rough stonework provided the occasional handhold, enough for an athletic horseman to climb up and gallantly return her hairbrush to Dorothea. She accepted it gracefully, and withdrew into her bedroom.

STILL NO LETTER. FORBID YOU GO WITH
FRENCH FAMILY.
STAY AT SCHOOL. FATHER

Dorothea smiled as she read the telegram. How kind of her father to order her to do exactly what she wanted to do. The school's timetable and their rigid supervision would crumble as the holiday approached. Her roommate was gone. If she played her cards right, she would have a few days of freedom before Madam Tours arrived with the handcuffs.

Mr Woodward was a man of firm beliefs. He treated the Sabbath day with respect, believing business should wait until the start of the working week. All day he wrestled with his conscience. Surely the Good Lord would understand a father's anguish? While Dorothea was throwing her hairbrush out of the window, Mr Woodward was in his study going through the unsatisfactory correspondence from France. There was Dorothea's letter asking for his permission to go on holiday with a French family. He was sure he had written to Dorothea to forbid it. If it were business, he would have a copy on file, but this was a family matter. In his hand was the letter from the school that he couldn't understand. It was supposed to tell him when term ended. If only Madam Tours were here to translate for him. The only part he understood was the bill.

Yesterday he'd sent a telegram demanding the date of the end of term. He might as well have dropped it down a mine shaft for all the response he'd got. Mr Woodward put his head in his hands and prayed for strength to get through the Lord's Day without demanding unreasonable special favours such as knowing where exactly on God's green earth his daughter was.

His household had regular habits. The servants retired early in the expectation of a sound night's sleep. That Sunday was to prove an exception. After midnight Mr Woodward grew desperate. It was technically Monday. He woke the gardener's boy and sent him stumbling off with another telegram.

STILL NO LETTER. FORBID YOU GO WITH
FRENCH FAMILY.
STAY AT SCHOOL. FATHER

On Monday there was no reply. He blamed the government, the weather, the French railways. Everything except Dorothea.

On Tuesday a telegram from Dorothea informed him that term ended on Thursday. Light dawned on Mr Woodward. Jeudi must be French for Thursday. He checked the letter. Those pesky people had no respect. In English the days of the week had capital letters.

Mr Woodward whistled through his teeth as he thought how close he had come to calling on Miss Hulme for a translation and advice. He knew she would be discreet but he preferred keep family matters private.

His relief did not last long. He began to calculate the distance between him and his beloved daughter. It was already past mid-day on Tuesday. He had to allow for delays on the railways and the sailing times of the ferries. He had an uneasy feeling that they had to wait for the tide. There was no time to waste. Mr Woodward reached for his hat; and Mrs Woodward for her smelling salts. The prospect of her husband venturing across the Channel gave her an attack of the vapours. Her shrieks brought the cheery maid running from the kitchen with a wet tea towel. She swatted her mistress's face with the cold cloth until pain and humiliation brought her to her senses.

This performance helped Mr Woodward to recover the power of thought. There was no need for him to go to France to escort Dorothea home. Was he not a captain of industry? His wealth was great, his pockets deep. When he wanted things done, people did them. Madam Tours had taken Dorothea to that wretched school. She could jolly well bring her back. He went to his study and rang the bell long and loud to show he meant business. The man servant, roused from a nap, was still pulling his braces up when he arrived.

The sleep of Madam Tours was disturbed by frantic knocking on her front door. Mr Woodward's telegram had arrived. At first, she demurred. Such short notice. The date was not convenient. The journey would take two days. The expense of her return journey must be covered. In all she drove a hard bargain.

Mr Woodward agreed to all her demands as long as she set off immediately. Madam Tours, a woman of her word, promptly did so. She arrived on Thursday to find Dorothea, like Goldilocks, asleep in her bed, with her trunk packed. Mr Woodward's joy was unconfined when a telegram confirmed that the obedient daughter had not gone gallivanting to the French seaside

Madam Tours' rejoicing was more cautious. She questioned Dorothea about the invitation from Hortense's mother that failed to materialise. Dorothea improvised with considerable ingenuity. Madam Tours was capable of writing to Hortense's family for an explanation. Her father was not. She offered her new chaperon several explanations. The family were in Paris, at their chateau, or was it their house by the sea? Hortense was in quarantine. There was scarlet fever in Paris. Measles. Or was it whooping cough? Madam Tours could take her pick.

The railway, the ferry and the firm hand of Madame Tours brought a reluctant Dorothea back to Atherley more quickly than she hoped. The town had not improved in her absence. No miracle had transformed it into a bright metropolis with a vibrant night life.

When the front doorbell rang at nine o'clock one evening John Truesdale laid aside his newspaper and gestured for Jenny to sit down again. The hour was late for Atherley and no caller was expected. Answering the door in such circumstances was man's work.

Edward Carter, now in his eighteenth year and a smart grey suit, stood at the foot of the steps. Sometimes, at the end of the day's business, he contrived to time his report to Mr Woodward so as to walk with Jenny on her way home from work.

'Good evening Mr Truesdale. Just thought I'd check. Make sure Jenny got home all right.'

'Aye.' John was taciturn.

Edward, still at the foot of the steps, could see an explanation was needed. 'I'm just back from Manchester. At the station they said there'd been an accident. Horse bolted. Young lady badly injured. Just thought I'd check as I'm passing. Make sure your Jenny's all right. On my way up to Mr Woodward's.'

John relented a little. 'Your boss keeps you busy. He's getting his pound of flesh.'

'Aye. I've to put the hours in but he's learning me a lot. It's a two-way street. I've got one brother apprenticed in the machine shop. A place at Woodward's is not to be sniffed at. He's a good employer. Tough but fair. Let me know when your Tommy's looking for a crib.' Edward Carter gave his disarming grin; he wasn't really joking.

'He's a few years to go yet,' said John.

'I'd best be off.' Edward put on his hat and turned to leave.

'Doesn't do to keep the boss waiting,' John called, glad of an excuse not to invite him in. The longer he could delay that young man from crossing his threshold the better, as far as he was concerned.

John settled back in his armchair and warmed his feet at the fire. A soft blanket of comfort enfolded him. He had eaten a good supper; his sexual appetite was regularly satisfied, and his family were in good health. Tommy had passed for the grammar school. There was no need to pay school fees for him or for Margaret and Jenny kept herself. For a change John was looking for ways to spend his spare money.

To make life easier for Anna, he suggested employing another servant to help the aging Hannah who took deep offence at the suggestion. After several days of fraught diplomacy Anna found a solution – Hannah's daughter, Bessie.

When Anna had been summoned to nurse her father, Bessie, then a girl of thirteen, had come to help her mother look after the children of the house. When the girl was old enough, the better wages in the mill lured her away. Now she was married with a child of her own. Some extra money would not come amiss. She understood her mother's way of working and could help her for a few hours a day with the heavy work. There was only one proviso; could she bring her daughter with her?

It seemed a good plan, but the apple had a worm in it.

Bessie arrived with an enchanting toddler with golden curls and a smile that occasionally dissolved into heart-breaking tears. She took one look at Anna, and held out her chubby arms to be picked up. Anna felt she had been chosen.

While Bessie scrubbed and heaved the furniture out to dust behind it, Anna played pat a cake and sang nursery rhymes with a bundle of cheerfulness who laughed for no reason and found delight in the oddest things: a creeping snail, a dandelion and pile of pebbles were all deserving of her concentrated scrutiny.

Most of all she demanded Anna's full-time attention until her mother came to take her home. When Anna waved goodbye to the child, she felt a visceral sensation of loss. Her arms and breasts ached. She told herself it was fatigue from carrying the child; the pain was muscle strain, not emptiness. For months the lie worked.

The truth will out. One day Anna threw herself on the bed and howled. She could deny it no longer. She wanted a child. It felt as if a great ravenous grey wolf had come to inhabit her body. The beast had a ferocious appetite that nothing could quell except to hold a small helpless human being in her arms and nurse it to her breast. The hunger woke her in the mornings and went to bed with her at night. It gnawed at her insides. It devoured her very being.

She tried counting her blessings. She had love, plenty of it. John loved her and she loved him. She already had a family. Her sister's children were a delight to her. The burden of her work was light; no rising in the cold and dark to spend long hours at a loom in a noisy mill.

The list brought her no comfort. Her heart's desire was forbidden. Her mind twisted and turned as she sought a way to beat her longing into submission. If she had a child it would be illegitimate. The law disqualified such children from inheriting and society closed its doors to them. The world was not kind to bastards in general. How would it treat the product of what some people regarded as incest?

The only relief she could find for her pain was in bed with John. She clawed and clung to his body with the ferocity and abandon of a tiger. He responded with vigour. They sent each other into soaring heights of rapture. Afterwards she would shed bitter tears as she washed his seed out with the syringe.

'I'd like to go to Manchester on Saturday,' announced Margaret with a blush. John stared at her in surprise. Margaret never went anywhere. She only took her nose out of her book to scurry to school or to church on Sunday.

'You cannot possibly go on your own,' he was quick to reply.

'I shan't be on my own. Miss Fossil and Miss Hulme are going. They have invited me to go with them.'

'Why?' John was suspicious. Were those redoubtable headmistresses white slavers in their off-duty hours?

'There's a meeting they want me to go to. They thought I would…,' Margaret hesitated as she checked her memory for Miss Fossil's exact words. She found them. 'Have my mind opened to new ideas. And it would be sensible for me to see the city. She hopes I will go there to study.'

John scowled but said nothing. Anna was more receptive to the idea. In her constant struggle to squash her maternal longings she relished the brief relief that any novelty brought her.

'You cannot have doubts about those headmistresses,' she scolded John. 'I cannot imagine anybody more respectable. Also, they know their way around. They are not like most women here who only know how to find the shops. They will know the art galleries, the lecture halls. It will be part of Margaret's education.'

John harrumphed for a bit, but not too seriously.

'I can pay my own train fare,' offered Margaret.

That's not the point,' he said testily. 'I am sure I can afford it.'

So, it was with her father's reluctant blessing that Margaret set off on Saturday. Jenny was at work, Tommy was out and Hannah had the day off, John and Anna took to their bed where they enjoyed some quite noisy lovemaking – a treat that was usually denied them. As John said, walls have ears.

'Get up, get up. Do your stuff,' Anna chanted as she climbed reluctantly out of bed.

'I brought up some hot water,' said John from his pillow. Anna's heart melted a little at his care for such a tender part of her anatomy.

'Could we go to Manchester? Have a day out? It's good to do something different, something new.'

'No reason why not. If you want to.'

'The first time I went it was to buy this wretched contraption.' Anna shook the syringe. A jet of water flew over the bed and landed on John's face. He laughed and wiped the dampness away with his big capable hand.

Anna did not laugh. She crouched by the bowl of water, wrapped her arms around her knees and wept. She sobbed as if her heart was breaking, as indeed it was.

In a trice John was with her, folding her in the warmth of his body, gentling her with murmured words of reassurance, kissing her hair and calling her his darling.

The floodgates opened. Anna's misery poured out. A man loved her; she loved him; she wanted his baby. She hated the necessity of having to keep washing the possibility away.

They went over all the old arguments again. To no avail. They did not have the means or the confidence to brave society's wrath. Their only hope, a bleak one, was for a change in the law.

In the end it was John who made the decision. 'I think I understand a little of what you feel, my dear. The same stirrings have gone through me. It is different for a man. But we both know it cannot be. We must not let it happen.'

It is difficult to look dignified when stark naked. John managed it. He spoke with the calm assurance of a man who knows the right thing and is determined to do it. 'I am torturing you. Every time we make love, I put you at risk and I add to your torment. I cannot bear to see you unhappy. We have to stop.'

Anna's sobs dwindled into hiccups. She dared not speak for fear of the low animal howl that wanted to escape through her mouth. She managed to nod her head in an and the instrument protected her from any possibility of physical contact with John.

Now the girls were older they stayed up later. Their presence helped to keep temptation at bay during that dangerous hour in the evening when they used to be alone together. Anna took to going to bed when the girls did. She would line up with them to have her candle lit.

There was a tricky moment the first time she did it. John kissed his girls' foreheads as usual. Anna took a step backward as she saw the anguish in his face. He wanted to kiss her, but not as he kissed Jenny and Margaret. Instead he held out his hand to her. She clasped it briefly. It was warm and dry and strong. The touch of it made her heart turn over. She wanted to press it to her breast and shed tears over it. Instead, she swallowed the lump in her throat and said as briskly as she could, 'Goodnight John.'

On the stairs Margaret said with surprise in her voice, 'That's the first time he's not warned us about the danger of fire.'

Jenny laughed, 'We really must be grown-up now. I know you are still at school but you are sort of employed, like me.'

'Not for long, I hope. God willing and a fair wind I'll be a student soon.'

Anna, behind them on the stairs, suddenly felt dismally old. They had a future they could look forward to. Anna saw nothing ahead but uncomplaining endurance. When they reached the first landing Jenny and Margaret took turns to kiss her cheek and bid her goodnight. As they set off up to the second storey, Anna was touched by their gesture of affection. She still felt old but now she felt loved.

A fair wind was indeed behind Margaret in her desire to be a student; it took the form of Miss Hulme and Miss Fossil. They had enjoyed the advantage of being born into wealthy middle-class homes where education, along with a secure income, coal fires and plenty of servants was an accepted feature of life. They were passionate in their endeavours to spread the opportunity to study as widely as possible.

Miss Hulme had been disappointed in her efforts to provide Edward Carter with the higher education his abilities deserved. His position as virtual head of a large family of boys, his father absent or dead, no-one was sure which, made his going away impossible. Even the doughty Miss Hulme shrank from asking his mother to part with him.

Also, she feared that the leap from barefoot child in a slum to mixing with the sons of the wealthy and privileged was a step too far for the lad. All in all, she believed he had found the ideal position as Mr Woodward's assistant. His quick mind and adept way of dealing with people and practical matters would stand him in good stead. She knew Mr Woodward would encourage him to follow the evening courses run by the Mechanics' Institute.

When it came to Margaret's future the ladies felt they were on firmer ground. Her father was not wealthy, but he was not poor; he counted as a member of the middle class. True, he was at the lower end as far as money was concerned but there was no question mark over his membership. The girl, if not exactly comfortable in society, knew how to behave.

Above all she loved to study. It was her enthusiasm for Latin that determined Miss Fossil and Miss Hulme to encourage her to go on to further study. The absolute uselessness of a dead language in the wider world did not deter Margaret one iota. Miss Fossil, however, felt it was her duty to point out this unfortunate fact to her.

'You see, Margaret,' said Miss Fossil, 'Latin is not much use in the world. But it is a help if you study the law.'

'Why?' Margaret felt she could be very direct with Miss Fossil.

'Lawyers use Latin phrases, such as sine die and habeas corpus. Probably so they can keep things secret from their clients.'

'I met a girl at the meeting in Manchester. She was studying law.'

'Good for her. She may study it but she will not be allowed to practise it. One day that may change. For the moment no woman can become a member of the Law Society.'

Miss Fossil conscientiously went on with her self-appointed task of discouragement. 'The medical profession also expects a certain knowledge of the language. The names of drugs, the parts of the body. There are a few women who have qualified as doctors.'

Margaret shuddered dramatically. Distaste distorted her face.

'I see,' said Miss Fossil. Just as well, she thought. It still needed immense determination and resources for a woman to overcome the obstacles the medical profession put in her path.

Margaret twisted and squirmed as she stood before Miss Fossil. She racked her brain. Was there no escape? In the end she burst out, 'Is there no way I can study Latin and hope to earn my own living?

'You would like to be independent one day?' In Miss Fossil's experience most girls just wanted to get married.

'Absolutely. It's the only sensible plan. My father keeps showing me the newspaper where it says there are a million more women in the country than men. He's trying to stop me frowning when I read. He says men don't marry girls who screw their faces up. I don't care about that, but there definitely are more women than men in this country. So, I plan to earn my own living. It's that or widespread bigamy.'

Miss Fossil loved her work as a teacher, but hesitated to press the career upon her star pupil. 'You could always train to be a teacher. Unless you can write a best-selling novel, I know of no other way a respectable girl can support herself apart from a good marriage.'

'Is it possible to teach Latin? In a girls' school, of course,''

'Of course. More and more girls' schools are opening all over the country. They want to offer the same opportunity to learn Latin that boys have had for centuries.'

Margaret remembered that as a child she had a picture of herself speaking Latin while a group of men listened respectfully. She knew better now. She would settle for a group of girls. 'That's what I'll do. I want to stick with Latin. How do I set about it?'

Miss Fossil reeled off a list of requirements. Margaret's father's agreement and support were essential. She would have to live away from home. Miss Fossil paused and looked searchingly at Margaret. Would that be an obstacle for her? Many girls did not like to leave their home. Margaret made it clear she was not one of them.

Miss Fossil returned to her list. The training would cost money and she would need living expenses for three years at least. Miss Fossil would look for scholarships, bursaries and the like. When the list came to an end Miss Fossil looked across her desk at her pupil teacher.

Margaret was undaunted. 'It looks as if I'd better start with my father.' She turned to take her leave.

'One last thing, Margaret.' Miss Fossil rooted through the papers on her desk. She found what she was looking for and handed it to Margaret. 'My old university runs a competition every year. Twenty lines of poetry in Latin. It would be good practice for you. See how you get on.'

When work was finished for the day Margaret and Jenny went to meet Anna in the drapery store to help her choose a fabric that would signal the end of mourning. Major purchases on this scale were rare; the women of the household wanted to share the pleasure. With an inward smile Anna considered choosing bright red. Until their recent vow of abstinence, she was what the world called a scarlet woman.

As they held fabrics up to the light and weighed the virtues of cotton, wool and silk, Margaret told them of her interview with Miss Fossil.

'I will need your help with father,' she told Anna. 'You know what a fuddy-duddy he can be.'

Anna promised to help while hoping to be spared the challenge of persuading John without kissing him. 'And I will need yours with him,' said Anna. 'Hannah wants to retire. Bessie's husband has had a rise and Bessie is expecting another child.' She cut off their congratulations with a brisk return to practical matters. 'The loss of Hannah will be a major upheaval in the household. You know how your father dislikes change.'

'We shouldn't grudge her retirement.'

'I expect she'll be busy helping Bessie. She will have two children to look after.'

'Yes. Her baby's due in a couple of months.' Anna pictured the golden-haired toddler who had fed her longing for a baby.

'Well I hope Hannah will give us lessons on how to make her scones before she leaves.'

'Agreed. Hers are something special.'

'This is nice,' said Jenny holding up a length of silver-grey silk. She rested it under Anna's chin. 'It would suit you, Anna with your dark hair.'

Anna, not Aunt Anna, she noted. The girls had always been meticulous in addressing her as 'Aunt'. It pleased her that Jenny had dropped the 'aunt'. Aunts were maiden ladies with grey hair and spectacles who disapproved of everything. 'Anna' made her feel like a friend rather than a relation. Her spirits rose. She had money in her pocket from the mean-spirited stepson. She pictured his face if he found out how frivolously she was going to spend it.

John listened carefully to Margaret's aspiration to study Latin and her account of Miss Fossil's efforts on her behalf. For all the close attention he gave to her, she finished without knowing his opinion of her admittedly bizarre ambition. He kept his face impassive, asked no questions and made no comments.

Some days later Margaret turned her thoughts to writing a Latin poem for the competition. Here her father proved unexpectedly helpful as she chewed the end of her pen and wondered what to write about.

John laid down his copy of Browning's poems. 'What did Romans write about?' he asked.

'Fighting. Honour. The countryside. Exile.'

He found a page in his book and passed it to her. 'Try that,' he told her. 'Imagine some poor Roman legionary, serving his time in the icy north, thinking of his beloved Italy, basking in the warmth of the sun and dreaming of the grapes he'd be harvesting.

Margaret screwed her face up and chewed her lip as she read 'Home Thoughts from Abroad.' John watched without comment; he had stopped blaming her excessive reading for her tendency to frown. It was, he had decided, just the way Margaret was made. He looked round the room for some fresh reading matter.

Anna caught his attention. She was sewing her new dress. It lay in her lap in silvery folds; she looked like a mermaid. John rose to find another book. He knew he shouldn't but he could not stop himself. On his way he brushed close to Anna. His face hovered above her fragrant hair as he murmured that he was looking forward to seeing her in the new dress. She jumped and blushed but said nothing.

In the hall John leant against the coat-stand to recover his composure. Dammit. He should not have gone so close or pictured her in the silvery dress - or without it for that matter. He couldn't have her, but he couldn't let her go. Was he just another selfish man who let the woman he loved ruin her life for him? Dear Living Lord let there not be another George.

The sound of girls' voices at the front door brought him back to the present. Jenny had been to the Mechanics' Institute. She walked back with Mavis who occupied the stool next to her at the Post office. Edward Carter usually accompanied them. John flung the door open just in case there was any surreptitious kissing. He did not regard Mavis who came from the grubbier end of town as an adequate chaperon.

Jenny was on her way up the steps, her face glowing. 'A speaker came from the Independent Labour Party.' Edward, at the foot of the steps lifted his hat to John. Jenny stood poised halfway between them. Their positions illustrated perfectly their relationship. Edward waiting to climb the steps and win the prize of Jenny, and John, guarding the door.

The thought unsettled John. He resorted to the kind of remark fretful fathers make. 'Bit of a waste of your time, I'd have thought,' he growled at Jenny. 'You won't have a vote.'

John struck himself several imaginary blows to his head in the hope of coming to his senses. What was the matter with him? He was still acting the deaf mute about Margaret's ambition, had made the kind of flirtatious remark to Anna that their agreement strictly forbade and now he was grumbling at Jenny for being female.

It was Edward who had the last word. 'Women may not have the vote yet, Mr Truesdale, but that day may not be far off.' He tilted his hat and set off down the hill.

Jenny came into the hall and hung her coat up. Seeing her so pretty and cheerful and God dammit so young, John had an unconquerable urge to spoil it all.

'You see too much of that young man. People will say you are walking out with him. That's what the girls in the mill do,' he accused her.

Jenny faced him, clear-eyed and confident. She knew, as he did, that 'walking out' implied a great deal of sexual liberty.

'Edward only walks home with us. Mavis won't let him sit near us if we're in the same class. It stops other lads talking to her. She doesn't like that.'' She laughed. Mavis was more relaxed about the conventions. John huffed in a bad-tempered and fatherish way. It was water off a duck's back to Jenny.

She tilted her chin to him and smiled. 'There's a talk on Free Trade this time next week. I intend to go.' She didn't say if Mavis or Edward would be going. It was clear to John that his opinion did not have much to do with the matter.

John's evening of clumsy blundering had no long-term ill effects on his family. Anna continued to run his house, mother his children and delight his heart if not his bed. Edward Carter continued to meet Jenny in public. They had grown bolder and progressed to naming places and specific times for meeting, rather than relying entirely on chance. Edward did not knock on their front door or try to cross the threshold of her father's house.

Margaret stopped thinking about her future; she was much too interested in the present. Home Thoughts from Abroad had set her mind whirring. She soon had twenty lines of Latin, comparing the warmth and ease of Italy with the icy wastes of Scythia. She slipped the finished work onto Miss Fossil's desk.

The headmistress was at the end of a particularly trying day. Mr Woodward had consumed a whole hour of her time, supposedly consulting her about building extra classrooms to accommodate the increasing number of applicants. In truth he wanted to talk about Dorothea who was newly returned from France.

It was not until supper time that Miss Fossil had time to look at Margaret's offering. She waved the paper at Miss Hulme, who was busy with her soup. 'It's brilliant. Quite simply brilliant.'

'Tell me about it,' said Miss Hulme through her mulligatawny. She remained determinedly ignorant about the Ancient World. She had better things to do with her time.

Miss Fossil rhapsodised about the accuracy and the elegance of the Latin.

'Show me,' demanded Miss Hulme. She glanced at the paper. 'Get her to copy it out again but not with her name on. Then you can do the necessary before you send it off.' Her commands met with a puzzled frown from Miss Fossil. 'For goodness sake, woman. The child has put her full name. She won't stand a chance. Just put her initials. If it is as good as you say, they will assume it was written by a boy.'

It is not known if Miss Hulme's strategy influenced the result. Margaret, or rather M J Truesdale was awarded the gold medal. There may have been a few suppressed smiles, a few embarrassed squirmings among the judges when the truth was revealed, but that is all. The gentlemen carried it off with smooth words and unruffled dignity.

Miss Fossil swung the gold medal on its ribbon and beamed at her protégée. 'You are made, Margaret,' she told her. 'You are sure to get a bursary now, and the university of your choice.'

'It will have to be Manchester. I don't want to go too far from home.'

'Your family. How do they feel about it? They will support you?'

'Oh yes,' said Margret airily. When you are floating on a cloud, you do not see the obstacles at your feet.

Tommy appeared that evening, waving the Atherley and Tilton Advertiser. Margaret's gold medal made the front page. The reporter was a trainee, a local boy, who was puzzled that the poem was in Latin. He had asked how to spell the word and whether it needed a capital letter. The newspaper was passed from hand to hand round the supper table.

John struggled to accept his girls were growing up. That one should leave home to go and live among strangers was a severe blow. Fears for her safety beset him. He knew the allure young female flesh held for men. How often had he registered births to girls of fourteen? Thirteen? Twelve even?

The two headmistresses sent him a note of congratulations. They offered their encouragement and support for the ground-breaking venture. Margaret would be home for the weekends they assured him. Still he hesitated, unable to share in the general jubilation.

In the evening by the fireside, Anna went through the arguments with John, to settle his fears at this great leap into the unknown. 'All the new universities admit women students,' she told him. 'It's only the old ones who are such sticks-in-the mud.'

'I suppose I might be a little bit jealous, that Margaret will be better educated than me.'

'Nonsense. You are a well-educated man, John. You read books and newspapers. You look at the world, you see what is happening and you think about it. That's the important bit, thinking about it, not just letting some nonsense that was out-of-date when Adam was a lad pour out of your mouth.'

'No-one will want to marry a blue stocking. Especially one who studies a dead language.' From across the room Margaret launched a dagger of a look at her father.

'It is an unusual choice of subject', Anna conceded. 'Margaret might not choose to marry. Much better that she should have work that interests her, than sit and twiddle her thumbs because she is a spinster.'

John fell silent. He looked across at Anna, her head bent over her embroidery. She must have thought marriage to George preferable to the single life. He knew the term 'old maid' struck terror into women's hearts. He did not want Margaret to be driven, by lack of opportunity, into an unsatisfactory marriage. His mind was made up. 'Yes. Margaret must go to university. I will not use poverty as an excuse. I will find the necessary money.'

Margaret leapt up to embrace her father. Anna, fighting the urge to join her in kissing him, found she had snapped her sewing thread and punctured her thumb with the needle. She sucked the drop of blood and watched enviously. If only she could cross the room and enfold John in her arms.

'It's a long time since the Truesdales were in the newspaper,' John remarked as he clipped the article out of the paper and slipped it into his copy of poems by Robert Browning. There it joined a similar cutting from the Atherley and Tilton Advertiser; it was yellowed with age. John gave a wry smile as he read the headline.

Atherley and Tilton Advertiser 5th June 1888

DARING THEFT OF BICYCLE ON THE SABBATH

He skimmed through the article. It came back to him as if it was yesterday. The bicycle he had bought in a moment of extravagance. Sunday in the park. Two little girls feeding the ducks. Only one of them his. The man with the moustache, joining the queue of men keen to try the elegant new machine. Such an improvement on the old boneshakers.

As he put the Browning back on the shelf he said to Anna. 'I was afraid they might dig up that old item about the bicycle.'

'People forget. The reporter was very young. He'd not remember. Most people have forgotten or have the sense not to ask. The only one I know who was crass enough to enquire, was Dorothea Woodward.'

Margaret pricked her ears up at the name. 'She's not been missed at school. It's a different place without her.'

'Is she finished yet?' asked Jenny. 'I hope it's an improvement.'

'She's been back a couple of weeks.

'About time too,' Anna remarked. 'She will find her mother much changed.'

Pls send Doctor. Missus very bad.

Mr Woodward frowned at the scribbled note from the housekeeper. He looked across his desk at the panting boy who had delivered it along with a strong whiff of the stables.

'Did you see Mrs Woodward yourself?' he asked.

'Naw. Housekeeper passed note through window. She don't let me into house.' He gestured at his boots to explain.

'So, you didn't see Mrs Woodward?'

A disappointed Mr Woodward shook his head. He had hoped for some corroborating evidence.

'Naw. I didn't see her. But I heard her. And Miss Dorothy too. Screaming and a wailing. Like world was coming to an end.'

'Thank you. That'll do.' Mr Woodward passed sixpence into a grubby hand. Get me a cab. Keep him at the door. Then you can get yourself a bite to eat.' He suspected the boy would go straight to the ale house.

Mr Woodward contemplated the note. It was not the first such message he had received from the housekeeper. Mrs Woodward had suffered greatly during Dorothea's absence at finishing school. She'd neglected her usual occupations of spending money and criticising her neighbours. The queen of the chapel had lost her iron grip. She moped about the house like a grey ghost that occasionally burst into fits of weeping.

Several doctors had been consulted. 'Hysterics,' they had decided. Well at least they agree on one thing, thought Mr Woodward as he examined their imaginative bills. If only one of them could have found a cure!

Mr Woodward was convinced the only cure was the return of Dorothea. And now his darling girl was back. She looked radiant. Her face more beautiful in some way he could not fathom. Perhaps it was her eyebrows. Her clothes and her way of speaking were elegant and refined. She was indeed finished; he had not wasted his money. She had been asleep when he left for his work in the morning.

He twisted the note in his fingers. What to do? It was a perfect excuse to go home to see his darling Dorothea. No more doctors he decided. He'd had a bellyful of them. He rapped on the glass of the window to summon Edward Carter. What was the point in grooming an assistant if you didn't throw work at him occasionally?

When Edward arrived, Mr Woodward issued instructions at him. Visit this. Inspect that. Speak sharply to Mr Tompkins. Get a better price for those three tons of…. 'When you've finished come up to the house and report to me.'

Edward had trouble not letting his jaw drop at this unprecedented list of jobs to be accomplished in the absence of his boss. Mr Woodward usually kept a close eye on things.

Edward quickly turned his expression of awestruck wonder into a brisk smile. 'You are taking a day off, sir?'

'Exactly. My daughter's home. From the continent.' What a thrill it gave him to say 'continent.' He grinned. 'Her mother has rather monopolised her. Now it's my turn. Catch up with all her doings in France.'

'Very pleasant, sir. Very pleasant.'

Mr Woodward took his hat from the stand and set off down the stairs. Just as he had instructed, the cab was waiting at the door of his office. The stable boy held the horse's head and the driver sat on the box with the reins in his hands.

'No need to rush back,' he told the stable boy through the cab window. He leant back against the leather seat and looked forward to arriving home. Whatever had upset his wife would be over. She would get better now. Dorothea was home. Dorothea. He rolled her name in his mouth. So pretty, so clever. Such a beautiful voice. She sang like an angel. He would ask her to play the piano in the evening. How he had missed music while she was away.

In the Coach and Horses, the stable boy was on his second pint. 'Never heard anythin' like it,' he told his audience. 'Well on Saturday night round our way. When my dad's had a drink or two and my mam's giving him an ear-battering. But in a posh house! You don't expect, do you? Screaming and hollerin. And words. Usin words like I never heard before in a lady's mouth.'

That evening it was with considerable satisfaction that Edward climbed the hill to his employer's house. The day's business had gone well. What had especially pleased him was the respect he had received. As Mr Woodward's representative chairs were vacated to accommodate him, refreshments offered, and forelocks tugged. He began to see the charm of a boss's life.

There was something different when he rang the bell at Mr Woodward's mansion. The housekeeper normally grunted, 'Oh it's you,' and pointed to a bench in the hall. There he would kick his heels until summoned. That evening she dropped him a bit of a curtsey, called him by his name and showed him straight into the study.

'Mr Woodward will be with you soon,' she told him. 'There's a few matters he's attending to.' She nodded her head at the bottle of brandy on the table. 'Purely for medicinal purposes,' she assured him. 'Mr Woodward had a bit of a shock. He says to help yourself.'

Edward saw there were two glasses on the table. Was the tee-total Mr Woodward testing him in some way? He considered pouring a drink and decided against it. It was Mr Woodward who had received the shock. Not him.

It was not long before Mr Woodward came, or rather, staggered into the room. He immediately sought a seat as if his legs would not carry him further. His face was drawn, the cheeks hollow and the eyes unnaturally bright. Round his lips the skin was chalky white as if someone had painted a clown's smile on his face.

Edward stood out of politeness. Mr Woodward pushed the brandy bottle across the table. Edward shook his head and waited for his employer to ask about the day's work. Mr Woodward said nothing but sat gazing into space for a long time.

Edward decided to take matters into his own hands and, still standing, began to report on the doings of the day.

Mr Woodward gave the appearance of listening, but asked no questions, and checked no figures as he normally would. The recitation of practical matters appeared to soothe him. He breathed more deeply and the ghostly whiteness round his lips began to fade. Edward came to the end of his account with a warning about the water level in one of the workings of the mine. The overseer was concerned about it. For a moment Mr Woodward gave Edward his full attention.

'You see to it tomorrow. First thing.'

'As you say, sir.'

'I do.'

Edward was amazed. Mr Woodward entrusting him with safety in the mine! The man must be very ill. He was always bragging how much safer his mines were than other collieries. Pride in his profession spurred Mr Woodward into action. He roused himself in his chair and gestured to Edward to sit. He poured himself a tumbler full of brandy and pushed the bottle across the table.

'You might like to take a sip of that, son, after what I've got to say to you.'. Edward sat as he was bid but ignored the brandy. Mr Woodward leaned forward and spoke in a confidential tone.

'My daughter is in urgent need of a husband. And I've got you in mind for the job'

'It's late for anyone to be calling,' said John when he heard the knock on the door. He rose from his chair. The others clustered behind him as he took his candle into the hall.

A cautious peep round the door, revealed Edward Carter with his hat in his hand.

'Sorry to be bothering you at this time of night, Mr Truesdale. Something very urgent has come up. I'm on my way back from Mr Woodward. The timing is his. I would not choose to come at this hour. I'd like a word with Jenny if you please.' He set his mouth and stared directly at John.

A stern warning to come back at a civilized hour was on its way to John's lips. His arm was tensed, ready to slam the door closed. Edward began to climb the steps. John froze. Was the lad going to muscle his way in to the house?

Anna intervened. She was perpetually grateful to Edward for helping Tommy at school. 'It's obviously something very urgent. I expect you'd like a word in private. We haven't another room you can use. We'll go back to the sitting room and you and Jenny can have the hall.' She took

John's arm and shepherded him away. 'I think all the proprieties have been met,' she told him, with authority in her voice, as she closed the door to the hall behind her.

Once alone Edward passed a hand across his forehead. Where to begin? He stuttered and floundered. Jenny, blessed with a quick understanding, took a few words and used the expressions on Edward's face, the gestures of his hands to fill in the gaps. She quickly worked out that Dorothea had returned from France in the family way. There was no accompanying bridegroom in tow. For a moment she almost laughed to think of her old adversary brought so low. 'So that's what they mean by finishing,' she said with a smile, unaware of the express train of a disaster that was rushing towards her.

Something in Edward's face made her regret the jest. His barging into her house at this hour meant serious business. With a cold feeling growing round her heart, a strange equation popped into Jenny's head.

$$\text{Dorothea} + \text{baby} - \text{husband} = \text{hasty wedding}$$

She put it into words to check. Dorothea plus baby, but minus bridegroom, equals a hasty wedding.

The next step in the calculation was Dorothea's horrified father searching for a replacement for the non-existent bridegroom and a way to limit the scandal.

The realisation that Edward, her Edward, was to fill the place of the missing bridegroom, exploded in Jenny's mind. She reeled. Of course, the Woodwards wanted Edward to be the husband; there was not a woman alive who would not want him. And there was no-one who wanted him more passionately than Jenny did.

She felt a bony hand reach into her chest and pull her heart out. She didn't scream, she didn't cry, she pressed her lips together and waited for Edward to confirm she had grasped the dilemma he was in.

'I've got a day to decide,' he said. 'A half share in all his business. My name on the door, the cheque book, the future contracts. Men work for years for much less.'

Somehow, she found a voice to ask, 'What's the alternative?' She knew the answer.

'Nothing said,' admitted Edward. 'It's muck or nettles as my mother would say. If I don't agree someone else will. Mr Woodward will find someone to marry his daughter. The new man won't want me around to remind him he was second choice. I'll be out on my ear before Christmas. And not just me. My brothers as well. We'll none of us get a job round here if Mr Woodward puts the black spot on us.' His eyes grew glassy as he contemplated his vision of disaster. He shook his head. 'I can't do that to my mam.'

Jenny took her courage in her hands. 'No. You can't do that,' she told him. She knew one day she might take some comfort from the generosity of her love.

'I had to speak to you first, Jenny. You understand.' He looked at her, long and hard.

She did understand. He was telling her without words that she was the one he wanted to marry. A tiny nugget of comfort in the disaster that surrounded both of them. She'd always seen Edward's life as an arrow, aimed high and true. Now its glorious flight was about to smash into the cliff face of marriage to Dorothea.

'Don't be jealous,' he told her. 'It's just business.'

'I know.' Jenny knew her worth. She would not deign to be jealous of Dorothea, the malicious, devious daughter of a sanctimonious mother and a criminally indulgent father. Yet here she was, letting him go into the Woodwards' hands without a weapon to his name. Think, she told herself. Think. It hurts less when you think. She ground down the emotion that threatened to overwhelm her brain. She scoured her mind for a smidgen of inspiration, some tiny blow to assert his independence.

'I tell you what, you tell him you'll do it if the business is called Carter Woodward. It sounds much better than

Woodward Carter. Get your name first. Show them who's boss.'

For the first time in that long and fateful evening, Edward gave his characteristic grin. But it was over. Her childhood dream of marrying the blonde Edward Carter she had hero-worshipped since she was a child was dead. It lay in tatters at her feet like the scattered leaves of autumn. She looked into the eyes of her beautiful boy to say farewell.

'We can still have our talks. I need to talk to you, Jenny. I don't know what to think about anything till I've talked to you about it. We can still be friends.'

Edward stepped forward, took hold of her arms and kissed her very hard. 'It'll always be you, Jenny.' There was much more he wanted to say but he bit his lip and was gone.

Jenny went back into the sitting room where her family awaited her. John took a breath to make a start on his inevitable interrogation.

Jenny, with Edward's kiss on her lips, came to a swift resolution. She didn't want anyone pitying her. She would take the bull by the horns and carry the dreadful blow off with a careless shrug of her shoulders.

'Well,' she said, pleased to hear her voice was functioning normally, 'that was a surprise. He came to tell me he's getting wed.'

John and Anna stared in amazement, their jaws slack.

Jenny took advantage of their silence. 'You'll never guess who. Would you believe it's Dorothea Woodward, newly returned from France?' She managed a disdainful smirk.

'Huh. The boss's daughter. Not very original, but effective,' was John's verdict. He could not keep the satisfied smile from his face as he returned to his newspaper. 'At least that'll stop him knocking at our door.'

Jenny slid away before they started to ask questions. She was up the stairs before her face collapsed and revealed the extent of her distress.

The staff were surprised when Mr Woodward failed to appear for work next morning. They knew he doted on Dorothea but his absence was unprecedented. They gathered in a small flock, looking for support. They turned to Edward for directions. He told them to get on with their tasks, and promised to deal with any problems on his return. First and foremost, he had to check a problem in the pit. The safety of his employees was always Mr Woodward's top priority. They understood; they were well-trained. They went off happily to their accounts and correspondence, murmuring their approval. 'Chip off the old block,' they agreed. It was Edward's first real taste of that heady substance – power.

Edward walked to the pit head, pulled on overalls and climbed into the cage to descend into the darkness and the heat of the mine. There he spent time on his knees peering at cracks in dim light and listening to the many and varied opinions of the miners. Though they failed to agree on a name for the problem they were united in identifying the solution.

A slightly grubby Edward returned to the office where he dealt with the mail, and the callers and all the little crises that occur when men, women and machines work long and hard. The end of the day took him by surprise; he had been totally absorbed by the tasks in front of him. It felt good being the boss; it might even be worth the price.

On his way up the hill he remembered that first encounter with Dorothea, when he escorted her home because she could not find the way. He had thought it a shrewd way to catch Mr Woodward's attention. Well he had certainly done that. Then there'd been the French conversation classes; she had shown she was quick with the language. And she could sing. Perhaps it wouldn't be too bad of an evening, after work, if she played the piano and sang. There was pleasure in music. He stopped his mind from thinking about the bedtime that would follow the music. She was ahead of him there.

Outside the Truesdale house he stopped for a moment and thought of Jenny. He removed his hat and held it briefly to his chest. It was not twenty-four hours since he'd climbed those steps and rapped on that door for the first, and last time. Common sense told him he had no choice. Bless her, she had made it easy for him to accept his fate. Goodbye, Jenny. And thank you. He pulled on his hat and set off resolutely up the hill.

At the Woodward mansion, the housekeeper greeted him even more effusively. She positively simpered before showing him to the study where Mr Woodward waited. There was no brandy on the table this time. They offered him tea. He refused.

When they were alone, Mr Woodward stared at Edward for a long time, willing him to be first to break the silence. Edward stared back.

'Well,' demanded Mr Woodward.

'I inspected the problem in the mine as we agreed. They are re-timbering about ten feet either side.'

'Good.' Mr Woodward looked to the ceiling for help from the Almighty in approaching the shameful subject of his daughter's urgent need for a husband. 'And the other matter?' he asked.

'Two things.'

Mr Woodward was taken by surprise. He leant back in his chair. He had not anticipated bargaining from the youngster. A straight yes or no, but not conditions.

'I am to be an equal partner?' Mr Woodward nodded. 'With my name on the door?'

'On the door, on the notepaper, on the contracts and on the cheque book.'

'Then I should like the firm to be called Carter-Woodward. It slips much better off the tongue than Woodward-Carter.' He could see the pain he caused the older man, but hardened his heart. Not nearly as much pain as I caused Jenny, he told himself. He thought of the jokes there'd be at his expense. People accepted seven- month babies but not when they were conceived in a different country. There'd be an awful lot of sniggering behind hands in the tap bar.

It seemed Mr Woodward had been following a similar train of thought. 'Aye. Best show who's boss.'

'Also, I should like to talk to Dorothea in private first. I want to be sure she agrees to this.'

Mr Woodward wanted to rise up and shout that the baggage didn't have much choice in the matter. She'd take the husband he'd found her as she had so singularly failed to provide one herself. The girl had to be made respectable. Lots of fathers would have shown her the door and packed her off to the Workhouse. Instead he swallowed his rage and got to his feet.

'She is waiting in the drawing room. You can have half an hour alone with her. That's all.'

Dorothea sat alone in the drawing room. She had spent the day considering how to greet her potential husband. Finishing school had taught her to prepare carefully for important meetings; she had not completely wasted her time there. The remembered image of Edward Carter as a young man of pleasant appearance consoled her a little. If she had to have a husband, better to have a handsome one. But compared with a smooth-mannered Polish count, he was as ignorant as a lumbering bear, fresh out of hibernation. There would always be a whiff of the slums about him.

Her father had a high opinion of this Edward's abilities. He might be handy with a slide rule and do logarithms but he would not know which spoon to use for soup. He would need considerable licking into shape before he could begin to compare with Aleksy. But first, she had every intention of testing out his other skills.

She had chosen her clothes with care, the deep magenta ball gown that showed off her black hair and her porcelain complexion. She reclined on a sofa with a book held open as if she were reading. Her silk petticoats settled round her thighs in a luxurious embrace. As she contemplated her next step, a cheering thought came to her. This was going to put that Truesdale girl's nose out of joint. Since she had to have a husband it was satisfying to snatch the one that post-office girl wanted. Spite made her smile.

She heard her father's footsteps in the hall and put on her contrite face.

Mr Woodward stood at the door and gestured at Edward. 'He'd like a word with you. You've got half an hour. I'll be in my study.' He left and closed the door carefully behind him.

Dorothea stirred on the sofa, her skirts rippling gracefully around her. 'I don't know why papa is being so careful of my reputation.' She smiled at him. 'It's a bit late for shutting the stable door. As you must know that particular horse has bolted.'

Edward gaped.

'Not what you expected?' Dorothea enquired with one of her elegant eyebrows raised. 'You thought I'd snivel and cringe with shame.' She gave a low chuckle and looked provocatively at him.

Edward spoke. 'To be honest I came to make sure you agreed with ...er.. the enterprise of your own free will. I'm not some rogue who would marry a woman against her will. I want to make sure that you agree. No-one has forced you into this.'

'That is thoughtful of you. I appreciate that.' Her manner was mocking. 'Let's put it this way. There was no more coercion than usual.'

'How do you think this arrangement will work, Dorothea?'

'I will keep my place in respectable society.' She pulled a face at the thought. 'I will have a comfortable home. We are sensible people; we should rub along quite nicely. If I am lucky and have a boy my father might come to love me again. He always wanted a son.' She looked bleak but not for long. A shake of her head sent her gold earrings swinging merrily, to lighten the atmosphere. They had been serious long enough. She tilted her head and looked up at

Edward through her eyelashes. 'And, of course, I will have a handsome husband.'

He chose to ignore the compliment though his cheeks flushed. 'Your father has told you the other side of the bargain? I don't want you to be under any illusions.'

'Of course,' she shrugged. 'You will have an equal share in the business. It is more than you could hope for even after years of honest toil. You will have half of everything. Except me.' She rose and moved towards him. 'You will get all of me.'

She stood close to Edward. He could smell her perfume. The best French with sultry overtones. It did something to his senses that the lavender fragrance of the modest maidens of the town had never done. He looked down at the cleft between her creamy white breasts and felt his eyes drawn irresistibly to them. She willed his hand to follow his eyes.

'Go ahead,' she murmured. 'It's only fair. If I were you, I'd want to try the goods before I bought them.' Somehow, he was kissing her breasts, so soft, so smooth and warm. She took his hand. He heard the rustle of silk as she hitched up her skirts and guided his fingers into that fabled place, he knew existed but had never experienced. She plunged a hand into his breeches and pulled out the tail of his shirt so she could grasp his manhood. He was a young man, there was no need to fondle or cajole; he was armed and ready for action.

They collapsed together onto the oyster damask sofa. She provided the guidance he needed. There they sealed the unholy bargain her father had made in a manner Mr Woodward had not anticipated. It was quickly over; it was Edward's first time. They adjusted their clothing and looked at each other.

'That wasn't so bad was it?' enquired Dorothea as if he had just had a tooth out.

'On the contrary.' He found he was grinning foolishly at her. 'I didn't know it could feel so good,' he told her shaking his head at the wonder of it all. He didn't love Dorothea. She was not particularly likeable. Yet the act, so quickly concluded, had sent the blood running round his veins with godlike vigour. Perhaps marriage wouldn't be as bad as he thought.

'Don't worry,' she told him. 'There'll be plenty more of that.' She checked his clothing for dampness, found none and rose to her feet. 'I suppose we should go and tell my father the happy news.'

It was in the interests of all parties to arrange the wedding with speed. A six-month baby would set the gossips on fire. They would work out that the hastily contrived husband could not be the father and that Dorothea's baby must have been conceived in France. Atherton did not take kindly to *foreigners*. As far as they were concerned *foreigners* started at the border with Yorkshire.

Mr Woodward could not face the humiliation of giving away his pregnant daughter in his customary place of worship. At the chapel he was a respected figure, held in high regard by the congregation. It was a Free Church, not a free and easy church, as the minister regularly pointed out.

'What do you think of a civil wedding?' he asked Edward. 'You're more of a modern man, bit of a freethinker. Heh?' Edward knew nothing about weddings whether civil or religious.

'The Registrar does the honours', Mr Woodward explained. 'In his office by the Town Hall. Very simple. None of the fol de rols the ladies like, though.'

'That'd be a relief.'

'No time like the present.'

A brisk walk down the hill took them to John Truesdale's office. Mr Woodward had no appointment but half an hour was quickly made available. Through Jenny, John had prior warning that Dorothea was to marry Edward. He was unaware of the complex calculations behind the decision. Jenny kept those to herself. She preferred Edward to be thought a rogue, rather than a dupe. Especially a dupe of Dorothea.

John kept his face professionally smooth. 'The marriage can take place twenty-one days after we have completed the formalities.'

'Twenty-one days!' Mr Woodward was aghast. 'That's three bloomin weeks.'

'The time is exactly the same in both church and chapel. Banns have to be called three times.'

'Is there no way to speed it up?'

'Only by a special licence.'

'How'd we get one of those?'

John had a moment of quiet amusement. He took care not to let it show on his face as he told Mr Woodward, a staunch Free Church man that he would have to apply to the bishop.

'Oh.' Mr Woodward stopped there. Not even for Dorothea could he stretch to such a level of hypocrisy.

Edward stepped in to smooth over the gap in the proceedings. 'The formalities, Mr Truesdale. What do you need to know?'

'Names, addresses. That sort of thing.'

When John asked Edward for his profession the young man glanced at his employer for guidance.

'He's an engineer, like me,' said Mr Woodward.

Pride flickered in Edward's heart for the first time in several days. It was almost worth being thrust into a sham marriage if he could be counted in the same profession as Arkwright, Stephenson, Telford and Brunel. His sense of having passed some mysterious test did not last long. The date of his birth caused a momentary blip in the proceedings.

'As you are not yet twenty-one, we shall need your father's consent,' said John.

'My father is missing. We have always assumed he was dead somewhere.'

'There is no death certificate?' John frowned.

Edward shook his head. 'My mother will give her consent,' he volunteered.

'I am glad to hear it. Unfortunately, her word does not count as far as the law is concerned.' John chewed his lip as he considered all the angles of the situation. 'No guardian, no uncle?' he enquired. Edward shook his head. John came to a decision. 'I shall mark it down that for you, Edward, there is no consenting party involved.'

Mr Woodward was more than happy to give his consent for Dorothea. No one thought it necessary to ask her.

'The ceremony is conducted with the doors open in the hours of daylight,' John assured them. 'An unwilling bride has the opportunity to flee.' The two older men chuckled complacently at the thought of such an unlikely event.

'You must have two witnesses,' John told Edward. 'You call upon them to witness that you take Dorothea to be your lawful wedded wife. It's very simple.'

Edward felt relief spread over his face. There would be no calling on God to bless this unholy union. It was not some mythical transformation of two individuals into one flesh. It was more of a business deal than a marriage ceremony. He could cope with that.

On the day of the wedding Dorothea was sick into the ornate bowl of the lavatory. As she knelt and heaved, she distracted her mind by studying the blue flowers painted on the white porcelain bowl and the decorated plaque that proclaimed the vessel to be called 'Cascade'.

'Wedding nerves,' said the maid, who recognised morning sickness when she saw it. She helped Dorothea to her feet, pulled the chain by its wooden handle and offered her a cup of tea to settle her nerves.

As Dorothea waited for the tea she wondered at her calmness, her total lack of emotion. Girls were taught to look forward to their wedding day with trepidation and excitement. Dorothea felt neither of those emotions. She was not an ignorant virgin about to face her first experience of sex. Nor was she a radiant bride, the centre of attention and surrounded by flowers. To placate her father, and the world, she had to have a husband; Edward would do nicely. The actual ceremony was a tiresome ordeal to be endured so that she could venture out into polite society. It had no more significance for her than wearing clothes or having her hair arranged. Marriage was simply a necessary step she had to take.

The maid went to wake Mrs Woodward. To her dismay her mistress would not get out of bed. The maid first coaxed with cups of tea and then threatened with Mr Woodward. To no avail. When summoned, the head of the household accused his wife of failing to support him on what was going to be the most trying day of his life. Mrs Woodward turned her head away.

Unable to move his wife, Mr Woodward called upon Dorothea, confident she would scold her mother into action; she always had that effect on him.

When the door closed and Dorothea was alone with her mother, she looked down at the sheet pulled tight over her mother's head. 'I don't blame you, mama. I'd do the same if I could. But I can't. I'm just going to grit my teeth and get it over with. Best not to come. There's nothing to see. You are not missing anything. I promise I won't make it difficult for father.'

The sheet snapped back. Mrs Woodward's cloudy eyes popped open for a second and fixed on her daughter. 'It's all my fault. I should have warned you.' Then the eyelids closed. Mrs Woodward pulled the sheet over her head, curled her knees up to her chin and went to hide in the world of sleep. She dreamt of tables groaning beneath the weight of a wedding breakfast, of new clothes rustling in tissue paper and wedding gifts of silver and porcelain. A wedding that would do her proud in Southport.

She remembered the early days of her own marriage. The great mound of her belly that was Dorothea. Then the hopes that failed. The sons, so longed for, who arrived in this world too early and left it too soon. I should have warned her. That's what they would say. In Southport.

The maid tiptoed in, drew back the sheet an inch or two. She saw her mistress open her eyes and turn her gaze to the bottle at the bedside.

'One spoon or two?' murmured the maid.

'Two.'

The maid poured out the laudanum and fed it to her mistress like a mother spoon-feeding a baby. She tiptoed out and closed the door gently behind her.

Downstairs in the kitchen the third gardener was drinking his morning tea. The maid came up behind him and ran her hands over his back. She aahed with pleasure as her fingers kneaded into the great ropes of muscle on his shoulders. The third gardener put down his mug and turned to embrace her with enthusiasm.

'Steady on,' she told him. 'We haven't got time for a proper jump, but we could have a really good squeeze.'

'Before the happy couple get back,' the laugh was deep in his throat.

'Aye. The happy couple.' She rolled her eyes to show her disbelief and thrust her hand down his trousers.

While Mrs Woodward languished in bed and the maid pleasured the third gardener in the kitchen, Dorothea and Edward were declaring themselves to be man and wife. Mr Woodward hovered over the proceedings in an agonising mixture of shame, guilt and wrecked ambition, quickly followed by straightforward relief when the deed was done. There was no going back now. He mopped his forehead with his handkerchief after he signed as a witness.

The other witness was Edward's valiant mother. Mrs Carter was old before her time from bearing a string of healthy boys. Hollow-cheeked and almost toothless, she could not write her name. John showed her where to put her mark.

Mr Woodward invited her to ride back with them in the carriage, in spite of Dorothea's scowl at the suggestion. He urged her to come to his home for refreshments, non-alcoholic refreshments, of course. A sudden longing for a glass of medicinal brandy came over him. He did his best to dismiss the temptation.

Mrs Carter refused his invitation with dignified politeness. She was moving into a new house; there was a lot to do. Her boys were helping her. Mr Woodward stifled a pang of envy. He offered her his hand, which she shook in a business-like way, and turned to leave the Registry.

'Let us drive you home,' said Mr Woodward, putting a hand on her arm to delay her. 'It won't take a minute and it threatens to rain.'

Dorothea scowled some more. Her eyebrows slithered about like slugs on damp slate but she said nothing.

'My mother's new house is most conveniently placed,' said Edward. 'We pass it on the way to yours, Mr Woodward.'

There had been no question of Edward and Dorothea having a house of their own. Mr Woodward blithely assumed his daughter would continue to live in the family home and her new husband would join them there.

Edward was in no position to argue. When all the contracts were signed, he was, on paper, a rich man but his wealth was tied up in the business. He had no capital though he would be in possession of a healthy income. It was not just to advance his own career that he had put his neck in the Woodward noose. He had done it to help his family. Already he had found the Carter tribe a better house than the slum they had previously lived in. It is amazing what you can do in twenty-one days if you put your mind to it and have credit.

Edward had chosen his mother's new home with great care. It was above the smoke and fog that engulfed the poorest part of town but did not have any great claim to gentility. No point in inviting enmity and mockery from neighbours. It was the first in a brick terrace where employed and respectable people lived. Best of all, it was at the foot of the hill on the road that led past Jenny's house to the Woodward mansion.

As Edward handed his mother out of the carriage, he looked with satisfaction at the home he was renting for her and his brothers. He could sit in the window of the front parlour and keep an eye out for Jenny as she walked to and from work. He might, just might, by chance, fall into step and walk alongside her.

He knew better than to explain his thinking to Jenny. She would resist. He would just let it happen and claim it was pure chance. Totally innocent. Once or twice a week. What's the harm in that? Public view. On our way home from work. I value your opinion. Our little chats are important to me. Edward smiled at the prospect.

Mr Woodward looked across the carriage at his new son-in-law. The lad didn't look too unhappy. He glanced at Dorothea; she was still scowling. And silent. Unusually so. She had spoken only to say the words of the wedding vow. What with her mother upstairs in a terminal sulk and Dorothea glowering like a basilisk, there would be no happy family celebration in the Woodward household that afternoon. A fierce longing to break his teetotal pledge swept again over Mr Woodward.

Matters did not improve for the trio after they arrived at what was to be the home they would share in the future. Mrs Woodward did not appear at lunch. The meal was an awkward occasion; the maid was the only one with a genuine smile. Dorothea displayed the table manners she had learnt at finishing school but none of their conversational ease. Even so, when she rose to leave, her father found that he was smiling at her.

Seconds later a great clash of chords bellowed out from the piano. Mr Woodward and Edward looked to each other in surprise. This was no Wesley hymn. This was heart-rending soul-stirring stuff. Father and new husband went to stand in the open doorway as Dorothea poured out her soul in a Beethoven sonata.

She looked so beautiful - the bloom of pregnancy was upon her. Tears came into Mr Woodward's eyes as he watched her play. She may have brought shame on the family name but she was still the apple of his eye, the treasure of his heart. He wanted to keep her close and keep her safe. What a fool he had been to let her go to France where she had fallen prey to their loose continental ways. This wouldn't have happened in Lancashire. There wasn't a man within fifty miles who would dare touch her for fear of his wrath.

Edward laid a hand on his arm. 'I don't know about you, sir, but I could do with a glass of medicinal brandy. It's not every day a chap gets married.'

Mr Woodward clapped him on the shoulder and led him to the study. 'Then perhaps we could pop down to the office and have a look at the plans for that new weaving shed. There's a couple of things I'm not quite happy about.'

It all happened very quickly. An offer came for Margaret to study Ancient Languages and Literature at Owens College in Manchester.

Jenny was aghast. 'Ancient Languages!' she exclaimed. 'You mean there's more than one of them.'

Margaret allowed herself a smug smile. 'There's Greek, of course. And Sanskrit. I might just take that if I get on all right with Greek.'

'What's this about you having an exhibition? I'm not having you make an exhibition of yourself. Not even for £50.'

Margaret smiled at her father. 'Don't worry. It's just another word for a scholarship. They give us £50 towards the expense.'

'That's all right then,' said John looking relieved. Further education was a novelty to his family. Proud though he was of Margaret's achievement, he found his first encounter with university deeply worrying; there were so many unknowns. It was not just the expense that alarmed him; there was a whole new vocabulary to be mastered. An exhibition that was not a public display but a gift of money was only the first of many puzzling new words.

Miss Fossil was beside herself with joy at her protégée's success. As soon as the term ended, she sat down one morning to invite the family to come to tea to celebrate. She stopped her hand from writing Mr and Mrs Truesdale on the envelope. There was, she knew, some kind of irregularity in the household. Its exact nature was not clear to her. In the end she referred simply to Mr Truesdale and any guardian or friends with an interest in Margaret's future.

John replied straightaway. Mrs Mainwaring, Margaret's aunt would accompany him.

Miss Fossil, who thought there was no time like the present, sent a reply suggesting that very afternoon. John's reply was delivered as Miss Fossil sat down to her lunch.

'The Post Office's working well', said John. 'We must tell Jenny.' On their way to Miss Fossil's for tea he and Anna walked through empty streets and past boarded up shops.

'It's like a ghost town,' said Anna.

'Wakes Week,' said John. 'The mills are closed and the mines are shut. Everyone who can, has gone away. They'll be streaming down the promenade in Blackpool by now.'

They climbed the three steps up to the front door of the elegant Georgian house that Miss Fossil shared with Miss Hulme. A grumpy maid showed them into Miss Fossil's comfortable sitting room.

'I'm guessing her young man is at the seaside and she's wondering what he's getting up to,' Anna speculated.

John said nothing. He knew from the spike in the birth rate that the mill girls could be very obliging in Wakes Week. Their good wages and steady work gave them confidence in their dealings with men. They frequently dispensed with the formalities of marriage to live 'tally' with a man. He got his marching orders if he failed to come up to scratch. John preferred to keep this free and easy attitude to matrimony hidden from his womenfolk.

Grumpy or not, the maid delivered Earl Grey tea and buttered scones. When the formalities were over, Miss Fossil and Miss Hulme both expressed their delight at Margaret's success. Indeed, Miss Hulme was slightly jealous of her friend's success. She had hoped the boys' school would have the honour of the first university place.

The two women sensed a certain hesitation in John and Anna. It had not occurred to them that Margaret's parent and guardian would regard a university education with suspicion rather than unalloyed glee. To reassure them, they tried to describe their own days as undergraduates. They started well, by describing the serious study, the conscientious chaperoning and the convent-like arrangements for living. All this was music to John's ears.

Nostalgia took hold of them. They wandered down Memory Lane. These two formidable women who had earned the respect of the hard-nosed businessmen and the even harder-handed labourers of Atherley grew positively skittish as they recalled their days at Girton. They took a brief holiday from being serious about the education of girls to revisit the glory days of their youth.

They described tea parties on lawns that swept down to the river and sherry parties in tutors' rooms. Mysterious new words littered the conversation: firsts and wranglers and playing something called lacrosse. John wondered if it was some kind of musical instrument. As they reminisced their voices, which they had softened to be more acceptable to northern ears, returned to their origins, the vowels clipped and the tone bell-like with the unmistakeable accents of the class with the habit of command.

Miss Hulme confided to them that she too had been the proud holder of an exhibition. 'Nat Sci,' she told them. She pronounced the abbreviation of Science as 'sigh' with the result that her guests were none the wiser. When they came to 'punting on the Cam' their visitors' incomprehension was palpable. The headmistresses realised they had lost sight of the real purpose in the meeting. 'To our moutons,' shrilled Miss Hulme which was not exactly a lot of help.

'Have you considered where Margaret will live when the new term starts?' Miss Fossil asked; she had re-discovered her tact and refrained from calling it Michaelmas. 'Margaret will not have time to waste going backwards and forwards from here,' she told them sternly.

John kept his face still and expressionless but mentally his jaw dropped as the reality of Margaret's leaving home hit him. As he grappled with the concept Miss Fossil ploughed on; she went full steam ahead.

'She has her exhibition of course, that will take care of the fees. I have made enquiries of the warden at the Women's Hall of Residence. There is huge variation in the level of the fees depending on the choice of room. From thirty-six guineas to an almost incredible sixty.'

Anna moved uneasily in her chair. She did not think Margaret would do well living among girls whose parents could afford such sums. Not without Jenny to protect her. She searched for a tactful way of suggesting something cheaper without embarrassing John. It proved unnecessary. Miss Fossil was ahead of her.

'Fortunately, I am in the position to be able to recommend an acquaintance of Miss Hulme.' The headmistresses had an inexhaustible supply of useful friends. 'A Mrs McKenna, she is a widow of great education, runs a lodging house for students. Perhaps six or seven girls, no more. Very clean and respectable. The girls have to be back by half past nine of an evening. They walk to the college in pairs. Mrs McKenna is very strict about chaperoning the girls in her care.'

John pursed his lips and nodded. He looked serious and judicial while doing everything possible to avoid accepting the suggestion. A stubborn resolve had come over him not to give his consent to Mrs McKenna's lodgings. He had no alternative plan. In fact, he had no plan at all; he just wanted to demonstrate to these forceful women that the final decision was his to make. He promised to let them know and took his leave with Mrs McKenna's address on a piece of paper in his pocket.

John and Anna walked back through the empty town and started to climb the hill home. There was no need to talk. They were both in mourning for Margaret. They realised she was leaving them.

'I didn't think it'd be like this,' said John. 'I thought I'd walk her down the aisle. Then I could hand her over to a husband and he could do the worrying.'

Anna smiled and took his arm. Now she thought about it, the conventional early marriage was an unlikely scenario for Margaret. About as likely as my marrying you, John, she thought grumpily. But she did not say so. Something swished against her skirt. She looked down.

'We seem to have acquired a companion.'

A small brown and black dog trotted alongside them. 'He looks sweet,' said Anna. The dog looked intently up at her. Anna sensed a meaning in its gaze. She did exactly what the dog had intended and fell in love with it.

'Do you think he's run away from his owner?' she asked John anxiously. 'Should we make enquiries?' She stopped and bit her lip. If the owner were found they would have to return him. Already the dog was a 'him' and already she was worried about losing him.

'I don't think so,' said John. 'Remember it's Wakes Week. They've probably just turned him loose.'

Anna was shocked by the thought. John forbore from telling her how the local vet dreaded the start of the holiday when people brought their dogs in to be put down. The whole family would be away at the seaside; there was no-one left to look after their pets. John could never decide which crime was the worse. The callous abandonment? Or the considerate murder?

As they reached the front door of their home Tommy was coming out. The dog sat neatly on its tail and gave Tommy the look. The teenager, bent down, swept it up into his arms and carried it into the house.

John was still outside, wiping his boots on the mat and calling out, 'Steady on now. Let's not be hasty. If you bring it inside, we'll never be rid of the damned animal.'

His words proved to be true.

With Tommy dancing attendance, Anna bathed the dog in the big white sink in the kitchen. It shivered a little but did not protest.

'There now,' Anna cooed to it. 'The water's warm. Not long now. And I've got a nice big towel to wrap you up in when it's all over.' She cradled water in the palms of her hands and trickled it down the dog's back. The whole business was deeply satisfying to her; it felt like bathing a baby.

After she had rubbed the worst of the wet off the dog, she handed him to Tommy who carried him into the sitting room and set him in front of the fire he had lit.

Anna felt the need to justify this unaccustomed extravagance. 'Summer evenings can grow quite chilly,' she told John. The dog curled itself into a neat little circle, put its chin on its paw and appeared to go to sleep. Every now and then it flicked an appraising eye at the two adults sitting on either side of the fireplace. Tommy stretched his adolescent length out on the hearthrug and with every appearance of perfect contentment watched the dog sleep.

John had been thinking over the events of the day. He realised that he needed to see the lodgings that had been recommended by the two headmistresses. He wanted to see the college building where Margaret would study, and trace the route, she would walk to get there. Then, when he thought of her, he could place her in a setting, like a precious stone in a ring, rather than have her floating free in space, like a ghost.

In venturing to visit Mrs McKenna and her lodging house he guessed he would encounter a woman who took no trouble to conceal her intelligence or modify her speech to her listener. She would be another blue-stocking, as such women were called. It would be good to have female support. Accordingly, he asked Anna to accompany him on a day trip to Manchester.

'What about the dog?' asked Anna. 'Who will look after him?'

'Tommy will. He can report him found at the police station. Someone may be looking for him.'

Tommy grunted. John took the sound to be agreement. Anna had a different interpretation. She guessed that Tommy would do no such thing. As well as heating up the water for the dog's bath, he had taken him a walk on a piece of rope and spent a long time watching him sleep. She agreed to go with John. Together they would inspect Margaret's lodgings as any careful mother and father would.

As they boarded the train, Anna remembered how she had gone alone to Manchester to discover how to prevent having a baby. It had been her first trip to the city. Her cheeks went red at the memory of the intense embarrassment she had felt. The sly looks, the nudges and the winks of the men. How determined she had been! Would she have been so resolute if she had known that love fulfilled would lead to a maternal craving so strong it threatened to devour her? The Fruits of Philosophy, for all its good advice, had not warned her of that particular peril.

Anna sighed as she sat at John's side in the train compartment. A stranger would take them for husband and wife. John looked at her profile and saw the pink in her cheeks.

'You are looking well today.' He wanted to add, 'My dear,' but knew it would be unwise. You can subdue passion; you cannot kill it. It will spring into vibrant life at the first hint of sunshine. With a skill born of practice he squashed the tiny fluttering of desire.

'Thank you.' Anna sought a light note. This was not the day for excavating their buried love affair; this was a day for Margaret. 'And you don't look so bad yourself, Mr Truesdale. You will need all your courage to face the widow McKenna. I fear she will be even more formidable than Miss Fossil and Miss Hulme combined.'

She was.

As the train steamed back to Atherley, they discussed their findings.

'You can be confident, I think, that Margaret will be quite safe at Mrs McKenna's lodgings,' said Anna.

John's guffaw was loud enough for the only other occupant of the compartment to lower his newspaper and stare disapprovingly.

'Absolutely,' John murmured quietly to make up for his previous outburst. 'I kept wondering where she chained the wolf hound. I bet she has one for the night shift in case someone tries to climb in through the locked windows.'

'Her hair was quite amazing.'

'Terrifying, you mean.'

'Mmm. Someone there makes good shortbread. Somehow I don't think it is Mrs McKenna.'

'Those pies in the kitchen smelt very appetising.'

'Tasty food is important. Margaret forgets to eat when she's studying. Sometimes she needs tempting.'

'If you say so.' John had a healthy appetite and assumed everyone else was the same.

'The whole house smelt right. They must open the windows to air it. That can't be easy when there is so much smoke and coal dust.' Anna was working through her Mrs Beeton's list of good housekeeping. 'The sheets were clean. They are sent to the laundry regularly.'

'What about the other lodgers?' asked John, who did not concern himself with such mundane details as the washing.

'We only saw one. Effie, wasn't it? She is a student. The others have gone for their summer holidays.'

'You mean the long vac.' John barked with laughter. Anna fell into giggles. The man in the corner rustled his newspaper in protest.

It was Mrs McKenna who had first used the expression 'long vac'. Effie had explained the phrase to them later as she showed them round the premises. 'When they say 'long vac' they really mean it,' she told them. 'It's the summer holiday and it lasts from June till October.'

As the train sped on Anna recovered her composure. 'Poor Effie. She has no home to go to when term ends. She stays in the house while Mrs McKenna goes off hiking in the Alps. I wonder she is safe there.'

John said nothing; he pictured the plump bespectacled girl in drab clothing.

Anna's thoughts about Effie were more positive. 'I imagine Margaret might find a kindred spirit in Effie.' She sat back. A possible friend was the finishing touch to the plan. She looked enquiringly at John.

'I don't think we need look elsewhere,' he said though it annoyed him to fall into line so meekly with the plans laid out by Miss Fossil and Miss Hulme. He pictured Margaret in Mrs McKenna's dining room. Effie was at the table. They were eating cottage pie. Other studious girls sat around the table, discussing Shakespeare's plays or Carlyle's unreadable History of the French Revolution. There was no need to keep a wolf hound on a chain in the yard. These were not the kind of girls who lured men into climbing through windows at night.

They walked home from the station. They agreed a cab was an unnecessary extravagance; economy ruled once again. John offered his arm. Anna took it, resting her hand on the warm and comforting wool of his coat. The memory of the last time they had taken this route alone together hovered over them. Then she had a secret plan in her heart and the syringe in her pocket. A shilling well spent. She wondered if it still worked. Perhaps it had grown rusty? When she had a moment, she might test it out.

Anna wondered if the fever for a baby had run its course. Perhaps, like chicken pox, it had come to a natural conclusion, leaving only a few scars and the memory of a dreadful itch. Could she risk its return?

She glanced at John. His profile was impassive in the light from the streetlamp. As usual his face gave nothing away. But Anna felt sure that his thoughts were going in the same direction as hers.

Margaret, who scarcely contributed two words about her day to the conversation at the family dinner table, proved to be a vociferous letter writer when she arrived in Manchester. She enthused about her work and the curious marks it earned. A β++ sent her into ecstasies. Jenny explained that a beta plus plus was almost as good as an alpha minus minus. The rest of the family were not much wiser but they understood that Margaret's work was going well.

'I never doubted that her work would go well,' said John. 'I was sure she would spend every hour God sent burrowing into her books like some small furry rodent. Just occasionally I think the girl might enjoy something other than dead authors and obscure languages.'

'She's certainly learning a lot of new words,' said Anna as she frowned at the latest of Margaret's letters. It was her task to read it out loud so that all the family could hear it. 'What in the name of all that's wonderful is 'badinage'?

'What!'

'Badinage. She writes here that there was a lot of badinage at the dinner table.'

'Probably stew,' suggested John.

'It seems some new students have arrived at Mrs McKenna's lodgings.' Anna paused. 'Oh dear.' Anna put the letter down in dismay.

'What's the matter?' enquired John, anticipating nothing more alarming than a bad mark or a missed essay,

'The new lodgers are men.' Anna read further. 'Oh! It's all right. They are students of theology. They are training to be clergymen.'

John held out his hand for the letter. His brow furrowed as he read. 'They have come to do Church History. They are Moravians, whatever that is.' He handed the letter back to Anna and chewed on these snippets of information. Perhaps Mrs McKenna should have a wolf hound somewhere.

'Ah. Bless her. She is such a good girl.'

'What now?'

'Mrs McKenna had to re-allocate the rooms to accommodate the two clergymen. She asked Margaret if she'd share with Effie. She agreed; it will save you half a crown a week. You know how careful she is with your money.'

John beamed his approval. Effie in the same bedroom was as good as a wolf hound.

'I thought she and Effie would make friends,' said Anna feeling smug. Her modest prediction had come true.

Jenny missed Margaret more than she expected. Margaret, with her nose in a book or staring wide-eyed into space with a pen in her hand, had always been there, ready to listen when summoned back from the Roman Empire to England in the early twentieth century. She was surprisingly broadminded; the hours she spent in pre-Christian Rome were a bracing antidote to the strict moral code the Victorians inflicted on the female of the species.

Deprived of Margaret, her usual confidant, Jenny thought of talking to Anna about the subject closest to her heart - namely Edward Carter. She feared she would not get the sympathetic reception she craved. Anna would have no choice but to follow society's line. A married man is forbidden fruit. Just as your dead sister's husband is.

John and Anna acted as if Jenny had successfully strangled her love to death on the day Edward took his marriage vows. They knew better than to stir the embers. Were they not experts on the subject of repressing feelings? Jenny put on a brave face and they accepted the surface she presented to them.

But it was not the end of the matter. It was surprising how often Edward ran into Jenny, on his way from his mother's or to the Woodward's mansion. Sometimes they would happen to meet in the churchyard. Jenny's excuse was visiting the grave of Florence, the woman who had saved her from the orphanage. It was a habit she had practised for years. Edward would claim he was taking a short cut to the Town Hall.

There was no surreptitious lovemaking, no lingering glances or chest heaving sighs. Their talk, or chats, as Edward liked to call them, were brisk and business-like. He could rely on Jenny to put her finger on the clause in a contract that bothered him, or provide a barbed remark to skewer his many critics through their uncharitable hearts. His meteoric rise to the top of Carter & Woodward had left a wake of jealousy and spite behind it.

In return he gave Jenny the career advice that no-one else supplied. She confided to him her ambition to train to operate the electric telegraph machines.

'Don't waste your time on the telegraph,' Edward told her. 'That's the past. The telephone has sounded its death knell. Money's the coming thing. There's a new course at the Mechanics' Institute. Commercial Finance it's called. A lecturer from Manchester Victoria University is coming to teach it. With a qualification in finance you could get a job in any of the businesses round here.'

Jenny said nothing.

'Most firms pay better than the Post Office,' Edward assured her, taking her silence for agreement. Success made him careless. 'You know you have to leave the Post Office if you get married.'

He might as well have shot her through the heart. The only man Jenny wanted to marry was Edward. Short of murder that was impossible. 'Think about it,' he urged as they reached his mother's house. He raised his hat in farewell and shouted from the top step as his mother opened the door, 'Ask your father what he thinks.'

Jenny struggled with the pain his unthinking remark about marriage caused her. When it was sufficiently subdued, she did think about the course he suggested.

John put down his newspaper and gave her his attention when she broached the subject. 'It's hard for me to think of finance as something you'd do from choice,' said John. 'I only think about money when I have to economise.'

'That's a very good reason for learning more about the subject,' said Anna with feeling. She had the task of putting John's economy drives into practice.

'But it would mean Jenny going out in the evening - alone.'

'Only twice a week.'

'Who would escort her home?'

'Surely there will be other girls there. It isn't far.'

John screwed up his face. His brow darkened. They could tell a 'No' was coming.

'I'll go,' said Tommy. 'It'll be a walk for the dog.'

'I'll go if Tommy can't,' offered Anna. 'As employers go, the Post Office are better than many, but I wouldn't like Jenny to be tied to them. There are not many other opportunities here.'

'The teacher is from Owens College. I can pay the fees. I've got savings.' Jenny knew her father would not deny her what Margaret enjoyed.

John got up and went to kiss her on the forehead. 'I pay for Margaret to go to university. I will pay for you.'

'You've come a long way from Miss Fossil's academy with its deportment and music lessons,' said Edward when she told him she had signed up for the course at the Mechanics' Institute.

'Don't forget the French conversation,' Jenny laughed and for a moment their eyes met as they used to. Hastily they both looked away as the image of Dorothea thrust itself between them.

'Wish me luck with the class,' she said as she started to leave.

'I might see you there.' He pointed a finger at his chest. 'Higher Mathematics. Tuesdays and Thursdays.' Edward turned away quickly, thinking he'd played his cards well. He didn't want her to see the grin on his face. Even so, he walked home alone that evening. Jenny felt he deserved punishing for keeping his intention to be at the Mechanics Institute secret until it was too late for her to back out.

He was unrepentant. His long friendship with Jenny – he still called it that – was deeply engrained in his being. He was determined to keep her close. He doubted Dorothea would mind even if some nosey busybody took it upon herself to report their random encounters.

Anna was a regular attender at Mrs Woodward's at homes. She had developed, if not a liking, an understanding of the woman. She saw that behind the sweeping judgements and frowning disapproval was an unhappy and uncertain person. Dorothea's absence had hit her mother hard and her return, once longed for, was a disaster. The sudden marriage and the identity of the groom had caused a furore among the local ladies who rubbed their hands with obscene glee at the toppling of the Methodist queen.

The ladies were confident that there was only one explanation for the marriage. Dorothea was pregnant. A theory is all very well. They needed proof. They wanted to cross-examine Dorothea, to grill her about dates and to identify the father. They were certain it was not the husband. Their investigations were frustrated.

Mrs Woodward cancelled her at homes for three months. She was too ill to receive visitors. Dorothea grew so bored she decided to take the bull by the horns and preside at the next one herself. The ladies arrived in droves. They found Dorothea, alone; her mother was keeping to her room. They murmured spurious enquiries about her health and did not listen to the replies. It was Dorothea they had come to see.

They inspected her with greedy eyes. It was not her stylish dress that interested them. It was the size of her waist. They wanted to calculate how far her pregnancy was advanced. Surreptitiously they looked for evidence. Dorothea smiled as she caught their glances to her midriff. She had laced her stays very tight that morning. It was hideously uncomfortable, but she was rewarded by seeing their puzzlement. She enjoyed watching them stew.

Anna was not looking for proof of the pregnancy. She had the evidence of Edward's late-night visit and Jenny's inconsolable sadness. What she saw was Dorothea looking heart-breakingly beautiful. A pain shot through Anna that squeezed her heart so tight she feared a savage shriek might escape her and shatter the china teacups. She recognised the emotion that had attacked her as the unworthy enemy it was. Jealousy. Pure and simple jealousy. Dorothea was pregnant. Anna was not, and never would be unless the world turned on its axis. Her days of fertility were numbered. One day she might find consolation in that inevitable fact. But just at that moment she did not.

Dorothea skilfully batted away the demands for details of her wedding. So sudden. So romantic. Almost an elopement. It's how they do things in France, she told them. No-one was qualified to argue with her. Quickly she brought the subject round to her time in finishing school. There she was on much safer ground. The refined cuisine, the continental manners. Such a shame men in England did not kiss ladies' hands as the French did, just brushing them with their lips. The folded lips and downcast eyes of her audience showed their disapproval. Kissing hands indeed! And the kissing had not stopped there!

Anna finished her cup of tea and handed it to the maid, who was watching Dorothea's performance with a smile on her face. 'Mrs Woodward?' Anna enquired. The maid looked puzzled. No-one thought of Dorothea as Mrs Carter; she was still a Woodward. 'I mean the older Mrs Woodward. Could I visit her? Just for a minute or two.'

The maid said she'd see. Minutes later she beckoned Anna to accompany her.

Mrs Woodward's bedroom felt stale and musty. Anna longed to open a window so a breeze could blow through the heavy brocade curtains and the sunshine play on the dark mahogany furniture. Mrs Woodward was dressed and sitting by her bed. It seemed to Anna that all the life had oozed out of the mother and into the daughter and her unborn child, leaving behind a withered shell.

Conversation was not easy. Mrs Woodward's malady had no medical name, no remedy and no symptoms she could describe. In desperation Anna started to prattle. The one topic she had in common with Mrs Woodward was daughters.

'Not mine really,' she gabbled. 'My sister's.'

Interest flickered in Mrs Woodward's face for a second, and was gone. A vague memory had stirred in Mrs Woodward's depressed mind. Once she had longed to know which of the Truesdale girls was the foundling. No matter. It was not important. Nothing mattered anymore. She lived in a dark abyss. If she looked up from the depths where she dwelt, she could see her husband and her daughter. They lived in a different landscape where the sun shone and there was talk and laughter. She was not invited to join them there.

Anna prattled on. A warning voice in her head stopped her talking about Jenny. The girl was too close to the new husband. With Margaret she was on safer ground. She told of her going to university.

'Do you miss her?' Mrs Woodward was not entirely without speech.

'Yes. I do.'

'I missed Dorothea when she went away to school in France.'

'That is a long way from here. I suppose I am lucky. Manchester is not so far. I might visit Margaret.'

'True,' said Mrs Woodward.

The cheery maid arrived. It was time for Mrs Woodward's medication.

Anna rose to leave. 'I hope I have not tired you,' she said to Mrs Woodward.

'I am always tired. My bones ache. Come again if you please.'

Anna nodded to show her agreement. There was nothing exciting to fill her days. Running the house, feeding the family and looking after a small dog were all very worthwhile but scarcely demanding activities. She could spare an afternoon or two for the unfortunate Mrs

Woodward. Whatever her malady was, it had affected her deeply; never once had she mentioned Southport.

The weeks passed. Christmas grew close and Margaret arrived home for the holidays. Or 'the vacation' as they now called it. With her came Effie, who had no home to go to. Margaret had written persuasively to ask if her friend could stay. After some hesitation John agreed.

As house guests go, Effie was one of the best. She knew when to talk and when to disappear discreetly. Within days she had found where the kitchen equipment lived and could produce a sharp knife or a soup ladle to order. The dog fell in love with her and learned to sit and stop barking when she raised a finger.

They soon discovered that, Effie had a talent for singing. A delighted Anna accompanied her on the piano. The spectacles and the lumpy shiny face were forgotten as they listened to her sweet voice. Such a treat after the tone-deaf Margaret and Jenny.

In the long evenings of December when the family sat by the fire, Margaret would open a book, arrange for the light to fall on the page and disappear into a world of her own. Effie would sit quietly with some anonymous piece of knitting, always ready to oblige, whether to run an errand, to listen or to talk.

Jenny was interested in her because she thought Effie's life must be even more blighted than her own. Since Edward's marriage, Jenny obliged her family by going through the motions of living while existing in a state of quiet despair. Brief encounters with Edward were the only relief from the monotony of her misery. Whilst these apparently random meetings provided a bright spot in a dark day, they also twisted the knife in her wound.

Effie was an orphan, shipped back from India when her parents died of cholera. An aunt in Manchester had taken over her upbringing.

'How would we manage without our aunts?' asked Jenny, looking appreciatively across at Anna.

'True,' said Effie, 'but mine died and Mrs McKenna took me in.'

Jenny had heard about Mrs McKenna. 'Margaret says she's...' Jenny was going to say 'terrifying' but Effie interrupted her.

'Let's just say she's a woman of firm beliefs.'

Even Tommy came out of his adolescent shell and talked with Effie. He wanted to know more about the university. Margaret, with her obsession with dead languages, was not the right source of information for him. He wanted to make a positive contribution to the world, not explore the past. His father could not help and his school masters had their own ideas and preferences. Effie was his best chance of hearing what he wanted to hear.

They agreed to take turns nursing the dog. When it was Effie's turn, she sat stroking its velvety black ears as he asked what subject she was studying.

'Geography.'

There was something in the way she said it that made him ask. 'Did you choose it?'

'No. It sort of chose me. I got an exhibition to study it. The trustees considered that the end of the matter. It was geography or nothing.'

'Which subject would you choose, if you could?'

'Something medical. The trustees wouldn't countenance it. Takes too long. Costs too much. Not a suitable subject for a young lady.'

'My school's very keen on engineering.'

'The college does a lot of that.' A glance at Tommy showed his lack of enthusiasm for the subject. She tried a different tack. 'You can combine it with medical studies. They track how disease is spread through the water and the sewage system. The different typhus fevers and cholera, dreadful illnesses. The study of morbidity they call it. Must be fascinating.'

'Could you change courses?'

'I doubt it. Margaret is lucky in wanting to do Latin. Professor Wilkins was the first to admit women. Other professors are not so enlightened.'

'What will you do when you get your degree?'

'I will train as a teacher for a secondary school. It's well paid.'

'Money makes a difference.'

'You can say that again. When I am twenty-five, I come into my trust fund. I can do what I want then.'

'And what do you want?'

Behind the thick lenses of her spectacles Effie's eyes went misty. 'What I'd really like to do is to buy a motor car.'

'A motor car!' Tommy gaped at the ambition of it. There was a boy at school who claimed his cousin had sat in one. Tommy had still not seen a car actually moving across the landscape. 'They are very expensive.'

'I know. They usually come from abroad. But there is somebody making them in Manchester. I've seen a few of them in the city. Lovely cars. The Royce ten HP.'

'Aitch Pee. What's that?'

'Horsepower of course.'

They both laughed at the idea of using ten horses to move one person. To console Tommy for revealing his ignorance on such a masculine subject, Effie handed him the dog who did not let the transaction disturb his slumber.

John and Anna found Effie could paint a fuller picture of university life than Margaret provided. Effie gave them a feeling of the buildings and of the people who formed the backdrop of Margaret's life. She gave them quick descriptions of the other lodgers at Mrs McKenna's.

They were amazed at the variety in the female students' backgrounds. They came from all levels of society - the self-taught poor on scholarships, the daughters of middle-class mothers, frustrated in their own ambitions, and the offspring of enlightened aristocrats who offered their girls the same opportunities their sons enjoyed.

'There's some interesting talk in the common room.'

'What's the common room?' asked John.

'It's where all the women students can meet.'

'Does Margaret go there?'

'Sometimes. Not often. She prefers the Christie Library.'

'Do you?'

'No that's just for students of Latin. I like going to the common room. At the moment all the talk is of votes for women.'

'I don't understand why a vote is so important? I won't have one for ages.'

'But you will have one. When you are old enough and pay rates,' said Anna' rattling her knitting needles as a form of protest.

'It would be nice to have our views considered. No Taxation without representation. That's what the Americans said. After all I expect to pay tax one day,' said Effie.

Margaret's head popped up out of her book like a tortoise looking out of its shell. 'One of our student's mother has just started a society to work for women's suffrage.'

'It's that law student, isn't it? The one who paints her eyebrows on.' Effie searched her mind for the girl's name.

Margaret supplied it. 'Christabel.' She returned to her reading.

'Her mother risked prison to defend free speech.' said Effie enjoying seeing the look of alarm on John's face.

'She must be a very odd woman,' huffed John.

'Oh. It turned out all right. The magistrates chickened out in the end.'

'Sensible men.' A sudden picture of Margaret in a coarse prison dress emblazoned with arrows popped into John's mind. He quickly dismissed it. Meek and mild, mousey Margaret was the last person to get into trouble with the law. John clapped his hands. 'Time for some music, I think.'

While Anna played and Effie sang, Jenny sat brooding. Effie had given her a glimpse of the wider world. A woman who risked going to prison. A girl studying law and painting her eyebrows on. Perhaps the world was not as fixed and rigid as it felt. A faint glimmer of light appeared on her horizon which had been deadly dark since Dorothea had snatched Edward Carter from her. It wasn't a plan, and Jenny could not put a name to it, but she felt a small seed of hope stir in her heart.

JANUARY 1901

Queen Victoria after more than sixty years on the throne died. Her death shook the whole country. The stores ran out of black crepe for mourning. The citizens of Atherly reacted in characteristic ways. Mr Woodward put on his bowler hat and quickly called a meeting of his free church brethren. The result was a notice in the local paper.

> From the Atherley and Tilton Advertiser
> 25th January 1901
>
> THE DEATH OF THE QUEEN
>
> A representative meeting of Non-Conformist ministers and the Free Churchmen of Atherley and Tilston has passed a resolution which has been despatched to the King, expressing their profound sympathy with the Royal Family and heartily assuring the King of the affection and loyalty of his Non-Conformist subjects.
>
> A United Memorial Service, representing all Free Churches is arranged for the day of the funeral.

John felt no need to advertise his loyalty, but enjoyed gleaning details from the pages of the London Times newspaper.

'By Jove. Madam Tussaud's were quick off the mark with their waxworks.'

'What do you mean?' asked Margaret, frowning over her copy of Horace.

'Well, they have an advertisement here that tells us they are open as usual. They already refer to 'Her late Majesty'. Poor Queen Victoria's body is not yet cold and they are offering a chance to gawk at His Majesty, King Edward the Seventh. They're not slow to spot a business opportunity. Oh. I see they will close on the day of her burial. They are not entirely without respect.'

'I'd love to see the waxworks,' said Jenny looking up from her needlework. 'Do you think we could one day?'

'Only if they move to Manchester,' said John and took refuge behind his newspaper.

'Oooooh!' Tommy gave a strangled groan of disappointment. He had heard about the waxworks, especially the scenes of horror and executions.

'It will be strange having a king,' said Anna. 'All my life it has been a woman on the throne. I've never known different.'

'I expect things will change with a new monarch,' Margaret speculated. 'Why, women might even get a vote.'

'We didn't get one when there was a Queen, an actual woman. What makes you think we'll get one with a man on the throne?' Jenny was scornful.

'I don't think the monarch has power over such things,' Margaret reasoned. 'They're not like the Emperor Augustus. Parliament decides who gets a vote.'

'A Parliament composed of men, voted in by men', said Jenny. 'I rest my case.'

'Be fair,' Anna intervened. 'Things are much better for women. You are too young to remember but the law was very harsh for women, especially married women. You couldn't own property. Everything belonged to the husband, including the children. Women were compelled to return to men who beat them. The court said it was their duty. Don't forget it was men themselves who changed those harsh laws.'

'Do you think the law has treated you fairly, Aunt Anna?' asked Margaret. Her quiet voice gave no hint of the sharp point her question contained.

Anna had a moment of panic. She hoped that Margaret was thinking of the Married Women's Property Act and the confused state of the laws of inheritance, rather than the Deceased Wife's Sister Act.

'No.' she said. 'It has not. The law has not been kind to me. I had to wait a long time for a sensible offer from that stepson. The law did not help me there. The amount was too small for a lawyer's fee but nonetheless it was an important sum to me.' Once again Anna thought how wise she had been in keeping her inheritance from her father in her own name. Only in dire need would she reveal its existence. That was the whole point of a nest egg, wasn't it?

The combination of gout and his distress about Dorothea had aged Mr Woodward. He no longer accompanied Edward to the office of a morning. He came in later and left early. He might nod his agreement when Edward consulted him, but seldom came up with a positive idea. He leant heavily on his stick and started to use the carriage for travelling into town.

'Something's knocked the stuffing out of the old man,' said Edward to Jenny when 'by chance' he met her walking home up the hill.

Jenny knew exactly what the 'something' was but refrained from naming Dorothea. 'How is Mrs Woodward?' she asked. 'Aunt Anna says she is much changed.'

'She's like a ghost. Scarcely comes to meals, scarcely speaks.'

'She used to enjoy going out in the carriage.'

'Not anymore. Mr Woodward has it on standby in case he needs it to bring him home. Some days we have to send a telegram for it to come and collect him.'

Jenny paused open-mouthed for a moment. An outrageous thought had come to her. Her voice squeaked with shock as her idea popped out of it. 'I think Mr Woodward should buy a motorcar.'

Edward was struck dumb. He gazed at Jenny with awe. Such a bold idea. And such a good one. It would be the first motor car in Atherley. It would silence the jeers and sniggering when that baby arrived with 'made in France' stamped on its forehead.

'I'm not doing myself any favours by suggesting it', said Jenny. 'I'll be flogging up this hill on my two feet and you'll be flashing past in a shiny new motor car.'

Edward treated her to his grin. 'How is commercial finance going? You are going to pass those exams with flying colours. There'll be a job going at Carter Woodward. We might interview a few other people, but the position has your name on it, Jenny.' He raised his hat and turned in at his mother's house.

Jenny walked home with her heart singing. She loved Edward so much she was happy with the crumbs from his table.

Edward's mother gave him a cup of tea and left him alone with his thoughts. She knew he was grateful for ten minutes when no-one made demands of him. As he drank his tea, he considered Jenny's idea of a motor car. What a girl she was! He had not intended to tell her about the job at Carter Woodward just yet. But he wanted to keep her close, didn't want her to go to Manchester as her sister had done. He knew in his heart and his mind that he wanted Jenny.

For a time, Dorothea had ruled his body. She had delivered on her promise to provide him with plenty of sex. Bedtime could not come soon enough. He could hardly wait to get the clothes off her and she obliged him with a freedom that made him gasp. As the weeks turned into months his desire sated. For all the pleasure of his senses there was something missing from the heart of their encounters.

Their mutual explorations were more like anatomy lessons than lovemaking. Their bodies were hot but their hearts were cold. As her pregnancy progressed, they both quietly sickened of the sport. By mutual agreement the frequency of their couplings dwindled. If asked he would have blamed the pregnancy but in his heart he knew differently. They nursed the pretence their appetites would return when the child was born. Edward doubted that life was so simple.

He was bracing himself to beam proudly over another man's child. Edward's many brothers had accustomed him to a vibrant family life. He hoped the arrival of the baby would soften Dorothea. She would grow less selfish, be kinder to her mother. He knew Mr Woodward would love a grandson. All his life he had mourned the lack of a son. Edward intended to be as good as a son to Mr Woodward. As an employer he was scrupulously fair. As a father in law he was more than generous.

He put down his cup and picked up his hat. He kissed his mother on the cheek, thanked her for the tea and set off up the hill with a swing in his step. He was going to give his father in law a surprise. And this time it was going to be a pleasant one.

It took some time for Edward and Mr Woodward to get their hands on a Royce 10 horsepower motor car. When they did the gout in Mr Woodward's leg prevented him from working the pedals. Edward to his delight had to master the technique of driving in double quick time. The laughably low speed limit in town allowed him to practise.

When they arrived in Atherley, the throaty roar of the engine brought out all the population who were above ground at the time. They cheered and helped push the car up the hill. Edward assured Mr Woodward that there would be a way to coax the vehicle up unaided. He crossed his fingers and hoped that was the case.

The Atherley and Tilton Advertiser sent a photographer. The proud new owners stood by their vehicle dangling goggles from their fingers as if they had just returned from exploring the Sahara Desert. The photographer became a frequent visitor. Each week there would be a photograph of the car. The car outside the Woodward mansion, the car outside the chapel, the library, the railway station.

Dorothea went into labour with a great deal of noise; she was not accustomed to bearing discomfort quietly. Edward took the famous motor car to fetch the doctor who arrived post haste with a bottle of chloroform. He disappeared into Dorothea's room and the shrieking stopped.

Some hours later the doctor re-appeared. In his arms was a baby with a shock of black hair. 'It's a girl,' announced the doctor with the air of one breaking bad news. Mr Woodward was so glad that Dorothea's ordeal was over that he would have welcomed a cat wrapped in a blanket.

Edward professed himself pleased.

Mrs Woodward produced a masterly piece of tact. 'She looks just like Dorothea did when she was born. Isn't that so, Kenneth?' Mr Woodward nodded.

The doctor normally handed a new-born into the arms of the father. On this occasion he dithered. Mr Woodward, the grandfather, was the most important man in the town. Everyone knew Edward was not the father, merely a hastily acquired husband intended to lend some respectability to the proceedings. As he considered this question an almighty scream came from the room behind him. In his surprise he almost dropped the baby. Mrs Woodward rushed forward to rescue it. The doctor turned back into Dorothea's room and the door slammed behind him.

Mrs Woodward sat down, pressed the baby to her chest, and rocked gently on her chair. Soon she was making noises, those ancestral sounds that women make to soften the shock to a child of losing the safety of the womb.

The men looked at each other.

'Perhaps, some medicinal brandy is in order,' suggested Edward.

'Most definitely.'

Several medicinal brandies later the cheery maid appeared at the door. 'Doctor says you can go to see Miss Dorothea now.' She winked at Edward as he passed her. 'You might like to take a glass of that for the doctor. He looks like he could do with it.'

They found the doctor much as they had left him. He stood outside Dorothea's bedroom holding a baby wrapped in a shawl. His face was white. 'I didn't realise it was twins. This time it's a boy.' Without a moment's hesitation he handed the baby to Edward Carter.

Edward looked down to see a head as bald and as pale as an egg. The tiny living thing squirmed and opened its eyes. They were as blue as Edward's own. He turned to Mr Woodward and held out the child for the older man to take.

'It looks as if one day it may be Carter-Woodward and Son.'

Tears streamed from the older man's eyes.

'Have you noticed? Margaret doesn't write nearly as often as she used to.' John asked Anna one Sunday.

'Well, of course not.

She is busy preparing for her exams.'

'She used to write all the time at first.'

'That's only natural. Then she made friends with Effie.'

'I don't suppose Effie will come this Easter. She doesn't have such long holidays now she's training to be a teacher.'

'I hope you don't expect me to write every week,' said Tommy, 'when I get there.'

'Only if the dog learns to read,' said John. They all chuckled. Tommy's fondness for the dog was a family joke.

'I promise,' said Anna, 'that if you write I will read your letter to him.' She rested her foot gently on the dog's stomach as it slept on the floor by her feet. With the point of her shoe she stirred the grey fur on its flank. He's going grey, she thought. Like me.

John's prediction proved wrong. Margaret and Effie came to stay. They saw little of Margaret; she spent her time with her books. She wanted a first-class degree. Her tutors encouraged her ambition to apply to Oxford or Cambridge. They claimed their graduates frequently found work there.

Effie was more relaxed about her studies. She already had her degree and had the promise of a position at one of the better schools in Manchester. Her path was laid out before her. There was only one problem, she told Tommy. The school was too near Mrs McKenna's to give her an excuse to buy a motor car.

'You could use it to go for picnics in the country. You could use it to come here,' said Tommy, who had ambitions of his own. If Effie had a car, he'd have the chance to drive it.

'Just one more year,' she said, 'and then I come into my own money.'

'I intend to be a student,' said Tommy. 'Tell me everything about it. I need to know before I go.'

Effie obliged. She confessed she didn't know much about the social life that would be available to Tommy. 'There are separate common rooms for men and women.' Tommy did not find that remarkable. 'And of course, there is a lot of activity in the city. Nothing to do with the Victoria University as we can now call it.'

'Such as?'

'Well there's lots of concerts and societies. I belong to a group. It's for women only.' Effie checked there were no family within earshot. 'We campaign for votes for women.'

Tommy knew his father always spluttered when he heard that slogan, so he kept his face straight and let no sound pass his lips.

'Margaret's not a member,' Effie rushed to reassure him. 'So, there's no need to worry your father. It's just me who has joined. I've no parents to fret about me and Mrs McKenna is all for it.'

John and Anna smothered Margaret with advice and reassurance before she returned to Manchester. She was not to worry about some silly exam, she was to eat well and go to bed early. There was a fruitcake in her suitcase in case of sudden hunger pangs.

'I am glad that Effie will be there to look after her. She is always so calm and sensible,' said Anna. 'Not like some of these young women. They are growing quite wild. Making speeches on street corners and chalking advertisements on the pavement.'

Jenny, like Margaret, faced examinations. Twice a week she had trudged off after work, to attend classes on Commercial Finance. At first it had been alarming. She was the only girl; the classroom was crowded with young men. Then the men had parted to make a passageway that wafted her to the front. 'It was like the Red Sea parting for Moses and the children of Israel,' Jenny told John. 'The lads whipped their caps off, folded them up and thrust them in their pockets. They shushed anyone who swore and escorted me home. All in all, they behaved like perfect gentlemen.'

When she wondered why she wasn't out enjoying the evening air after being stuck behind a Post Office counter all day, it was Edward Carter who urged her to keep going.

'You've got grit. Stick it out. Get your qualification. Then you can come and work for us. You'll be the first female finance officer in Atherley. It can't be done any quicker. Even so, people will talk.' Edward warned her. 'They daren't say it to my face. It's you they'd go for.'

Jenny already knew that when there was trouble, people would find a handy woman to blame. Even Dorothea was subject to this golden rule. Although she appeared to shrug off an illicit pregnancy by producing the perfect family, a girl and a boy, from a single foray into childbirth, the townspeople of Atherley would not forget that her father's money had bought her a husband.

In public Dorothea paraded her children with pride, stroking her daughter's glossy black hair and running her fingers through her son's crisp curls. In private she ignored them, an arrangement that suited Edward, her parents and the stern nanny. In the many hours she was free of childcare and domestic duties, she worked at her music. An expert from Chetham's in Manchester was consulted. On his recommendation she took piano lessons and spent hours on vocal exercises.

Dorothea longed to display her talents. Opera might find an appreciative audience in France, but she doubted it would find one in the drawing rooms of Atherley. The townspeople would not rise to their feet crying 'Brava'. They would talk of her brass neck in making herself the centre of attention when everyone knew her father had bought a husband for her. They would sneer behind their hands at the fancy foreign songs.

When Mrs Woodward suggested she join the chapel choir, Dorothea curled her lip in scorn. A few weeks later and desperate to perform in public, she had second thoughts. Religion, like marriage, would provide her with a cloak of respectability. Accordingly, she started going to choir practice. There she had a rare moment of gratitude, thanking God that John Wesley wrote such splendid hymns.

Word of her sweet and powerful voice spread among the musical fraternity. Two strangers appeared one morning at the chapel. They gave their full attention to the service, tipped their hats to Mr Woodward, and presented him with their cards. A letter soon dropped through his letterbox to prove their credentials; they represented a Manchester choral society. Would Mrs Carter consider joining them? For the Messiah.

Dorothea played her cards well. She demurred. What about her children? How would she travel? Would other women be there? By the time she finished Mr Woodward was begging her to join the choral society; his desire to display his beautiful daughter burned as bright as ever. Handel's Messiah was not Dorothea's favourite piece but its place at the heart of northern religion made her participation more than respectable; it was a civic duty.

The Messiah was a triumph. Dorothea's ambition grew; she wanted a wider audience. How could she bring the good people of Lancashire to listen to her music, without it being in a place of worship? What she needed was a good cause, a charitable enterprise, that would attract attention throughout the towns and villages. Perhaps even in Manchester itself.

She soon found one. The colliery band was enjoying some success in brass band competitions. They would do better if they had new instruments, new uniforms, a place to rehearse etc. etc. Her father immediately donated £5. Dorothea set about raising more by holding musical evenings in the family mansion.

The local gentry sat on spindly chairs in the drawing room and listened to her playing Schubert. So keen was he to help, Mr Woodward relaxed his views on alcohol and allowed wine to be served to his guests. A significant increase in donations was the result.

Following the success of the recitals in their home Dorothea broached the idea of giving performances in public. Her parents, re-invigorated by their grandchildren, raised no objection. A respectable matron with two children in support of charity was a different matter from a young, single woman drawing attention to herself. Soon there was not a spring fair, a school prize-giving or a church fete, but Dorothea would appear and the sound of music would fill the air.

Edward, the businessman, welcomed her campaign. Jenny had taught him the value of the art of distracting people. Dorothea's fund-raising created good will among his employees and turned attention from his meteoric rise. He was about to advertise for a finance office, a position Jenny was now qualified to fill. Eyebrows would be raised and winks exchanged if, or rather when, a woman was offered the job. Edward had already planned the perfect smokescreen. He was going to install the telephone in his offices

When Jenny handed in her notice, Miss Titterington took her to the Post Master's office for a formal farewell. He still resembled a walrus and his memory for names had not improved.

Miss Truesdale is leaving us,' said Miss Titterington with an edge in her voice. The walrus rested his chin on his flippers and looked sadly at Jenny.

'They keep doing it, Miss er... I blame the dowry. Six years is not long enough.'

'Miss Truesdale isn't leaving to marry. Miss Truesdale is going to be the finance officer at Carter-Woodward. The biggest employer in town.' Miss Titterington couldn't hide the triumph she felt at this female success.

The walrus sucked in air. He let it out. 'You are like me,' said to Jenny. 'Numbers talk to you. Listen to them and you won't go far wrong.' He wafted a flipper. They were dismissed.

Jenny was sad to say goodbye to Mavis and Miss Titterington. She would be the only woman in the Carter-Woodward office. But not for long. The firm was busy building a cloakroom with a flushing toilet.

'It's an investment,' she told Edward when he had pulled a face at the expense. 'Think of your wages bill. Women work for less. Except me,' she said and turned on her heel, flicked her skirts at him and walked away.

Jenny was home early that day. She knew her father was perturbed about her new job so she put her pinafore on and announced she would do the cooking. Her father wouldn't bother her in the kitchen. He seldom ventured into that female stronghold. He turned to Anna for reassurance.

'Jenny won that job fair and square,' Anna told him. 'Mr Woodward himself appointed her. If people want to gossip, let them. We know Jenny is a good girl. She would not come between a husband and wife.'

'She could work for someone else. Old Jenkinson at the bakery was saying how he couldn't get anybody to do his books.'

'And how much will he pay for the privilege?'

'Not as much,' John grudgingly admitted.

'Jenny will have a proper salary. Paid monthly.' Anna felt a glow of pride at the girl's achievement. 'And next year, if Margaret trains to be a teacher, she'll be the same.' She looked at John expecting to see satisfaction in his face. No more fees to pay. His expression was rueful. It dawned on her. The girls would be financially independent. They were moving beyond his control.

He changed the subject. 'What's all this about a telephone? Whatever that is.'

'It's a machine you talk into. You can talk to people miles away and they can hear you.' A smug smile spread over Anna's face. 'Jenny will have one in her office.'.

'What for? She could just send a telegram.'

'Mr Woodward is very shrewd. I am sure if he thinks it a good idea, other people will.'

'I can't see it catching on.' John shook his head in puzzlement and returned with relief to the world he knew well. 'Bessie came into the office today. You remember her?'

Anna did. And Bessie's golden-haired toddler. And the desire for a baby the child had ignited. She managed to mmm in agreement.

'Bessie came to register her mother's death. Hannah. Our Hannah's died. Bessie said she had helped her with the washing. Then sat down with a cup of tea. Sighed and went to sleep. Never drank the tea. Never woke up.'

'How was Bessie?' asked Anna.

'She was sad, of course.'

'Hannah was a godsend when the children were little.' The memory of a trusted servant and a lost wife and sister passed through the room on silent feet.

Anna rose. 'I had better tell Jenny.'

Jenny cried when Anna told her about Hannah who had stood in as a mother after Anna had left. After their meal they sat at the table and thought of Hannah and her scones. A peaceful death at the end of a life of hard work. It could be worse, they decided before turning to practical matters. When was the funeral? Who would attend? Should they tell Margaret?

'Her exams are finished.' Anna counted the days out on her fingers. 'We'd better wait till she's back from that interview at Cambridge. I will write to her in a couple of days. Don't want to upset her before then. There'll be time for her to come for the funeral.

As it happened Margaret did not go to Hannah's funeral.

The afternoon post brought a letter from Margaret. Anna read it out loud.

Dear All,

To put it mildly my trip to Cambridge was not a success. The porter at the college directed me to the professor's staircase. I was so nervous I could not remember the number of his room.

Fortunately, a young man, who was also a student of Classics appeared. He knocked boldly on the right door and flung it open without waiting for permission.

The don was hunched over his desk beneath a tangle of wild white hair; it sprouted from every orifice in his head.

'Name,' he barked.

I told him. Silence. He continued to pore over his book.

I added that I had an appointment. A junior lectureship. Finally, I had his attention.

'Do I know you?' he enquired.

'We have never met,' I assured him.

He raised his eyes to heaven and slammed his fists on the table. He mouthed some words. I guessed his meaning. I put on my frostiest face and lifted my chin.

'Professor Wilkins,' I began, intending to remind him of the letter my dear Professor had sent on my behalf. I got no further.

'Of course, I don't know you,' exploded from his lips, as if I was some strange creature newly arrived from the moon. 'I meant your people, of course. Do I know your family?' He stretched out a claw and pulled Professor Wilkins' letter from a hodgepodge of

documents. 'Truesdale,' he read when he had adjusted his spectacles.

Suddenly I was interesting. He turned to look at me.

'Any connection to the Somerset Truesdales? Made a fortune in sheep.'

For a second, I considered telling him I was one of the northern Truesdales and we had made our money in cotton. I missed the moment. The ball was now in his court. He hurled it back at me.

'School,' he snapped.

*I did not think he would treat Miss Fossils' academy for young ladies with the respect it deserved. It was at that moment I decided I would **not** go to Cambridge.*

'Yes,' I told him in the clearest and most penetrating voice I could find. 'I did go to school. It was the only school for girls in our town. Fortunately, my father could afford it. Without that school I could never have gone to university. I would never have got my degree. And yes, I do have a degree in Classics. It was awarded to me by the University of London. I am more fortunate than the young women who study here. Although they may pass all the examinations, this university will not, to its shame, award them a degree.'

I rose to my feet, very conscious in such a masculine domain, of the rustling of my skirts. 'I will trouble you no further. I withdraw my application. Good day.'

I swept out, skirts swishing. The trouble with sweeping out is that you have no idea where you have swept to. The same young man, who had braved the door of the lion's den, found me and escorted me to the station.

I managed to wait until I was back at Mrs McKenna's and with Effie before I started crying. When I did, I didn't seem able to stop. Poor Effie spent hours drying my tears. Then I took to my bed, pulled the covers over my head and decided to hibernate.

As a result of this childish weakness I did not open your letter until too late to come to Hannah's funeral. I will write to her daughter to give her my apologies and condolences.

Apart from missing Hannah's funeral, I have no regrets. I will not work in an institution that treats my sex with such disrespect.

Jenny wondered if the lectureship at Cambridge already had someone's name on it, and that Margaret's attempt on such a prestigious stronghold was doomed from the start. She had a sudden pang of conscience. Carter-Woodward had interviewed two other candidates for the position that Edward had promised her.

'Did they pay her travel expenses?' she asked.

'It doesn't say,' said Anna.

Jenny felt slightly better. Carter-Woodward had paid the unsuccessful candidates travel expenses and half a day's pay for time lost. A fair exchange for the token interviews designed only to minimise gossip and make her new position acceptable to other employees - and her family. She didn't know much about Cambridge dons except that many of them were clergymen and were not allowed to marry. Perhaps that explained things.

To take her mind off the subject she went into the kitchen to make scones, as a memorial to Hannah. Her parting shot to John and Anna was to point out that if they had one of the new telephones, they could talk to Margaret directly. They could ask her how she was, instead of just speculating.

She had just put the scones in the oven when the doorbell rang, and the dog barked. It was the telegraph boy. He handed the buff envelope to Tommy who loped off to hand the message to his father. The telegraph boy kept his place on the doorstep.

'You might want to send a reply,' he muttered.

A warning bell rang in Jenny's head. The news must be dramatic. Telegraph boys had ways of finding out in advance the contents of the envelopes they delivered. She rushed into the sitting room to find her father white-faced, Anna dissolving into tears. Tommy looked nonplussed.

Jenny grabbed the telegram from John's hand and scanned it quickly. She looked round for a pencil and paper, wrote a brief message and pressed it into the telegraph boy's hand with a sixpence.

Back in the sitting room Tommy wanted to know what was going on. 'The telegraph is from Effie. Margaret has been arrested. She is in Strangeways Prison. Effie is very worried about her.'

'S'trewth,' said Tommy.

The power of speech returned to John and Anna. They wanted to know whatever had happened, and why and where and how. There were no answers to these questions. All they had was the telegram with its bald statement.

MARGARET ARRESTED AFFRAY. HELD STRANGEWAYS. NOT WELL. PLEASE COME. EFFIE.

Even at such a stressful time the economical Effie managed to confine herself to less than twelve words.

'You sent a reply,' said John. 'What did you say?'

'That we would come tomorrow. It is too late to set off today.'

For the first time Anna spoke. 'You know what she's like. She's not eating properly. First her exams and then that dreadful trip to Cambridge. Her nerves must be in a frightful state. The news about Hannah must have been the last straw.'

Jenny's hands flew into the air. 'The scones! I forgot the scones.' She rushed into the kitchen to rescue them.

The next day three people with strained faces and a basket of scones, two apples and a pork pie, waited for the early train for Manchester. John sent Effie a telegram with their time of arrival. Jenny restrained herself from mentioning again how useful a telephone would be in such circumstances. This was not a day for scoring points; it was a day for working together.

As they rocked along in the train, each wondered what the meek and mild Margaret could have done to be arrested. John was sure it was a case of mistaken identity. Anna guessed that kind-hearted Margaret had intervened to protect a badly treated child. Jenny kept her suspicions to herself. She added Margaret's mistreatment in Cambridge, to the proximity of the Pankhursts and came up with something to do with votes for women.

Effie was looking even more unkempt than usual. Her hair strayed from her bun, her hat was askew and there was something about her clothes that said they had lain in a heap on the floor all night.

They huddled round her in a corner of the station, while she described how distraught Margaret was on her return from Cambridge. 'It was the injustice of it that enraged her.'

'I bet that Pankhurst girl has something to do with all this,' said John.

'No,' said Effie with surprising firmness. 'It was me. It was my fault. It was my group's regular meeting. Obviously, I wasn't going to leave Margaret alone. She insisted she would come. Said it would be good for her.

Just being in a room with women who were doing something about the injustice to our sex would console her.'

John looked round nervously at the word 'sex'. Never before had he heard that word pass a woman's lips.

'We made plans to advertise the next meeting. We write on the pavement or a wall in coloured chalk. It's very effective. And cheap. The next day I let Margaret sleep late. When I got back, she'd gone. She had taken my chalks.'

John had done enough listening. He bundled the women into a hansom cab. He climbed onto the step and spoke face to face with the driver, to save shouting 'Strangeways Prison' and embarrassing himself before the passing shoppers

The driver was a professional. He kept his face straight. 'Right you are, sir.'

Close in the cab, Effie continued. 'Word came from the police. They'd arrested one of us. And she wasn't eating.'

'Why? Why arrest Margaret? And not the others?' asked John.

Effie looked embarrassed. She kept her eyes down as she told him. 'She chose the wrong place.'

'The wrong place? Where's that?'

'She wrote it on the wall of the office of the Registrar of Births Marriages and Deaths.'

The breath left John's body with a great whoosh. He flopped back on the upholstered seat of the hansom cab and turned his eyes to heaven. The three women waited for the anger to suffuse his face. It did not happen. He slapped his knee and started to laugh. It was not just a chuckle, but a hearty belly laugh that went on till the tears came to his eyes.

'The Registrar's office. Nice bit of irony there,' said John and wiped his face with his handkerchief. He rapped on the roof of the cab and shouted, 'Stop. Change of plan,' to the driver. He searched his pockets to check he had his business card and leapt out of the cab. Inside, the women, wide-eyed with shock, struggled to hear what John was saying to the driver. A fist thumped against the cab door, a shout at the window and John was gone. The driver flicked the reins and the cab lurched into motion. The three women clutched at each other for reassurance. Where were they going?

'We're there', announced the cab driver and pointed his whip at high brick wall. It loomed over them like the cotton mills in Atherley but without the tall windows that let in the daylight for the mill hands to work by.

It was Effie who recognised Strangeways prison. She also knew which door to use. Had she been here before?

'No. But we swap information.'

A matron in a rough brown dress, took them to a small reception room and indicated a bench where they should sit. She took refuge behind a wooden counter. Effie, made brave by feeling she was to blame, asked to see Miss Truesdale.

'Truesdale', muttered the matron and ran a grubby thumb up and down a sheet of paper. The name rang a bell in her mind, but she could not find it on the list of current inmates. She abandoned the attempt, went to the door and shouted something incomprehensible down the long corridor. She returned and sat in silence behind the counter.

Jenny lasted a few minutes before she jumped to her feet. 'We have brought some food for her.'

'Third division prisoners are not allowed food from outside.'

Jenny sat down with a thump and a frown on her face.

Clogs clattered on stone flags. Keys rattled and doors clanged.

'Prisoners dinner time,' explained the matron. She laid heavy emphasis on that shocking word 'prisoner', and clamped her jaw shut at an ominous angle.

More footsteps in the corridor. Leather soles this time. A man's voice. Young, cheerful and Irish, something about missing his dinner. The matron's lips curved; it was almost a smile.

Anna decided this was the moment to intervene. She smiled at the matron and leaned confidentially on the counter. 'We've come such a long way,' she began, playing the part of the anxious mother. 'If you could just check how she is. Tell her we're here. You know how it is. Children. Always a worry. And she's such a slip of a thing. A gust of wind could blow her over.' She heaved a great sigh.

Anna's gamble paid off; the matron had children of her own. 'Truesdale, you say. She's not on the list. I believe the doctor saw her this morning. He'll have gone for his dinner now.' The matron heaved herself to her feet and made for the door. 'You will have to wait.' She paused at the door. 'I don't suppose you've got a pork pie in there.' She indicated the basket.

'Never travel without one,' said Jenny and handed it over.

The matron had not exaggerated when she told them to wait. An hour passed.

'Some dinner,' muttered Jenny. 'I am starving. Do you think we could share a scone?' They were brushing away the last crumbs when the matron returned.

'Doctor says, as you are here, you can take her home with you. No court date's set. He says he won't be responsible for her. Wait while I go and get her.'

Suddenly, Margaret was with them, in her own clothes, not prison uniform. Even so, the stench of the institution arrived with her; it was the smell of engrained dirt, sour air and despair. Their greetings were subdued, relieved, rather than joyous.

The matron simply opened the door and waved them out. She stood back and took a moment to watch as the frail figure, formerly prisoner Truesdale, stepped back into the world. The girl had refused her food so politely. None of that throwing it at the wall. She'd passed her meal on to her neighbour. The matron smiled with satisfaction. Some days things just came together nicely. A new young doctor, the dinner hour and a tasty looking pie. He had signed the slip without a murmur.

The girls clustered protectively round Margaret while Anna paced about wondering what to do next and where on earth was her father?

'We shall have to take a cab,' said Jenny as if she hailed one every day; she did not expect many cabs to come to Strangeways Prison

'But where do we go? And what about your father?' asked Anna.

'We cannot wander around Manchester looking for him.'

They huddled at the edge of the pavement where the cabs drew up. Effie's voice quavered as she asked if anyone had money. They looked round at each other. Anna and Margaret shook their heads. Effie and Jenny found a few shillings in their purses. Did they have enough to pay for a cab?

The cab driver listened as they counted their money. He said nothing but answered their question by driving forward to pick up a more promising passenger.

'You must eat something,' Effie was saying to Margaret who was looking very white. She seized the remaining scone from the basket and pressed it into Margaret's reluctant hand. 'I know it's not ladylike to eat in the street but ladies aren't supposed to end up in prison.' Preoccupied by their own problems, they did not notice the cab draw up or the man who dismounted.

'On this occasion, you should do as your friend says, Margaret. I don't always agree with her but this time she is right.'

The new arrival was John.

Anna and the girls felt their composure falter. The weight of the burden they had carried all day was lightened and they leant gratefully against the steadying male presence of their father, sometime lover and friend. This time the driver waited as John helped them into the carriage, tucked in their skirts and closed the door. They settled back in the cocoon of safety he had built round them and let out the breath they had been holding for many hours.

John paid the driver at Victoria station and produced their return train tickets. from his wallet. They all agreed Effie should come with them; she had ways of getting food into Margaret, a notoriously reluctant eater.

On the train, John found his role of hero who rescued damsels in distress was short-lived. Where had he been, the women demanded. Why had he abandoned them and sent them to venture alone through the gates of a prison?

'It's obvious. I went to see the Registrar whose office my daughter had vandalised.' He could speak freely. The compartment was empty. There was something about the aroma of Margaret that repelled other passengers.

John tried to look nonchalant. 'I showed him my card. We talked business for a bit. When he told me about the writing on the wall, I had to come clean. Admitted it was my daughter, offered to pay for the damage. I explained she had just had a great disappointment in life and was temporarily disturbed.'

Margaret did not raise a protest at her father's diagnosis but snuggled closer to him. 'The Registrar rather assumed the cause of the upset must be a young man. I didn't disillusion him. Next thing I know he's offering to drop the charges.'

'I had to strike while the iron was hot,' added John. 'I persuaded him to tell the police that he couldn't be bothered with all the paperwork. They felt the same.' A collective sigh of relief went round the compartment. It was official. Margaret was not a criminal.

'It seems you went quietly, Margaret.'

'I was pleased to see the policeman. Some men had started to shout things at me. It wasn't very pleasant.'.

It was Jenny who injected a chilly note into the general jubilation. 'Exactly how did the Registrar tell the police to drop the charges?'

John had the grace to look sheepish as he admitted the Registrar in Manchester had a telephone machine on his desk. 'Fortunately, the police station has one as well. Just the main police station that is.'

'And the police telephoned the prison,' said Jenny looking sly. 'You see. I told you they're a useful device.'

'Not so fast, Jenny. As it happens the prison doesn't have a phone. The police had to send a telegram. And that's why they released Margaret.' John sat back, folded his arms and looked smug.

An uproar of protest broke out among the ladies. They claimed it was a victory for diplomacy and a pork pie.

It was late when the weary and bedraggled party arrived in Atherley. Margaret's most urgent need was for a bath but that had to wait till the morning when the fires were lit and the water heated. Margaret and Effie took mugs of cocoa upstairs. They whispered to each other well into the night.

Within a couple of days, the family gave the impression that the incident had never occurred. Margaret began to recover the weight she had lost as the result of her frantic studying and her day in gaol.

'It must be nice having a sister,' said Effie as Jenny delivered a plate of toast to Margaret who was busy with a book.

'Oh, we're not really sisters.' Margaret spoke without thinking and immediately clapped her hand over her mouth.

The information Dorothea had plotted so hard to acquire was handed to Effie as a gift. The family comforted Margaret who felt she had done something wrong and Effie who felt she had been prying.

'It's not a secret,' declared John. 'Not from you, Effie.' He would be eternally grateful to the girl who warned him of Margaret's imprisonment. 'It's just that we don't think it is important.'

Jenny picked up her sewing and went to sit next to him. 'Tell us the story, Papa. You know I love to hear it.'

John leant back in his armchair and began the well-rehearsed story. 'Well, it must be nearly twenty years ago.' He looked across at Jenny who nodded her agreement. 'My father had died and left me a small inheritance. I'd read about the new designs for bicycles in the newspaper. Some even had these new rubber tyres. I thought it would be just the thing for getting to work.

'That Sunday I wheeled it down the hill to the park. It created quite a stir. No-one had seen anything like it. Every man and his dog wanted a turn.'

He turned to Margaret. 'You were going to feed the ducks. This little girl trotted up. Her curly red hair was hidden by her sunbonnet.' Jenny bobbed her head as she made her entrance into the story. He turned to Margaret. 'You shared the crusts. The two of you were busy feeding the ducks. Then a man in a suit asked if he could try the bike. Said he had a new job. Just the thing for getting to work. I must have hesitated. I didn't know him, but he pointed to the little girl. I assumed she was his. So I let him have a go.

He was a natural. Looked as if he'd ridden a bike before. Set off at top speed. Then there was a bit of a hullabaloo. A little boy chased a duck and fell in the water. I helped to get him out. The next time I looked, the bike and the rider had gone.'

John paused. 'Then there was you.' He stroked Jenny's vivid hair. 'Florence was so happy to have two girls. She said the stork had made a special delivery in answer to her prayers.'

'It was in the newspaper,' said Tommy and lifted the copy of Browning's poems from the shelf and passed it to his father who took a faded clipping from its pages and handed it to Effie. The others had seen it many times.

Atherley and Tilton Advertiser 5th June 1887

DARING THEFT OF BICYCLE ON THE SABBATH

Mr John Truesdale, Registrar of Births, Marriages and Deaths was the victim of an outrageous robbery in the Memorial Park on Sunday. Mr Truesdale was testing out his new safety bicycle. Many men in the town expressed an interest in riding the novel machine. Mr Truesdale kindly allowed a person unknown to him to take a turn on the bicycle. The man headed for the park gates and was soon on the road to Manchester.

The constable was informed and quickly gave chase. He was not able to apprehend the thief. It is doubtful whether the police horse could have caught him so great was the speed of the machine. The man left behind a small child.

The mayor, Mr Kenneth Woodward, said afterwards that the council might consider supplying the police with bicycles. The council would consider whether any resulting increase in efficiency would justify the cost to the local taxpayer. The child is a girl of two or three years old. Mrs Truesdale has kindly offered to look after her while enquiries are made.

'Fair exchange is no robbery,' said John with a smile. 'I'd much rather have Jenny than that death machine of a bike. You see now, why I am so suspicious of new inventions,'

'What surprises me,' said Effie, 'is the way they leave the little girl to the end. If I was writing for that newspaper, I would have the abandoned child as the headline.'

'That wouldn't have suited Florence,' said John. She used to wake up in the night afraid someone would come to claim our Jenny back.'

Effie wondered what had happened to the man with a brown moustache. She pictured his desperate cycle ride and the guilt that would torment him for abandoning his child.

A letter came from Professor Wilkins to tell Margaret that her first-class degree was now a reality. Unfortunately, no suitable junior lectureship was available in his department. If she wished to continue to study in Manchester, he was confident there would be a place for her on the teacher training course.

He forwarded a letter. It came from the young don at Cambridge who had rescued her on the stairs. The hairy professor had let slip Professor Wilkin's name. The young don wanted the young lady to know he thought it grossly unfair to deprive women of qualifications they had earned through hard work. His own sister had suffered such a fate. He hoped he would be allowed to call on her if ever he came to Manchester.

The two letters did much to restore Margaret's bruised ego. As she smoothed out the paper of the letter from Cambridge a slow smile spread over her lips.

'You know, I just might write back and thank him.'

A frown crinkled the normally cheerful creases on Effie's face. 'I don't think that's such a good idea. You don't want to encourage him.'

'Just a letter of thanks. That's only polite.'

'He might come to Manchester. He might call on you!'

'He won't know where I live. I don't know where I will be living next year.' Margaret only thought in academic years.

'How about another year at Mrs McKenna's?'

'Do the teacher training, you mean?'

Effie grew cunning. 'It would keep you in Manchester. In the professor's eye. If a lectureship came up, you'd be bound to hear about it.'

Effie's plan worked. Margaret decided she might as well go teaching. There was not much demand for Latin in the workplace. Not like Jenny and her commercial finance.

She had missed the deadline for applications, but, as Effie said, a first-class degree opens many doors.

John had hoped for a year off paying fees, before Tommy became a student; he was in his final year at school and was keen to study medicine.

'If she can't earn her own living after this then heaven help her,' said Jenny to console her father. The subject of money was much on her mind. She had the promise of a healthy income and few outgoings. Yet she had set off to rescue her sister from prison with one shilling and sixpence in her purse, some scones and a pork pie.

She had not considered the cost of the hansom cab, the price of the train tickets or paying a fine to free Margaret from prison. Such expenses, though perfectly foreseeable had not crossed her mind; these were things from the world of men. She had blithely assumed her father would have enough money in his pocket to pay them, as indeed, he had. I am going to have to shake my ideas up, Jenny told herself. Commercial Finance officer with Carter-Woodward is most definitely the world of men. The first thing I am going to do is to open my own bank account.

John agreed to shoulder the burden of supporting Margaret while she studied to be a teacher. 'There is one condition,' he told her - and Effie for good measure, 'There is to be no more writing on walls or attending meetings run by that Mrs Pankhurst. Understood?'

'Absolutely. Doesn't seem right to break the law when you're a teacher.'

'Setting a bad example to young people?'

'Exactly. To be honest we've gone off the WSPU. The Pankhursts are moving to London to campaign there. We might join the NUWSS.'

'What on earth is that?'

'That's the law- abiding party. Mrs Fawcett started it; she knows how Parliament works. She helped her husband when he was an MP.'

'Blind Fawcett?' Anna looked up from her book. 'He was Postmaster General. Before my time. People still speak of him with respect.'

Anna thought of Mr Fawcett, who had among other things arranged for postal workers to have paid holidays. He wouldn't be married to the kind of wild woman Mrs Pankhurst seemed to be. She thought John might have been a little harsh in his ban on the girls' political activities. 'I don't see why you shouldn't go to meetings. But no more getting into trouble with the police.' She shook a warning finger at them.

'Agreed.'

When the young people returned to their studies Anna's sole companion for most of the day, was the dog. She grew restless, fussing about details and criticising the new maid till she left in a huff. She started trying new recipes no-one liked and grew dis-satisfied with her wardrobe but lacked the energy to improve it. Her only consolation was visiting Mrs Woodward who was busy with her two grandchildren.

Now that she never made love with John, the company of the twins cheered her without arousing an overwhelming desire to have her own baby. It was her reward for abstinence. Jenny was at home in the evenings now her classes at the Mechanics Institute had finished. Her presence made it easier for Anna and John to control their passion.

In November 1906 Effie came to help celebrate Jenny and Margaret's twenty first birthday. No-one knew the exact date of Jenny's birth but it seemed only fair that both girls achieve their majority on the same day. 'To be honest,' said Jenny, 'I think I've been a grown-up for years.' No-one contradicted her.

'Strange to think we were schoolgirls when the century started and we are fully-fledged adults now,' said Margaret.

'What can we do now, that we couldn't do before?'

'Get married without asking papa.' They laughed at the idea.

'As if,' said Margaret, 'I'd consider marrying a man who lacked the courage to face my father.'

All Jenny could think of was a married Edward Carter approaching her father to ask for her hand. She wanted a ringside seat at that encounter. The fireworks would fly.

'You be careful, Jenny,' said John as if he'd read her thoughts. 'You have to prove you are over twenty-one or have my consent to get married. If I don't like the chap, I'll withhold it.'

'You could buy a car,' said Effie, who had every intention of buying one herself.

As John and Anna listened to what they now knew was called badinage they felt old. The self-denial they had practised for so long and so well, was in danger of leaving them with no secret to keep. Sometimes they felt they had succeeded in killing their love.

'One day,' thought Anna, 'Jenny too will leave home. A young man will come calling for her, knocking on the door and offering to take her out to a church social. Next, she'll be engaged and then married. What will happen to me then? How can I continue to live here with John? It was the children who gave my presence legitimacy. Without them, I will be some kind of frightful spinster aunt. John will grow tired of economising to pay Tommy's fees and my keep. Some wealthy widow will set her cap at him. He is well-preserved, still quite a catch. What will become of me then?

She mulled over the events of her life. Raising her sister's children was the most rewarding of the many duties that had fallen in her path. Nursing her father had been both a duty and an escape route from the danger of her love for John. Then she had of her own free will married George. She blamed her mother who always proclaimed it was better to have a second-rate husband than none at all. Anna seriously doubted anyone believed that now. She was sure Jenny and Margaret would not subscribe to that particular Victorian doctrine. They were modern young women qualified to earn their own livings.

A shiver ran down her spine; she felt exposed to the chilly and unpredictable winds of fortune. All that stood between her and total poverty was her tiny secret nest egg

1907

Once you have decided you are an adult, you put away childish things. When you earn your own living you no longer need your parents' permission. You might ask their opinion but only on the understanding that you won't be tied by their answer.

When the newly adult Margaret, returned to work in Manchester in January, she and Effie faced a choice that tormented their tender consciences. They had promised Anna, not to break the law, but temptation came to them in the form of a poster inviting members of their Suffrage Society to take part in a 'United Procession of Women' in London.

In the quiet evenings in their shared room they debated the pros and cons of the enterprise. How exciting to be part of the first ever march organised by women for women. They were sure it would be peaceful as the law-abiding Mrs Fawcett was in charge. They picked over the words of their promise to Anna. She'd agreed they could go to meetings. A procession, they argued, was just a meeting outdoors. Anna had not specified that the meetings should take place in Manchester. There was nothing to stop them going to London. They'd promised to avoid getting arrested. The police did not arrest you for walking down the street. It was a free country. In short, they did everything except consult Anna and John. They did not ask because they knew the answer would be a resounding No.

The chairman of their Suffrage Society was in charge of the project. 'I must warn you,' he said while giving them a piercing stare, 'you will not be chaperoned. Your relations may find that very shocking.' Two girls who worked in a textile factory fell into giggles.

'Don't make us laugh. Our sweethearts are coming. They want us to do it in style.'

Margaret and Effie's scruples melted away like snow in the sunshine. If these girls could travel to London with their sweethearts, surely the two of them could go without outraging public opinion?

Now he had fulfilled his duty by pointing out that a women's march was an unprecedented event, the chairman became business-like. 'Let's find out how many are going. Then I can get a discount on the train tickets. If there are enough of us, we can have our own compartment.'

Early in the morning of 7th February Mrs McKenna handed them sandwiches for the journey. 'Don't forget your umbrellas,' she urged them. 'It looks like rain.'

'That's because we are in Manchester,' said Effie. 'It always rains in Manchester. It won't in London.'

Late that night Mrs McKenna, who had been waiting anxiously for the return of her two intrepid lodgers, heard the doorbell ring.

'Don't tell me you've lost your keys,' she said as Margaret and Effie stood on the doormat.

'No. We thought we'd warn you so you could put some newspaper on the floor.'

Mrs McKenna advanced her candle. The two figures on the doormat were wet, very wet. Their clothes clung strangely tight to their bodies. Mrs McKenna lowered her candle. From the thighs down their skirts were caked with mud, Effie lifted the hem of her skirt and held out a foot. Her boot was hidden by a thick layer of brown mud.

'That'll be mud from London, I assume. London, where it doesn't rain.'

They stuffed their boots with crumpled newspaper and set them by the kitchen fire to dry. It took hours on Sunday to make their clothes ready for work the next day. As they busily brushed, dried, polished and ironed Effie suddenly said, 'It was worth it though. Wasn't it?'

'Yes,' said Margaret. 'The first women's march ever. And we were there.'

'Along with a few countesses in their carriages.'

'And a few men. The Manchester lads did it in style. That electric cab. All crammed in and shouting like glory.'

They chuckled at the memory of the cab with streamers of white, green and purple flying from its windows. Effie fished the damp newspaper out of her boot and waved it in the air. 'With so many of us the press cannot ignore us this time.'

'They'll probably laugh at us and call it the Mud March.'

Just as the girls maintained a discreet silence about the women's procession, so did Edward Carter about a meeting with a solicitor, newly arrived in town. 'Remember,' he said as he left the young man's office, 'no notes.' He drove to his mother's house, perched on the lower slope of the road that led past Jenny's home and up to the Woodward mansion at the top of the hill.

Mrs Carter, accustomed to the comings and goings of her many sons, made him tea and left him to his thoughts. Edward sat at the front window and looked at his expensive car parked incongruously outside the modest home he rented for her. When he put his empty cup in the kitchen sink, she was peeling a great pile of potatoes for several hungry sons' supper. She smiled as Edward gave her his wry smile, but asked no questions. Her boys had trained her well.

The car took the hill in its stride and turned into the leafy drive of the Woodward mansion. Edward found Mr Woodward strolling round the empty paddock. 'I miss the horse,' said Mr Woodward. 'It was pleasant to come out here and stroke his nose. Sort of soothing.'

They walked past the old stable now converted into a garage. 'That worked well,' said Edward. 'Goes well with the main house.'

'Aye. Bit of a faff getting the same bricks. Worth it in the end.'

Edward pointed to the far end of the paddock, where there was a stand of silver birches. Now there was no horse to graze the undergrowth was busy invading.

'Do you know who owns that land?'

Mr Woodward scratched his head. 'Not sure. It's probably part of the original estate. It might even be me. '

'I'd like to buy a piece of it. Build something like that.' He gestured at the converted stables.'

Mr Woodward turned to him with a question in his face.

'I think we could do with another car. And until your leg gets better, we need a chauffeur to drive it.'

'Mmmmmm.' Mr Woodward's response was cool.'

'He can drive Dorothea to her concerts. She's getting lots of invitations. Doesn't do to turn them down; they'll stop coming. You know how happy singing makes her.'

Mr Woodward looked uncomfortable. He did not like to be reminded of the impairment that prevented him learning to drive the car.

'He could take you and Mrs Woodward out with the twins.'

Mr Woodward warmed to the idea.

'I'll take responsibility for the project. Pay his wages. It's time I contributed more. Took responsibility. I'd like to own a bit of land, put down some roots.'

Mr Woodward offered his hand. 'We'll get the lawyers on it. Check the owner. Sort out a price.' Edward took his father-in-law's hand and shook it.

As John read his newspaper that same February, it was not the Mud March that grabbed his attention. His newspaper was no longer a pleasant companion for his leisure hours; it was a despatch from the battle front. The hoary old subject of the Deceased Wife's Sister Marriage Act had come out of its stable for another run round the block.

It had already reached its Second Reading. That sounded hopeful. Presumably it had passed the first one. The Church of England could not decide if there was a Divine Prohibition on the matter. The Free Church was confident there was not. John, a member of the Church of England, considered defecting to the Methodists as a reward for reducing his illicit lovemaking with Anna from the foul crime of incest to a mere carnal sin.

Spring came. Lord R Cecil spoke long and eloquently of the right of clergymen to refuse to marry such couples. John felt his fist clench and pictured the violence that he would want to inflict on any vicar who refused him. And who was this Lord R Cecil to be so careful of other people's consciences?

'Are you all right, John?' asked Anna, looking up from her embroidery. 'You've gone a funny colour.'

'It's nothing. Something in the news amused me.'

'Do tell.'

'It's man stuff. You wouldn't understand.'

Anna pursed her lips. She wanted to say, 'Try me,' but refrained. John busied himself looking for some snippet of other news to divert her. He did not wish to raise false hopes, given the slow and tortuous ways of Parliament.

The Letters to the Editor gave John some crumbs of comfort; he and Anna were not alone in their predicament. Holman Hunt, a famous painter, wrote to give the bishops a lambasting. 'A scheming minority' and '16 agents of Ecclesiasticism,' he called them.

Three days later an Eleanor Cecil wrote to the paper about the monstrous injustice of not consulting the large number of women involved. John was deeply suspicious of the writer. She must be some connection of this Lord R Cecil who had so much to say on the subject. Wife? Sister? But the lady had a point. John glanced at Anna. She was sitting with a skein of wool draped over her wrists while Jenny wound it into a ball. They were deep in conversation. This was not the moment to ask her opinion. After all this was the nineteenth time the question had come before Parliament.

Even with the new Liberal government's massive majority, it had as much chance of passing as women had of getting a vote. The Honourable Members always found ways to avoid doing what they didn't want to do. Even if the repeal of the Dead Wife's Sister Marriage Act made its way through the House of Commons, the elephant trap of the House of Lords awaited it.

At the beginning of the summer holiday, Margaret and Effie came to visit. They talked about following in the footsteps of the redoubtable Mrs McKenna, by going to France for a walking holiday. John and Anna endured a brief panic; it was an open secret that Dorothea Woodward, as she was then, came home from France 'in the family way'. Common sense quickly re-asserted itself. Margaret and Effie were not silly, inexperienced and undisciplined girls.

They are young women, thought John, not really girls anymore. Margaret had recovered the flesh she had lost; she was no longer so white-faced and tense. Anna commented on the improvement.

'Isn't it strange?' said Margaret. 'When you teach, you learn so much. I never used to feel confident. As a teacher I have to give the impression of knowing what I am doing. So, I act confidently. As a result, I feel confident. I don't know how it works.'

'It must have worked at your interview.'

Margaret beamed. She had been appointed to a prestigious girls' school to teach Latin. 'To be honest there wasn't a lot of competition. There are not many female Classics graduates looking for work.'

'They are all in London. Heckling politicians and going to prison,' said Effie.

'Are you envious?' asked Anna with a sudden suspicion in her mind. Perhaps the trip to France was a decoy. Perhaps they really meant to go to London, break windows and set fire to letter boxes.

'Nooo.' Effie lengthened the syllable to show her scorn. 'The Pankhursts have fallen out with us Liberals. We're sticking with Mrs Fawcett. No violence.'

Anna was reassured by Effie's statement. For all her scrubbed and sensible appearance, she thought, Effie was a bit of a dark horse.

What Anna did not know was that the young don from Cambridge would be passing through France on his way to the Dolomites. The girls just might find their path crossed his.

Tommy paid a quick visit home to play a football match. He did not see much of the girls. He could not stay long; he had to go back to finish dissecting his corpse.

'All right for some,' said Jenny. She checked her appearance in the hall mirror and fixed her hat with a pin. 'Some of us have to go to work.'

'I notice you go with a smile,' said Effie who didn't miss much.

'That's right.' Jenny smiled some more. She couldn't marry the man she loved, but she could work with him. It surprised her how comfortable she was in the office with Edward. Their work involved complex calculations which effectively kept passion at bay. Jenny found numbers soothing. They were either right or wrong. None of those awful decisions to make.

The comings and goings of the young people diverted John from the slow progress of the Deceased Wife's Sister Marriage Act. In August the bill had its Second Reading in the House of Lords. Did that mean John could propose to Anna? He dithered. It would be like throwing a bomb into the delicate structure of their relationship.

He continued to scour the newspaper. Another Cecil had written to the Editor. An H Cecil this time. He – or was it she? – declared the relationship to be as 'immoral as concubinage or bigamy'. John was overtaken by a roar of outrage that he could not restrain.

'What is so exciting in the paper?' Anna demanded.

John looked for a diversion. 'They are thinking of buying the Cullinan diamond for the King.'

'Why?'

'Because it is incredibly big.'

Anna looked unimpressed. 'No good as a ring then.'

John's control snapped. He rose on legs that decided to quiver and shake in a ridiculously girlish fashion and went to put his arms round Anna. It was a bear's embrace, sprinkled with tears. Shocked though she was, Anna did not push him away.

'Oh, my dear. Are you unwell?' she murmured in his ear and pulled him closer. The warmth of him. The bulk of his shoulders. The bristles on his chin. She forgot his distress in her delight in his closeness

It took some time to explain the hope he had not dared to share. 'This is the nineteenth time this has gone to Parliament,' he cautioned, 'and I am still not sure if the stupid bloody law has changed.'

'It says, "carried amid cheers".' Anna held the newspaper close. She could not find her glasses. 'That sounds pretty conclusive.'

'We should wait for confirmation before we say anything. Not to the family. Not to anyone.' The habit of secrecy still held them in its grasp.

At the end of the month The Times published a letter from the Archbishop of Canterbury. The law had received Royal Assent.

'That is all the assurance I need,' said John and went on his knee. 'My dear, my darling Anna will you marry me? I have wanted you for so long, I cannot believe that at last I have the right to ask you that question.'

For answer, Anna wrapped her arms around him and pressed him to her heart.

When Jenny came home from work, she was quite overcome by the news. 'Such a surprise!' she kept saying.

'I suppose you think we are too old for this sort of thing,' John complained.

Jenny struggled to explain. 'No. I just never thought about you having such feelings. You took such good care of me, and Margaret, and Tommy. And now the dog, and Effie. I didn't think there'd be any love left over.'

'Love isn't an exact quantity,' said John. 'It doesn't come in pint bottles like milk.'

When they were alone Anna expressed her amazement that there had not been even a whiff of suspicion in the household.

'I don't suppose they looked very hard,' said John. 'Too busy with their own lives.'

'Exactly as it should be.'

Jenny, who regarded herself as an expert in the art of hiding forbidden love, wondered if she had concealed her love for Edward as thoroughly as John and Anna had hidden theirs. A tiny speck of hope flickered in her heart. The law now allowed John and Anna to marry. Perhaps one day society would extend the same right to her and Edward.

The prospect sent her so dizzy, she did not hear her father calling her name.

'Jenny. Are you listening? Will you go to send the telegrams?'

Now he was sure the law had changed, John became brisk and business-like. 'First, we must tell the rest of the family. Margaret and Tommy. Ask them to come tomorrow. It's Saturday. There won't be classes.'

'And Effie,' said Anna. 'She is as good as family.'

'I can do better than that,' said Jenny, reaching for her coat. She ran down the hill and arrived breathless at the Carter-Woodward offices. The watchman let her in and gave her a taper to find her way to her office through the dark building.

'Nothing wrong is there Miss? Just, the boss came not ten minutes ago.'

'He must have forgotten something. We'd have heard the hooter if there was an accident at the pit.'

With the help of the taper and a faint light through the window in the door of Mr Woodward's office Jenny found her desk, her telephone and Mrs McKenna's number. The redoubtable landlady had been one of the first to install one in her home. She answered it with such enthusiasm Jenny jumped and dropped the earpiece.

'There's no need to shout, Mrs McKenna. Let the wires do the work.' It took some time to get Effie to the phone; when she arrived, she was her reassuring self. Yes. They would all come. She would personally guarantee Tommy's presence. Could Jenny say why they were summoned?

Jenny rang off. It was the happy couple's privilege to break the news.

The click of a door closing, a shadow falling on her desk. 'I'm sorry, Mr Woodward. I'll pay for the call. I've never done this before. It's an important family matter.'

'I should hope so, Miss Truesdale. Or as it's out of office hours can I call you Jenny?

It was Edward. He waved a sheaf of papers to prove his errand and listened as she quickly explained about John and Anna. 'That's a very heartening story.'

Jenny rose, all flustered. 'I have to get back. They'll be wondering where I've got to.'

'Will you let me drive you home? It is much quicker.' He took her silence for consent. 'Keep your taper going. You'll need it. My car is at the back.' He went to Mr Woodward's office and turned off the gas light. Then he took her elbow and guided her to the door. When they reached the car, he pinched the taper out, pulled her close and kissed her. 'I haven't done that since the night I came to tell you I was going to marry Dorothea. I want to do it all the time. Now get in the car before I do it again.'

The business with the starting handle kept him out of temptation's way. As he drove past the nightwatchman's hut, he wound the window down and shouted, 'I'm taking Miss Truesdale home. I made sure all the lights are out.'

That night Jenny wished she kept a diary. There was so much she wanted to write in it. Today the man who is not strictly speaking my father told me he is going to marry the woman I think of as my mother. How strange is that? For a moment she thought of the man who rode away on the bicycle. She watched him disappear over the horizon of the past and turned to more important matters. Edward kissed me. For the second time.

Margaret, Tommy and Effie sat in a row on the train and tried to guess why they had been summoned by their father.

'Jenny was most mysterious', said Effie. 'Just said she couldn't say. The line went dead. I'm sure she just switched it off.'

'Perhaps we are having gaslight at last.'

'Or a flushing toilet. I know Jenny is very keen on them now she has one at work.'

'As long as the dog's all right,' said Tommy. Medical school suited him. He played football and had developed some impressive muscles. His hair flopped over his forehead and his brocade waistcoat hung open in the fashionable manner.

'Jenny would have warned you if it was the dog,' Effie assured him. 'I definitely got the impression that it was something pleasant.'

They stopped talking as they tackled the hill. 'Gosh. I'd forgotten how steep this is,' said Margaret as they arrived home. 'Our part of Manchester is deliciously flat.'

At the house the dog demonstrated he was in good health by greeting them warmly, as did the smell of something roasting in the oven. Anna looked lovely in her best silver-grey dress. It was Jenny who wore the pinafore; it had been agreed she should do the cooking that day.

To their surprise, John offered them sherry and bid them all sit. The chairs were set in a semi-circle as if he had an important announcement to make. They sat with their tiny glasses and looked at each other. Their eyes fell on Jenny. Had she abandoned all hope of Edward? Was she getting engaged to some other young man? If so, where was he? And why was she the one wearing a pinafore?

John took centre stage and rested his hand on Anna's shoulder, something he had never done in public before. The young cast about in their minds for an explanation of this unusual behaviour. Tommy leapt to his feet. 'Aunt Anna! You're not getting married again.'

Silence.

Anna took a breath. 'As it so happens, I am.'

The fashionably dressed football player, who had sliced through a human liver without flinching, was a small boy again with only a blue rabbit to comfort him. He flung out his arms and went to embrace her. 'Please don't go away again.'

Anna returned his hug with interest. 'I am not leaving you,' she said and enjoyed watching the puzzled expressions on their faces.

John stepped forward. 'I am pleased to say that your Aunt Anna has agreed to marry me.' It took some time for them to work it out. When the light dawned, they gave a throaty roar of wordless delight. It soon developed into expressions of relief, delight, surprise and belated congratulations.

When the young had relieved their feelings, John took charge of the proceedings again. 'I have loved Anna for a long time, but the law prevented us from marrying. Now that law has changed and so at the first opportunity, I am going to tell the world how much I love her by making her my wife.'

He smiled at her in wordless happiness. He turned to the Margaret and Tommy to say, 'I like to think your mother would give us her blessing. Anna has been a mother to all of you.'

They gave voice to their approval and waved their sherry glasses in the air.

'Now I think about it,' said Tommy, 'it's a bit late for our parents to get married. Quite shocking really.' He pinched his face to express disapproval. 'It wouldn't do in Southport.'

They all howled with laughter. John launched into a long explanation of the tortuous ways of Parliament which lasted until Jenny appeared looking hot and bothered to say lunch was ready.

After lunch, they agreed to leave the dishes to soak. John and Anna, who had a mysterious errand to do, suggested that the young people took the dog for a walk. The fresh air would help them process the news and sort out their thoughts. Margaret was puzzled about the law against the marriage in the first place.

'Oh, it's all that one flesh business,' said Effie with a casual wave of her hand.

'Explain,' demanded Tommy.

It gave Effie great pleasure to explain the out-dated ideas on matrimony. She was always on the lookout for opportunities to convert men to a more rational way of thinking. 'When the church marries a man and a woman, they claim they become one flesh. One flesh with one voice. Obviously that voice is a deep male one.' She looked round, waiting for signs of outrage. She was disappointed. They simply nodded to show they were listening, so she continued. 'If you really are one flesh then your wife's sister is your sister, so…' Her voice trailed away. Not even Effie could say the word incest in the presence of a man. Tommy went pink.

One thing still irked Jenny. What's this about clergymen refusing to marry them? Perhaps they'll have a civil wedding. Papa being a registrar.'

'He couldn't do his own wedding.'

'They could go to a different office. How about that one where you wrote on the wall?' Tommy found the idea amusing. Margaret did not.

'The Romans wouldn't have this problem,' said Margaret to change the subject. 'The priests did what you told them while the gods waited in the wings. If they disapproved of your goings-on, they struck you down with a thunderbolt.'

'They should just go to the church, show the vicar the bit in the newspaper and get married,' said Effie.

'They'd still have to call the banns.

'What are they?' asked Tommy.

Did you never listen in church? You know the bit where the vicar gives notice that so and so, spinster of this parish is going to wed so and so.'

Tommy sucked in his cheeks and tried to remember anything from his time in the church pews. 'No.'

'They do it three times. In case one of the pair already has a wife or husband.'

Tommy's face froze. 'So, everyone will know they are going to marry.' A terrible thought struck him. 'But they are living in the same house. People will think they are.... You know.'

'For a medical student you are very mealy-mouthed,' said Effie. 'You mean they might anticipate matrimony.'

Tommy flushed. 'Yes. I don't want people saying things like that about Anna. I don't want them even thinking it. I always think of her as my mother.'

The girls showed they understood. 'I'll be there as chaperon,' said Jenny.

'Ah. But you won't do,' said Margaret. And Tommy agreed. Even Effie admitted that under the circumstances a female chaperon should be a relative by blood.

When they returned to the house, John had another announcement to make. He and Anna had been to see the vicar; they wanted to be married in church to prove that their union was not only valid in the eyes of the law. It was also sanctioned by the church. After all it was the church that had caused all their problems in the first place. The vicar would be calling the banns the following day. John had interrupted him writing his sermon and enjoyed watching him scuttle about filling in the forms.

No bridegroom spends the night before his wedding in the bride's home. John was even more scrupulous than Tommy, of Anna's reputation. He felt chivalry dictated he should move out straightaway. He had arranged lodgings, down the hill, at Mrs Carter's. Edward's mother had a bed to spare; one of the many Carter boys was away busy, building a bridge, crewing a clipper or pacifying an unruly colony.

Anna and Jenny would remain at home. With so many able-bodied men a mere hundred yards down the hill they need not fear for their safety. John planned to come home for the occasional meal; he had doubts about Mrs Carter's cooking.

Four weeks later John and Anna were married. Tommy asked for the privilege of leading her to the altar. Margaret, Jenny and Effie provided a colourful flock of bridesmaids each in their own dresses. When Tommy arrived at the chancel steps, with Anna in her grey silk dress on his arm, he gave the vicar a reproachful look for all the years this happy occasion had been delayed.

Mrs Mainwearing became Mrs Truesdale and if anyone was scandalised, he – or more likely she – kept her opinions to herself. The door between the bedrooms was ceremonially unlocked and that night the happy couple took official possession of the big bed.

They lay together, filled with pleasure at being able to share a bed, openly and legitimately. They could take comfort together without fear of discovery, a simple pleasure that had been denied them for so long.

'It will be wonderful not to have to get up and use that horrible syringe,' said Anna. 'I hated having to leave you.'

'No more keeping secrets. Tiptoeing about in fear of being heard. Jumping when you hear a door creak. Terrified there might be a baby.' John took her hand, kissed it gently and made it into a fist with his. He waved it in a gesture of defiance. 'Isn't it wonderful. We can say to the world. This is us. Man and wife. These are our children.'

'They are rather a mixed bag,' Anna reminded him. 'Two are yours. My only contribution is through my sister.'

'And the time you spent raising them.' John shook her fist at the world again. 'They are our children. Jenny is ours.'

'Can we count Effie? She has no other family and she fits in beautifully.'

'There might be further additions,' said John.

'True. The girls are of an age to marry.'

'I wasn't thinking of husbands. Would you mind a baby, if one came?'

'Well as you are thinking of the future, husband of mine, I suggest we set about installing some modern plumbing.

Perhaps we could skip gas lighting. It is a bit smelly. And go straight to electric lights. Queen Victoria is long dead. Any child of ours will be born in this glorious twentieth century to a world of motor cars, aeroplanes and telephones.'

'And votes for women,' said John, kissing her neck. Their minds soon turned to other matters and nature took its course.

Dear Reader,

Thank you for sticking with the Truesdales. I am not the only person who would like to know what you think of their story. It is always good to have a recommendation – or a warning – from a fellow reader.

Don't be modest. It is easy to publish your thoughts to the digital world. Many people already have a platform they are happy to use.

If you don't do technology you can always spread the word through your local bookshop, newsletter, parish magazine or the good old grapevine.

If you'd like to know what happens next look out for *Spinning Jenny*.

Thanks to Lucy Savage-Mountain for her cover design, and to Lesley Upham, Rebecca Stubbs, Heather Rosser, Liz Harris and the members of the Oxford Chapter of the Romantic Novelist Association for advice and encouragement